L'Auberge

JULIA STAGG

HODDER

First published in Great Britain in 2011 by Hodder & Stoughton
An Hachette UK company

First published in paperback in 2011

1

Copyright © Julia Stagg 2011

A CIP catalogue record for this title is available from the British Library.

ISBN 978 1 444 70823 3

Typeset in Plantin Light by Hewer Text UK Ltd, Edinburgh

Printed and bound Clays Ltd, St Ives plc

Hodder & Stoughton policy is to use papers that are natural, renewable
and recyclable products and made from wood grown in sustainable forests.
The logging and manufacturing processes are expected to conform
to the environmental regulations of the country of origin.

Hodder & Stoughton Ltd
338 Euston Road
London NW1 3BH

www.hodder.co.uk

For Mark
My very own chef in a French restaurant

I

'Sold? What do you mean it's sold?'

Josette pushed her glasses back up her nose, batted away the dangling strings of *saucisson* which were obscuring her view, and peered intently at the source of the biggest news to hit the commune of Fogas since ... well, since the curate had been found in a compromising position with Madame Sentenac by none other than Monsieur Sentenac, wielding a rifle and a manic look. The curate, abandoning both his mistress and his mission in a split second, had jumped out of the window and fled, leaving the church without a priest for the last twenty years.

But this. This was much bigger.

'I mean it's sold,' said the taller of the two women across the counter from her.

Josette watched as Véronique, postmistress of Fogas, made the most of her dramatic pause, shifting the baguette she was holding to her left hand, knowing better than to place it down on the glass display-case filled with hunting knives, and carefully, slowly, brushed the excess flour off her cardigan. The minute she'd walked in the shop, eyes dancing and her lips curved in a mischievous smile, Josette had known there was gossip to be had. And that Véronique would make the most of telling it.

With a final adjustment of the small cross that hung around her neck, Véronique resumed her tale.

'It's sold, and the first round of paperwork has already been signed.'

A sharp gasp from the only other witness to this incredible news, if you discounted Jacques that was, demonstrated Véronique's uncanny ability to unearth the facts of village life when the likes of the woman next to her, Fatima Souquet, wife of the deputy mayor of Fogas, had yet to hear a whisper.

'But how can you be so sure?' questioned Fatima sharply, her barely disguised annoyance amusing Josette.

Véronique smiled craftily and leaned in to reveal the tricks of her trade. 'Because I was just up at the town hall and overheard the mayor talking on the phone to the solicitor! The *compromis de vente* was signed last week and in less than a month the Auberge des Deux Vallées will have new owners.'

As one, the three women turned and looked out of the shop window at the imposing stone building perched on the river bank at the end of the village, wisteria winding out of control up to the gutters, shutters hanging off, a general air of neglect permeating the whole.

'But that's not all,' continued Véronique, her voice taking on a sombre tone. 'The new owner is *not* the mayor's brother-in-law.'

This was too much for Fatima, who whipped round, her face a picture of astonishment.

'That can't be true!' she declared. 'It was a done deal. His brother-in-law has even had business cards made.'

'Pouff!' Véronique blew air out from between her pursed lips, dismissing Fatima in an instant. 'Lot of good they will do him now. He was outbid at the last moment.'

And that was when Josette felt the first twinges of anxiety. If Véronique was right, as she usually was, then this could only bring trouble to the commune, the mayor's wrath being legendary. The thought made her glance at Jacques who was loitering in the darkest corner of the shop as always, his white halo of hair glowing against the shelves of tinned cassoulet, firelighters and shoelaces, and her heart constricted. Trouble was the last thing he needed. He looked so helpless. And so annoyed. But then she couldn't be sure if his scowl was at the latest news or the presence of Fatima Souquet in his precious épicerie.

'Ah well,' she sighed, polishing the glass above the knives absently with her sleeve in case that was the root cause of Jacques' displeasure. 'At least the Auberge will reopen and the restaurant can only be better than the last one.'

'Ha! That's what you think,' announced Véronique as she played her trump card. 'The new owners are ENGLISH!'

Fatima reeled back and in her surprise, grabbed the glass display-case for support. But she escaped without rebuke. Josette was too busy trying to stop her jaw from dropping to reprimand her.

The Auberge had been sold to the English. How would the commune ever recover?

Merde, merde and double merde. Serge Papon slammed his arthritic hand down on the steering wheel one more time causing the car to swerve precariously across the narrow road leading down from Fogas to La Rivière. With an expertise born of frequent rages and even more frequent drink-driving, Serge pulled on the steering wheel, jerking the car in towards the mountainside before it could slide over the edge and into the ravine below.

Someone was going to pay, that was for sure. He'd wooed Gerard Loubet for the last six months, determined his brother-in-law's offer for the Auberge would be accepted. He'd even waived this year's commune taxes for the old fox, sure that the

3

Auberge was as good as his. And now Loubet had gone and sold it out from under him and retired to the Med. But what was worse, he'd sold out to an Englishman.

Pah!

Fuming at the audacity, Serge negotiated the car around the Romanesque church that marked the start of La Rivière with rather less skill than usual, almost scraping against the wall on the tight bend.

Based as it was at the meeting point of the two valleys leading down from the mountain villages of Fogas and Picarets, La Rivière bound the commune of Fogas together. Over the years it had often served as peacemaker between the two villages in the age-old struggle for power, possibly arising from the fact that to go from one side of the commune to the other, it was necessary to descend to La Rivière and go up the other side. But with the mood Serge Papon was in right now, it was going to take more than geographical diplomacy to calm him.

The post office came into sight, closed after the morning's business, and Serge ground his teeth as he passed. No doubt the postmistress, Véronique Estaque, had taken no time in spreading her gossip and the entire commune was probably laughing at him right now. And he still had to break the news to his sister, a task he wasn't relishing.

Serge clenched the steering wheel even tighter, and thrust his bulbous head towards the windscreen.

He'd show all of them. He was mayor of Fogas, with all the power of his elected office behind him, and he wasn't afraid to use it.

He swung the car around the last bend and slammed on the brakes at the give way sign. As he glanced to his left to check for traffic, his eye was caught by the metal sign on the building down the road, swinging in the slight breeze.

4

Auberge des Deux Vallées.

Serge Papon glowered as though the building itself had somehow offended him.

With a growl he turned on to the main road, muttering as he went.

Someone was going to pay.

The aura of shock that still suffused the dim interior of the épicerie following Véronique's revelation was shattered by the sound of gravel hitting the window as a car pulled up sharply outside.

Josette was the first to react.

'It's the mayor!' she hissed, her hands flapping at the two women with whom she'd been gossiping. They both snapped to attention and jumped apart, Véronique acquiring a sudden interest in the cheese cabinet with its half-rounds of Bethmale and Rogallais and Fatima immersing herself in the blocks of firelighters. Josette just had time to register Jacques' frown deepen even further at Fatima's proximity when the door crashed open and the mayor entered, clearly not in the best of moods.

'Pastis!' he barked at Josette and strode through to the room next door which served as the village bar, ignoring the two women who were trying their best to blend into the walls.

Josette followed him through and started getting his drink ready while the mayor fumbled in his jacket for his mobile phone before pulling out the chair nearest to the fire and collapsing into it with a sigh of frustration. He jabbed at the phone, needing several attempts to get the number right, a combination of stubby fingers and a vain refusal to get glasses, and then held the phone to his ear.

'Christian? Christian?' he shouted. 'Get yourself down here straight away. An emergency meeting. . . . what? I don't care if you've got your arm up a cow's arse. Get down here now. And bring that idiot Pascal too,' he added, hanging up on the objections still issuing from the phone.

As Josette carried the tray with the mayor's drink over to his table, she caught a brief glimpse of Fatima's pinched face through the door to the shop. No doubt she was furious to hear her husband Pascal described in such terms and having Véronique as a witness wouldn't have helped, thought Josette as she placed the glass of pastis on the table. She put a jug of water down next to it, spilling it slightly as she suddenly noticed Jacques sitting in the inglenook behind the mayor, oblivious to the roaring fire, his frown now replaced with a slight smile. But the mayor didn't even look up. He simply pulled the glass towards him, added a slosh of water and took a long gulp of the opaque liquid, his shrewd eyes narrowed, deep in thought.

Christian Dupuy grabbed his car keys from the shelf and headed out, his mother's voice following him through the door and across the yard and seemingly floating back to him from the white mountain peaks ringing the horizon.

'The man is a rogue, Christian, pure and simple. Whatever scheme he's up to now, you want no part of!' she admonished, snapping her tea towel at a couple of hens who were trying to sneak into the house.

'Yes Maman,' Christian murmured as he eased his large frame into the Panda 4×4. He really ought to get a bigger car, he thought, as he wedged his knees under the steering wheel. But with the way farming was going there was little chance of that this year.

'She's right you know,' his father chipped in from the barn where he was tinkering with an old tractor, bits strewn out on the ground around him. Christian watched as he placed another part on a growing pile and knew that his father would head to bed tonight claiming to have fixed the machine, but that the pile of discarded parts would be no smaller.

'But seeing as you're going down there, can you pop into town and buy a fire extinguisher?'

With a raised eyebrow, Christian looked at his mother who put her hands on her hips in defiance.

'So I had another accident. At least I caught it in time.'

Christian smiled in resignation and turned the key in the ignition. Unfortunately, more and more these days he felt like he was the parent in the relationship and his parents were the children. His mother's inability to cook a meal without a kitchen fire was a liability and the fact that his father knew more about radical left-wing politics than farming was less than useful in the day-to-day running of the farm. And they wondered why at forty he was still single.

With a sigh he put the car in gear and pulled out on to the road down to La Rivière, debating whether to go against his political convictions and acquire shares in the company that made the fire extinguishers he had to buy on a regular basis. At the rate his mother was going, it would produce a better income than farming!

He passed through the village of Picarets, his eyes drawn to the magnificent panorama before him, the small houses hugging the hillside as the valley dropped away, and the larger mountains on the horizon, the true peaks of the Pyrenees, standing majestically behind them. No matter how often he drove down this road, the view inspired him. But as the car turned from the mountains and headed into the woods that led to the valley below, his thoughts turned to Serge Papon.

What on earth was up with him that meant Christian had to drop everything and head to the épicerie?

★   ★   ★

Josette had just served the mayor his second pastis when the shop door opened, heralded by a sound like a stifled burp from the ancient bell positioned above the door. The bell was getting less and less predictable, alternating between a repertoire of rude sounds or no sound at all. Knowing it was time to replace it, Josette had so far put off the task for sentimental reasons. Especially as she could no longer ask Jacques to do it.

'Bonjour,' Christian called out as he appeared in the doorway of the bar and swept the much smaller figure of Josette up into an embrace.

'About time,' muttered the mayor, his bad temper made no better by the pastis already consumed.

Christian ignored him, keeping hold of Josette's hands and studying her face intently.

'How are you?'

'OK . . . OK . . .' she managed, glancing over at Jacques who was in the inglenook, smiling broadly now at the arrival of Christian, the son he had never had. 'Some days are better than others.'

Christian nodded.

'Well, let me know if you need help with anything.'

'Of course,' she lied and gently removed her hands from his and headed into the shop before his kindness could overwhelm her.

Sitting on a stool behind the shop counter, Véronique had made herself comfortable, clearly having no intention of leaving just as things were getting interesting. But seeing Josette enter she immediately stood up.

'Here, have a seat Josette,' she said, gesturing at the now vacant stool. 'I'll get the drinks sorted next door. You look shattered.'

Josette smiled, knowing Véronique's offer was mostly genuine but also motivated by her insatiable desire to have her finger on the pulse of Fogas's politics. But Josette sat anyway. She had to admit, she did feel tired as she took off her glasses and massaged her temples. Maybe it was the thought of the oncoming trouble in the commune. Whatever the cause, it was making her acutely aware of her sixty-seven years and a few more on top.

'Where's Fatima?' she enquired, suddenly realising the shop was empty.

Véronique nodded towards the window, her mouth twisted in irony.

'Prepping her husband for the coming meeting as always.'

Sure enough, Fatima had Pascal cornered up against the municipal noticeboard at the end of the alley leading to the post office. Out of sight from the bar, she was frantically gesturing as she drilled home her instructions. Pascal meanwhile had the look of a man whose mental faculties were being stretched to the hilt as he simultaneously tried to memorise everything his wife was saying and tried to dodge the quantities of dog shit that littered the ground, threatening his highly polished shoes.

Having finished her pep talk, Fatima stood back, releasing Pascal from his dog-induced hell. With a final check of his image in his car window, he smoothed back his hair and strode towards the bar, choosing to enter it directly from the front rather than through the épicerie.

Josette chuckled to herself. Poor Pascal. He still avoided the shop if he could, never having been a favourite of Jacques, who'd made no attempt to hide his contempt. As far as Jacques was concerned, Pascal Souquet represented the worst of the second-home owners in the area who claimed local heritage because their parents were born in the commune and they'd spent every summer holiday here as children. While this in itself was no problem, the majority of the people who moved

9

back to live in the area in the houses they'd inherited were conservative in outlook and wanted nothing in the commune to change, reluctant to accept that for the young people, change was essential. Without it, the commune would not be able to support them.

Thus when Pascal had used his network of fellow second-home owners to secure his election as deputy mayor, Jacques had been dismayed. His fears had been somewhat allayed by the appointment of Christian Dupuy in the other deputy position, thereby providing a balance to the self-serving ambition of Pascal and his wife and the endless political scheming of the mayor. But still Jacques had feared for the future of the commune.

As Josette watched Fatima position herself in her car so she could see into the bar, she wondered if his fears had had any foundation.

'You're late!' grumbled Serge as Pascal entered the bar, Pascal's fingers barely touching his hand in the kind of effeminate handshake that Serge despised. If his hands weren't so riddled with arthritis he'd crush his deputy mayor's hand so hard that Pascal's ostentatious signet ring would leave a lasting imprint.

Unaware of the dark thoughts swirling through the mayor's mind, Pascal turned to Christian, gave the same ineffectual greeting and pulled out a chair, dusting it off carefully before he sat down and casually crossed one immaculately attired leg over the other.

Serge could feel his anger rising. It was bad enough dealing with the mess over the Auberge but having to deal with this jumped-up dandy on a daily basis was more than a man could bear. His grip tightened involuntarily on his glass of pastis as he tried to calm himself, breathing in through his nose and out through his mouth as he'd seen his wife do in her yoga practice.

Good light in, bad light out. Good light in, bad light out. Good light in . . .

'Serge? Are you OK?' Christian was addressing him, a slight look of concern on his face as the mayor brought his focus back to the bar and the matter at hand, a good deal calmer.

'Yes, urm, so, hrmmmmmmmmp.' Serge cleared his throat and took one last gulp of pastis, signalling Véronique as he did so. 'Pastis, beer and a kir,' he ordered before the other two could object. He was damned if he was going to drink alone.

'We have a problem, a big problem,' he started, cutting to the chase now he was assured of Pascal and Christian's attention. 'The Auberge has been sold to an outsider.'

Serge watched his audience react and knew instantly that Christian was hearing the news for the first time. Pascal, however, had clearly been primed by his ferret of a wife who'd been in the shop with Josette and Véronique earlier. Well, that was no problem. Christian was the one who was harder to handle and he was at a disadvantage not having known what was coming. Serge was confident he could pull this off.

'But I thought your brother-in-law was buying it,' Christian stated, visibly nonplussed and thrown by Pascal's knowing smirk.

'So did I,' growled Serge. 'So did I! But Loubet, may he rot in hell, pulled a fast one and sold the Auberge to a foreigner. Regardless of the impact on the commune.'

'Impact on the commune?' queried Christian, pulling back as Véronique delivered the drinks, trying not to notice the shape of her backside as she leaned across the table to give the mayor his pastis. He dragged his eyes back to the mayor, but knew that Pascal had seen and was smirking even more, damn him.

Christian scratched his head to cover his confusion and decided then and there that he needed to get out more. If he was starting to covet Véronique Estaque of all women, with her pious ways and hideous dress sense, then he really was in a desperate state.

'You're welcome,' Véronique said sarcastically as she walked off, causing Christian even more confusion until he realised she was referring to the lack of gratitude for the drinks rather than his misplaced lechery.

Ignoring Véronique in the way he ignored all women, Serge continued. 'Yes, impact on the commune. The sale of the Auberge to foreigners will have a profound effect on Fogas.'

'In what way?'

'Because the restaurant will fail,' interjected Pascal with the air of someone talking to a retarded child. 'And the good people of the commune will have nowhere to eat.'

Serge sat back and watched this development with interest. So, Pascal had been well schooled by Fatima. Clearly she knew the line the mayor was going to take and was determined her husband would be on side. Now why was she doing that, he mused, and stored the question at the back of his mind for further analysis when his wife was snoring beside him and he couldn't sleep for the pain in his hands. For now, he had to keep his wits about him if he was going to manoeuvre this to the outcome he wanted.

'But why is it a given that the restaurant will fail just because they are foreigners?' demanded Christian.

'Because,' Pascal replied in his lofty manner, 'the new owners are English!'

Christian looked at Pascal and then at the mayor, and then reached for his beer.

'Shit!' he exclaimed. 'That is a problem.'

Serge lifted his drink to his lips to conceal his smile of satisfaction. This was going to be easier than he'd thought.

*　　*　　*

Several hours and many pastis later, Josette shut the door of the bar behind the mayor and his adjuncts and started to close up for the night. Through the glass she could see the twinkling lights of the commune of Sarrat on the mountainside across the river, clustering pinpricks of civilisation. By contrast, in front of the bar the road out of La Rivière disappeared into the night and the looming mass of the Cap de Bouirex. Josette could just make out the silhouette of the Auberge where it sat at the end of the village, beyond the illumination of the last street light.

So, things were afoot. According to Véronique, the mayor had called an extraordinary meeting of the Conseil Municipal, the elected governing body of the commune of Fogas, to be held tomorrow evening at the town hall. He had a plan up his sleeve but would it be good for the commune, Josette wondered.

She sighed and turned the locks on the door, making sure that the bolts at the top and the bottom were secure. And suddenly Jacques was beside her, looking down the road at the Auberge.

'Well,' she said to him, 'he's up to his old tricks again.'

Jacques didn't reply but just continued staring at the Auberge.

'But at least we have Christian as deputy mayor now which should help keep things from getting too out of hand.'

At the mention of Christian he nodded his head.

'So, I'm off to bed. I'm really tired. I'll see you tomorrow?'

At this Jacques turned towards her and Josette knew he was trying to tell her something. She smiled to cover her frustration. It was so difficult. Losing him had been bad enough. But having him back on these terms was almost worse.

She walked to the back of the bar and started up the stairs

to the empty double bed that seemed to have grown bigger over the last six months.

In the darkness of the bar below Jacques kept up his vigil at the window, looking out into the night and the trouble he could see coming.

2

The woodpile was warm; about the only place that was, sitting as it did in the direct sunlight that barely managed to crest the hill opposite the Auberge in mid-November. She was well hidden and quite content. The wood smell tickled her nostrils and the buzz of a late bee caught her ears but she didn't move. She was making the most of this unexpected surge of warmth.

'Tomate. Tomate!'

She twitched her ears but remained with her eyes closed.

'Tomate. Food.'

One eye opened, a slit of green in the sunlight, vivid against the black and white fur.

'Come on, Tomate, or I'll be late back to school.'

Chloé Morvan dropped her school bag to the ground in frustration and started walking towards the woodpile, shaking the plastic container of food as she went. She knew where the cat was. She was always in the same place and always played hard to get. Reaching up over her head to the top of the stack of wood, Chloé thrust her short arm into a small crevasse between two large logs and felt her fingers touch warmed fur.

'Lunchtime Tommy,' she said as she stroked the only bit of cat she could reach with her fingertips.

Withdrawing her arm, she opened the plastic container and tipped some dry cat food into the bowl on the ground. And as always, the sound of the pellets falling on to metal provoked a response. First one paw, then the other, the cat stretched herself out of her hiding place and yawned widely, her pink tongue curled back against the roof of her mouth. She surveyed the world with a quizzical look as though unsure it was the same one she'd left behind that morning when she'd closed her eyes; then her gaze settled on Chloé and the purring began.

'Are you sure we're allowed to do this?' Lorna Webster asked, keeping her eyes glued to the road in front as she posed the question. Even a sideways glance at Paul and she would be sick. Not for the first time she wondered about the advisability of someone as carsick as she was moving to live in the French Pyrenees.

'The estate agent seems to think there's no harm in it so I don't see why not,' Paul replied. 'Besides,' he laughed, 'it's almost ours anyway. Only three more weeks to go!'

Lorna grinned despite the nausea. Insane. That was the only word for it. The whole thing was just insane. And then, just as quickly as they had formed, the bubbles of laughter inside her evaporated and were replaced with pure fear. The kind of fear that had kept her awake for the last week as the magnitude of their decisions started to become apparent. Currency exchanges, insurance, bank accounts, estate agents, lawyers, removal companies, legal documents, most of it in French which neither of them had a great command of. What were they doing? No, rephrase that. What the FUCK were they doing?

'You OK? Am I going too fast?'

Lorna shook her head and swallowed to get rid of the foul taste that had risen up her throat on the tide of her anxiety. Paul squeezed her hand.

'Not much further now,' he said, as he took yet another

bend, trees on both sides of the narrow road, clinging to the mountainside on the right and to the steep river banks on the left. Lorna kept her gaze straight ahead and wondered how anyone could ever know where they were on this road. It all looked the same as it snaked its way up the valley away from St Girons, the views confined to the sides of the mountains which enclosed it. She gripped the edge of her seat as she felt the sickness wash over her again and then the car turned the final bend and they were propelled out of the gloom of the forest and into the sunlight as the valley widened in front of them. And there it was, the November sun bouncing off the old stones like a giant spotlight.

The Auberge.

And unless Lorna was mistaken, someone was cavorting around the garden doing somersaults. With a cat.

A car looks like a car no matter which way up you are. Normally, the sight of one wouldn't have disturbed Chloé from her routine. But the sudden arrival of a car in the drive-way of the Auberge just as she was suspended upside down in mid-air was enough to make her miss her landing in surprise and fall flat on the grass with a wallop, narrowly missing Tomate. She lay there, blinking furiously as her mind tried to catch up with her prostrate body, the cold seeping up from the ground into her bones.

'Oh my God, are you OK? Can you move? Have you broken anything?'

Chloé focused on the face that was hovering above her upside down. A woman, about her mum's age, with straight black hair, the kind of hair that Chloé coveted, the kind of hair that didn't have a life of its own and didn't have to be tamed before school every morning, was leaning over her and asking her something but Chloé couldn't understand a word of it.

Clearly she'd hit her head and dislodged something when she fell because she could see the woman's lips moving, she could even hear sounds, but none of it made sense. She shook her head to try and re-lodge the thing that she'd dislodged but instantly felt dizzy, so she gave up and lay back on the grass.

On the up side, she would no longer have to go to school. On the down side, Maman was going to go spare.

'Is she OK?' A man now appeared above her.

'I don't know. Her eyes are open but she hasn't spoken. We'd better call an ambulance.'

'What's the French for "hurt"?'

Chloé sighed the sigh of a martyr as she accepted that her universe had changed forever. So she could no longer communicate with the world at large. At least she could still become a trapeze artist and fly high above the crowds in a purple leotard, her straightened black hair streaming our behind her as she swung a hand's breadth away from the arching canvas of the big tent, carried aloft on the roars of the people below . . .

'You . . . are . . . OK? You . . . are . . . ill?'

At the touch of the man's hand on her forehead, Chloé suddenly regained her powers of comprehension.

'You . . . are . . . OK?' he asked again in a way that reminded her of Gerard Lourde at school in the special class where the teachers spoke really slowly and used small words.

'Yes . . . I . . . think . . . so,' Chloé replied, doing her best to help the man out.

The man smiled and said something to the woman, who smiled down at Chloé too. And then the man put his hands under Chloé's arms and gently lifted her on to her feet. She felt the horizon wobble a bit but it was nothing a trapeze artist couldn't handle.

Tomate had reappeared after the fright of Chloé nearly landing on her and was winding around her legs, eager to resume the game of acrobatic chase across the grass. The woman bent down and rubbed Tomate's head, making the cat purr like a Ducati.

'Is . . . this . . . you . . . cat?' asked the woman.

'She . . . lives . . . here,' Chloé explained.

The woman seemed surprised. 'Here? The Auberge?'

Chloé nodded.

'Name?' asked the woman, smiling at Chloé.

'Chloé.'

At which point the woman leaned over and tickled Tomate in the exact place that was guaranteed to make her roll over and over on the ground like a dog.

'Hello Chloé . . . Hello Chloé,' said the woman as she rubbed Tomate's belly.

Chloé sighed for the second time that day. These two were really 'special'.

'No,' she said with a hint of exasperation. 'I'm . . . Chloé.... she's . . . Tomate!'

'You . . . Chloé? OK. OK. She . . . is . . . Tomate?'

The woman was finally nodding in comprehension while the man started to shake Chloé by the hand.

'Hello Chloé. I'm . . . called . . . Paul.' He grinned at her and she felt herself grinning back even though she was more used to cheek kisses than hand shakes.

'My . . . wife. She . . . is . . . called . . . Lorna,' he continued, indicating Tomate's new friend.

Chloé was just wondering whether they would be able to go any further with this conversation when there was a shriek of tired brakes and her mother's dilapidated ex-police van shuddered to a stop at the end of the road up to Picarets. Maman jumped out of the van, leaving it running, and ran across the main road to the Auberge, her thick red plaits bouncing as she covered the short distance to the fence.

'Come on Chloé or you'll be late for school . . .' she shouted, her voice falling quiet as she suddenly realised that Chloé was not alone.

'Oh, hi,' she said, advancing towards the three of them. 'Sorry. Didn't mean to shout. You must be the new owners. Hope Chloé hasn't been bothering you? It's just that she comes down to feed the cat in her lunch break. Hope you don't mind? Claude at the estate agent's said you'd be dropping by but I thought she'd be out of your hair by then . . .'

Chloé looked at Paul and Lorna as Maman drew breath. Their faces were contorted into the same expression that Chloé had seen on Maman's face when she tried to give Chloé a hand with her maths homework. They clearly needed help.

'Look Maman, slow down, all right? They're "special",' she explained.

'What do you mean, "special"?'

'I dunno. Like Gerard Lourde at school,' she said with a shrug.

Maman gave a laugh and ruffled Chloé's hair.

'They're not "special", love. They're English!'

Chloé wasn't sure what the difference was but Paul and Lorna had caught the word English and were nodding vigorously so maybe Maman was on to something.

'Hello, I'm Stephanie, Chloé's mum,' Maman said, holding out her hand. '*It's . . . nice . . . to . . . meet . . . you.*'

Hearing English, Lorna's face relaxed into smiles as they introduced themselves and next thing Paul was explaining something to Maman which involved lots of gestures and the odd word in French and suddenly Chloé realised she was the topic of conversation.

'No!' she exclaimed suddenly, making Paul stop in his tracks. 'No . . . need to worry, Maman. I just fell over that's all,' she said, pulling Maman's focus back on to her and away from Paul's attempts to explain what had happened. He was still making circles in the air with his finger, trying to get across the seriousness of the fall.

'You fell over?' Maman asked with tight lips. 'Is that it? Just a fall? You weren't . . .'

'No Maman, OK? I wasn't. I don't . . . I wouldn't . . . I just fell while I was chasing Tomate.'

Stephanie stared into Chloé's eyes, searching for any dishonesty.

'You know how I feel about you doing somersaults, Chloé. I don't want you doing them. You understand?'

Chloé nodded, not understanding at all. It was the only thing Maman was strict about, the only thing they really disagreed on. So using the logic gained in her nine years on the planet, Chloé simply did them out of sight, using neighbours' lawns, Christian's fields and the garden at the Auberge. How else was she going to achieve her dreams?

Satisfied with whatever she saw in the depths of Chloé's eyes, Stephanie reached out and pulled her daughter to her so all Chloé could smell was incense and shampoo and potting soil. She peeked out under Maman's arm and she could see that Paul had stopped his gestures and Lorna was smiling at her.

'Did you bang your head?' Maman asked, finally releasing her.

Chloé nodded and rubbed her scalp through her thick mop of curly black hair where a huge bump had already formed.

'Does it hurt?'

'Yes.'

'How much?'

'Enough not to have to go back to school . . .' Chloé tried her luck.

Stephanie put her hands on her hips and smiled, shaking her head in mock despair.

'OK. No school. But you can help me pot up some new cuttings, all right? Now get your things and let's leave these people in peace.'

Chloé turned away to hide her grin and walked over to where she'd dumped her stuff, the cat following her. As she reached down to pick up her bag, Lorna approached her.

'Nice . . . to . . . meet . . . you . . . Chloé,' she said. 'And . . . no . . . say . . . Maman . . .' and then she made a looping gesture before placing a finger on her lips and winking.

Chloé laughed, glad to have a co-conspirator. She swung her bag over her shoulder, shouted goodbye to Paul and followed Maman out the gate towards the waiting van.

An afternoon off school. Not as good as a lifetime off school but better than nothing.

'They seem really nice,' commented Paul as the battered van performed a laboured U-turn and headed back up the mountain towards Picarets, Chloé waving at them from the passenger's seat.

'Lovely,' agreed Lorna, waving back until the van disappeared around the bend, leaving a strong smell of exhaust fumes in its wake. She let her arm drop to her side and hunched her shoulders against the chill of the early afternoon, feeling like Chloé and Stephanie had taken the warmth of the sunshine with them. For a few moments there as Lorna and Paul had tried to communicate with Stephanie with her stilted English and their monosyllabic French, Lorna had seen how they could belong in this community. Now she felt like an outsider again.

And how come their French was so crap? Why had it proven so difficult to construct the simplest of sentences, sentences they would have had no problem with in their French classes back in Manchester? It was so frustrating and Lorna suspected it wasn't going to get any easier in the foreseeable future.

'Come on,' Paul said, throwing an arm around her shoulders and turning her towards the Auberge. 'Let's go and inspect our new home. I'll get the torches, you grab the notepad and we'll see if the cat wants to join us.'

As if sensing she was the subject of the conversation, Tomate wandered over to them, her purr audible from a distance.

'Tomato! Funny name for a black and white cat, don't you think?' mused Paul as he opened the boot of the car to retrieve the torches.

Lorna laughed, not having thought about it before now. She reached down and tickled Tomate under the chin, producing even more noise from the cat. They hadn't expected to be acquiring a pet as well as a home and business but Tomate was a definite bonus.

Collecting her notepad from the car, Lorna followed Paul and the cat around the back of the building to the small patio that separated the Auberge from the river. The concrete was covered in a thick mush of dying leaves from the vast ash tree that dominated the river bank and the plastic chairs and tables were strewn around, victims of the autumn storms. They leaned on the fence and watched the water tumble noisily over the weir which stretched across to the opposite bank with its empty fields and scattering of houses.

When Lorna and Paul had first seen the property in June the sun had been dancing off the water, the trees green and lush around it. But it was the tatty 'For Sale' sign hanging drunkenly on the front door that had really caught their attention.

'Tempted?' Paul had asked with a laugh as they drove past, their eyes greedily drinking in the magnificent building, the winding river and the fields stretching out in the distance. Lorna hadn't replied. More than anyone, Paul knew her dream was to quit her job working in a school canteen and open her own restaurant. But no matter how they'd approached the figures, they didn't add up. Paul and Lorna simply couldn't afford it.

Clearly though the Auberge had made a lasting impression. Not long after, they'd stopped for lunch in a mountain village and had stumbled upon a small restaurant which looked nothing more than someone's house. Opting to eat outside, they'd taken one of the few available tables under the trees on a narrow stretch of garden next to a stream. They'd sat there, languid in the afternoon sun, watching the waiter, who was more like a farmer on his lunch break than a professional *serveur*, make his slow way to and from the kitchen. Paul had suddenly exclaimed, 'You could do this!'

'Do what?' Lorna asked, bemused.

'This!' Paul gestured at the tables around them. 'You could run a restaurant like this.'

Lorna followed his gaze, taking in the mixed clientele of workmen and tourists, all sitting contentedly under parasols as the waiter delivered a basket of bread here, a carafe of wine there and stopped for a chat now and then. No one was complaining about the leisurely service and the gentle buzz of conversation was accompanied by the hum of cicadas and the burble of the small stream near by.

'Yes . . .' Lorna agreed hesitantly. 'Yes I could. But how would you find work?'

'I'd be like him.' Paul nodded at the man plodding back to the kitchen. 'We'd be a team.'

Lorna laughed drily. 'You'd get bored in no time!' she said, not daring to believe he meant it.

'Maybe. Maybe not. It might give me the time I need to concentrate on designing websites.'

Recognising the earnest tone in his voice, Lorna took a moment to let it all sink in. With redundancy looming in the worsening economic climate, Paul had been trying to develop his own IT business but with a full-time job, it had been hard to allocate time to it. Becoming a part-time waiter, however, hadn't figured in his plans.

'You're really serious?' she finally asked.

'Yes.' Paul smiled slowly and leaned back in his chair. 'Yes! Having seen that Auberge for sale back there, I think I am!'

The meal had passed in a blur. Lorna had barely registered the succulent steak or the exquisite chocolate mousse and her wine had remained almost untouched. She'd been too busy estimating the cost of the ingredients, counting the number of diners and calculating possible profits. Paul had roughed out some figures on a napkin and based on his redundancy pay-off and the sale of their house, they'd worked out that it was feasible. It all depended on how much the Auberge was.

When they'd finally raised their heads they'd realised that lunch time was over and the waiter and his wife, the chef, were sitting at a small table deep in conversation with what were clearly regulars. Lorna had felt excitement run down her spine. That could be Paul and her sitting there, at ease after their work, part of a community.

'Here's to our Auberge!' she'd said, raising her neglected glass of wine.

'To our Auberge,' intoned Paul with a grin. 'We'd best call the estate agent and make sure we can afford it now!'

And so they had. They'd been astounded by the price. It was almost too good to be true. After viewing the Auberge and realising its full potential, they'd returned to the UK and immediately put their house on the market. The four months it took to sell seemed like an age. But finally, in October, with Paul's redundancy payment in the bank as well, they'd been in a position to put in an offer. To their delight, it had been accepted.

In the long days and sleepless nights that followed, it had been easy for them to imagine living in the Auberge and setting up a new life as hoteliers in the beautiful building on the river bank. Now, even though winter had barely started, the river was flowing a lot faster and the trees were bare, uncovered branches stretching towards the cold sky. It all seemed a lot bleaker. And a lot more real.

Shivering slightly, Lorna turned her back on the river and took her first proper look at the Auberge since arriving. It was far removed from the welcoming photograph she'd had on her computer screen for the past five months, windows thrown open by the estate agent, the light soft, the warmth almost tangible. Today, the stones on the north-facing rear of the Auberge looked grey and hostile, the windows closed over with peeling shutters and dead tendrils of ivy covering the walls.

It just needs a bit of TLC, Lorna told herself firmly. And before she could lose her nerve, she crossed the patio to the flight of steps leading up to the back door.

Things would be better once they got inside.

'Oh my God. What the hell have we done?'

Back out on the patio an hour later, Paul flopped on to one of the plastic chairs and put his head in his hands, feeling for the first time since they'd had their offer for the Auberge accepted in mid-October that they'd bitten off way more than they could chew. He heard Lorna come up behind him and felt her hands rest on his shoulders, giving them a soft squeeze.

It had been awful.

When they'd entered the large dining room that took up most of the ground floor, their first impression had been the smell. It wasn't damp. It was more cloying; a combination of the musty old odour of neglect and the over-sweet stench of dead mouse. In the weak winter sunlight struggling through the holes in the rotting shutters they could just about make out the thick layers of dust coating everything, the cocoons of spiders' webs draped from wall to ceiling to woodburner and the mouse shit that littered the surface of the huge French dresser.

Already feeling disheartened, they'd moved across to the kitchen door. As Lorna pushed it open and poked her head inside, something darted out over her foot and scuttled off into the shadowy corners of the big room.

Lorna shuddered, trapping a scream in her throat. 'Tell me that was just a mouse!'

'Definitely. Just a mouse,' Paul lied, carefully watching the area around his feet in case the rodent was followed by any of his even larger mates. 'Knew we should have made the bloody cat come in!'

Instinctively moving closer together for moral support, they entered the kitchen, Paul switching on his torch to combat the gloom. He swept the beam across the stainless steel counter to the right of the door, pinpointing more piles of mouse droppings and a stack of plates, the dull sheen of old grease visible on their surfaces even in the dim light of the torch.

'Environmental Health would have a fit in here,' Paul stated, staring at a mass of something furry and blue resting on a wooden board.

'What is it?' whispered Lorna.

Paul shrugged. 'Bread? Whatever it is, even the mice haven't touched it!'

Lorna shook her head in disbelief. 'You'd hope their culinary skills were better than their hygiene.'

'Hmm, don't count on it.' Paul crouched down and gestured at the rows of catering-size tins on the shelf below, picking out the labels with the torch.

Spaghetti Bolognese sauce, boeuf bourguignon sauce, coq au vin, ravioli ... there were even several huge tins of the regional dish cassoulet with its haricot beans, sausages and duck legs. So much for the famed French home cooking. It looked like it had been usurped by the tin-opener in this restaurant.

'Would we use them?' Paul asked.

Lorna bent down to get a closer look, noticing the obligatory dusting of mouse shit and a thick layer of grease. She gave a wry laugh and turned one to Paul. 'It's out of date.'

'By much?'

'Only two years ...'

'Jesus! All of them?'

'Most of them. Some are only a year out,' she added drily.

Paul whistled softly. 'The food must have been awful!'

Lorna nodded in agreement, contemplating what this meant for them as new owners and her as the chef. Fully aware of just what they were undertaking, trying to compete with the French in the culinary stakes on their home turf, she was somewhat relieved to think that the previous owners hadn't excelled at the art. Surely the locals would be overjoyed to have a restaurant that served authentic home-made food at last, using vegetables and herbs from the garden she planned to create and locally sourced ingredients.

Compared with these tins of mass-produced, processed food, Lorna was certain that her simple recipes would go down a treat. She felt a rush of adrenalin as she imagined the dishes coming out of her kitchen: pan-fried salmon steaks with fennel and leeks in a vermouth sauce; chicken breasts marinated in lemon, rosemary and thyme and of course, lots of garlic; Toulouse sausages slow cooked in cider served with sage mashed potato ... as her mind wandered, Lorna's nostrils began to twitch at the aromas her thoughts were

28

conjuring. It was only when Paul interrupted her reverie that she realised they were twitching at something else entirely.

'What on earth is that awful smell?' he asked with a grimace.

Lorna sniffed tentatively and sure enough, the general smell of decay which they'd noticed when they'd walked in had been replaced by something a lot stronger. And a lot more offensive.

They both straightened up and turned towards the furthest end of the kitchen, following the bad odour as Paul's torch picked out a grill plate covered in centimetres of baked-on black crust and a chip pan, the lid left off and a drowned lizard just visible in the murky depths of the oil. They stared down at the dead reptile for a few seconds in mute awe, Lorna racking her brains to remember if the Auberge had been this neglected when they'd visited in June. Or maybe they'd just had a bad case of rose-tinted glasses?

As they moved away from the chip pan and towards the fridge, the smell became overpowering.

'Shit! What the hell IS that?' Paul wrapped his arm over his nose in self-defence at the unbearable stench.

'I think it's this.' Lorna pulled on the handle of the huge catering fridge, opening it and then closing it again in record time as a fit of coughing took her breath. It had been enough to afford her a view of the black gunk that oozed over the shelves and the thick mould that covered the fridge from top to bottom.

'You'll get that clean in no time,' Paul offered half-heartedly. Lorna shot him a look and turned to go, having seen very little yet, at the same time, more than enough. Her dreams of producing mouth-watering meals in this kitchen suddenly seemed a long way off.

Retracing their steps across the big room, which was now

like a cosy living space compared with the chamber of horrors in the kitchen, they headed out into the hallway and towards the stairs. Paul led, his torch beam bouncing off the hunting scenes hung on every available bit of wall space as he made his way up. Hounded stags, wounded wild boar, fleeing isards, the stairway was a procession past a succession of dead or dying beasts of the forest. Then, as Paul reached the top of the stairs, he swung the light in front of him and jumped in shock.

'CHRIST!'

Instinctively rearing back from the monstrosity, he lost his balance, the torch tumbling from his hands as he grabbed wildly at the banister rail to save himself from falling down the stairs.

'What? What is it? Are you OK?' Lorna was beside him in an instant.

With a shaky laugh, Paul picked up his torch and aimed the soft yellow light on to the wall at the top of the stairs.

'SHIT!' Lorna squealed, as the glass eye of a mounted stag's head stared back at her. 'Oh my God, that's . . .'

'Awful?'

Lorna nodded, dumbstruck by the moth-eaten head with its one glass eye and broken antlers, hanging drunkenly on the wall.

'I don't remember that from last time, do you?' she asked.

Paul shook his head. 'It's not something we'd forget really, is it? Wasn't there a photo there or something?'

'Yes, you're right. It was a photo . . . an aerial photo of the Auberge.'

'Well Monsieur Loubet must have decided to take it with him and leave us this instead. Can't see he'd have much use for a stag's head on the Mediterranean!'

They laughed nervously, the sound echoing loudly in the empty corridor and making them start once more.

'Let's have a quick look at the bedrooms,' Paul suggested, trying to sound less jumpy than he was. 'I want to get up into the attic while it's still light.'

Reluctant to turn her back on the beast at the top of the stairs, Lorna sidled after him, feeling vaguely foolish but totally justified.

It didn't take long to take stock of the seven bedrooms and the laundry room lined up on either side of the corridor. Apart from quantities of garish wallpaper and woodworm-ridden wardrobes, possibly from the Napoleonic era, the only potential problem was the mattresses. When they'd visited the Auberge before, all the beds had been made up with crisp linen and colourful throws. Now they were stripped of their covers and the mattresses were showing their age in numerous stains and the odd broken spring. Several of the bed bases were also suspect, one held together with rope and another propped up on bricks where a leg had been severed.

By torchlight, Lorna added to her growing to-do list. She was starting to think she'd been somewhat optimistic bringing only one notepad. Especially as the laundry room had merited an entire page, most of the sheets too old or too stained to be put back into service and the towels more bald than fluffy.

'You ready for the attic then?' Paul asked as Lorna finished writing and stuffed the notebook back in her pocket.

'God yes. It can't be any worse than we've already seen.'

Paul swung open the attic door and promptly stood back, giving Lorna a twisted smile.

'Not so sure of that!'

Lorna followed the light from his torch as it disappeared into the dark of the stairway, but not before it had illuminated the thick mass of spiders' webs that spanned the doorway.

'Ladies before gentlemen,' Paul whispered in her ear, giving her a gentle push in the back.

'Thanks for nothing,' she muttered, brushing the dust-covered strands aside with the handle of her torch.

Together they crept up the stairs, crouched over to avoid the worst of the webs, until they were standing in the long stretch of attic, the skylights in the roof making their torches redundant at last.

'Doesn't look much of a living space right now!' Lorna commented as she swept her eyes over the rough flooring and the arching rafters covered in soot and dirt, the underneath of the slates visible above them. They'd estimated that it would be at least a year before they could start on the renovations needed to turn the huge space into living accommodation for themselves. Until then, they'd have to make do with one of the bedrooms on the floor below.

'No, but it's going to be great.' Paul walked over to the nearest skylight and stood on tiptoe to get a better view through the small pane of glass, smoky with age. 'Look! You can see the high peaks from up here,' he announced excitedly, standing back to let Lorna see and stepping straight into a puddle.

'What the . . . ?' Paul stared down at the sheet of plastic underneath the window where the water was pooling around his feet, its function suddenly becoming very apparent.

'There must be a leak,' he stated, feeling the wood around the window with a growing sense of panic. 'Here. Feel that. It's sopping wet!'

But Lorna wasn't listening. She was looking in horror at the attic floor and the countless discarded fertiliser bags strewn around in what they had thought was a haphazard jettisoning of unwanted packaging.

'Oh shit!' they cursed in unison.

*　*　*

Glad to be outside once more, Lorna gave Paul's shoulders one last squeeze and then sank into a chair beside him, not sure that she had any encouragement left to give.

'Christ. How can a property deteriorate so much in five months?'

Paul grunted, his head still buried in his hands, his eyes staring vacantly at the carpet of dead leaves beneath his chair.

'Well, at least we know the worst of it now,' Lorna continued, trying hard to sound more upbeat than she felt. 'And the leaks will hold until we take possession next month.'

After checking the slate roof, they'd identified four major ones that needed urgent attention, a more detailed inspection of the bedrooms below revealing rusty stains on the ceilings and sagging plaster. Knowing there was little they could do immediately, they'd scoured the attic looking for something more suitable than a plastic sheet to place beneath the holes but had found only long-sprung mouse traps and even more quantities of mouse shit, testimony to the ineffectiveness of the traps.

In the end the solution had been obvious. Half an hour and one full bin bag later, four hastily emptied catering tins of out-of-date Bolognese sauce stood proudly under the worst of the leaks.

'We'll turn it around you know,' Lorna said, leaning into Paul. 'It'll just take time.'

'And a fuck of a lot of money!'

Lorna looked at his bowed head and slumped shoulders.

'Do you want to pull out of the sale?' she suggested. 'It's not too late. We'd lose our deposit but maybe that's better than going through with it?'

As if sensing their change of heart, Tomate jumped up on to the arm of the plastic chair that Paul was sitting in and rubbed against him, wailing into his ear at the same time.

Paul raised his head, instinctively reaching out a hand to stroke the cat.

'I don't want to pull out. At least, I don't think I do. I don't know . . . It's just so different from when we viewed it in the summer. I mean it's the roof . . . the oil tank . . . everything! How could we not have noticed it all before?'

Lorna nodded. She knew exactly what he meant. When they'd descended from the attic, their inspection of the cellar had only served to add to their problems. Apart from two freezers left in a similar state to the fridge in the kitchen, they'd also discovered a small but potentially lethal leak in the gigantic oil tank that straddled one half of the huge space. Lethal because of its proximity to the ancient boiler. As an engineer, Paul knew that both would have to be replaced. And he had a good idea as to the cost.

'And that's not even mentioning the mouse shit!' Lorna added with a grin.

Despite himself, Paul burst out laughing, the sudden noise surprising the cat who jumped from his lap and bounded across the lawn.

'Yeah, the mouse shit. Even in the bloody till!' He shook his head in amazement and stood up, holding out his hand to Lorna.

'You're right,' he said, pulling her up into an embrace. 'We'll work it out.'

Lorna let out a sigh of relief as she buried her face in his fleece. Despite all the problems they'd encountered, she still felt sure that they were doing the right thing.

'Come on then.' Paul pulled away and reached for the bin bag on the floor, full of Bolognese sauce. 'Let's get the keys back to the estate agent before he goes home for the night.'

Together with the cat they walked around the Auberge towards the gate. Just as they reached it a battered Panda 4×4

34

came down the road opposite, turned out on to the main road heading towards the village and tooted merrily at them as it passed by, the driver waving as he went. Catching only a glimpse of curly blond hair, Paul and Lorna waved back.

'Well that's a good sign!' Paul said as he dropped the bin bag in the bin. 'We'll need the good will of the neighbours if we're going to make this place succeed!'

They got into the car and drove off towards St Girons, leaving the cat ensconced once more in the woodpile. She put her head on her paws and wondered what the remainder of the day would bring.

3

'Idiot!' Christian smacked himself firmly on the forehead. 'Stupid idiot!' He hit himself once more for good measure, the slap resounding in the tinny interior of the car.

It had been instinctive. Pure and simple. And yet so stupid. And it proved beyond doubt that he, Christian Dupuy, was not cut out for all this subterfuge.

What had he been thinking of?

Bluetongue. That's what had caused the slip-up. He'd spent the day at a Farmers' Union meeting in Foix, the departmental capital, listening to various experts talking about the recent outbreaks of the disease in the department of the Ariège and the financial impact it was having on farms all around the area. Was it any wonder then that he'd been so preoccupied that when he'd pulled out on to the main road and seen a figure at the Auberge gate, he'd waved. It was an automatic reflex for a man used to knowing all his neighbours.

So that was it then. He was now as deceitful as the mayor. There he was waving at a man while en route to a meeting that had been called to put him out of business.

Christian scratched his head as he was wont to do in times of stress. And these were stressful times. Cattle and sheep stocks across the region had been decimated by the onslaught of bluetongue in the late summer and early autumn and the impact was hitting everyone in the pocket. So far he'd been fortunate and the disease had passed by his small farm in

Picarets. But still he'd had to invest in an expensive round of vaccinations and the cost had eaten into what little profit he'd hoped to make.

And now the mayor had him playing games.

Totally disgruntled, he crunched the gears changing down as he approached the épicerie and pulled up outside rather more sharply than he'd intended. He turned off the engine and looked over towards the shop window where he made out the figures of several people inside.

That was all he needed. Véronique Estaque. He could see her leaning on the counter, the material of her skirt pulled tight, outlining her shapely frame. And he felt his palms start to sweat.

God what was wrong with him? Surely with all that was going on, his brain had more to concentrate on than the curve of Véronique Estaque's arse?

He dragged his eyes away and decided to wait a few minutes before entering the épicerie. Desperate to look anywhere but in the shop window, he glanced back along the road to the Auberge which was glowing in the late afternoon sun.

Was it right, what they were doing, he wondered, his honest soul tormented by the devious nature of the plan outlined by the mayor the night before. He'd woken in the early hours that morning, his mind racing, and had lain awake weighing up the pros and cons of the proposed action until the aged cockerel had roused him from his bed. And he'd had to concede that the mayor and Pascal had a point, even if their solution was somewhat drastic.

It was the restaurant that had swayed him. He'd dined there at least once a week and had savoured the food, devoid of the ashy, carbon aftertaste which typified the fare he was offered at home. His mouth started to water at the thought of Madame Loubet's sublime Bolognese sauce and her traditional cassoulet, the recipe for which she guarded jealously. In his humble opinion, nobody could beat her superb home cooking. Least of all someone English.

So the action they were about to undertake was necessary. Because if the restaurant failed, the commune would suffer, financially as well as gastronomically, as a sizeable proportion of the commune's income was derived from the *taxe professionnelle* that the restaurant had to pay. And being brutally honest, there was no way the restaurant would succeed with an Anglo-Saxon at the helm.

With a face set to combat the distaste he felt at the approaching meeting, Christian opened the car door.

Might as well get on with it, he thought.

'Shhhurrrelytherre'shhhgottobeshhhomeotherrrwayofrr resolvingthishhh?'

Annie Estaque paused to take breath and slurped her false teeth back into her mouth, giving Josette time to notice Christian walking dejectedly towards the shop door, his normal smiling countenance now weighed down by a frown.

'Well if there is, here's the man to think of it,' said Josette as Christian slouched in through the door.

'Think of what?' he asked, bending down to kiss Annie's leathery cheeks, creased and lined from a lifetime of farming.

'Think of some other way of sorting out the mess over the Auberge. Véronique was just giving us the gist of what was said last night and Annie doesn't think much of the mayor's plan.'

As if underlining the point, Annie snorted and then hacked into the sleeve of her cardigan.

'For goodness' sake, Maman!' Véronique sniffed in disgust, a rare blush of embarrassment staining her face as Christian bent to greet her.

38

'So?' asked Josette, as Christian planted kisses on both her cheeks.

'So what?'

'So have you got any better ideas?'

Christian leaned heavily on the counter, as much to take the weight off his feet as to avoid hitting his head on the lengths of *saucisson* suspended from the ceiling.

'It's a difficult one.'

Annie snorted again.

'Don'tseewhat'sshhhodifficult. TheAubergehasbeensh hholdandtherrre'snomorrretoit.'

Véronique nodded, in rare agreement with the woman she was normally mortified to call her mother.

'It does all seem a bit unfair, ganging up on the new owners like this. It's almost like bullying. And the mayor's proposal is extreme to say the least.'

'But you don't understand,' protested Christian, turning pink under the piercing stares of the Estaque women. 'If the restaurant fails it will really hurt the commune financially. And given the nationality of the new owners, it's highly likely to fail. Everyone knows the English can't cook!' His voice took on an incredulous tone. 'Who in their right mind is going to eat there?'

'Huh! The last one was no great shakes and yet the mayor made no move to intervene.'

Christian looked genuinely puzzled.

'What was wrong with Loubet's restaurant? The food was great!'

Annie and Véronique both broke into peals of laughter causing the fading blush on Christian's face to renew in strength. Josette smothered a grin as he turned to her for support.

'Why are you all laughing? It was a good restaurant.'

'It was shhhit!' Annie burst out, for once the combination of her broad accent, false teeth and fast pace of speech proving no impediment to comprehension. 'OldmadameLoubetkne wbuggerrrallaboutcooking!'

'But . . . but . . . I thought her cooking was really good.'

Véronique laughed again, causing Christian's face to really flare.

'Of course you did. And no wonder when you have to suffer your mother's cooking. She's the only woman I know who thinks carbon is a condiment!'

Christian raised his hands in defeat. There was no arguing with that.

'OK. You've made your point. So what do you propose?'

'I'mnotprrroposinganything.' Annie picked up her shopping bags, preparing to leave, having already said far more than was usual for her when it came to commune affairs. Though undisputedly related despite Véronique's attempts to disown her in public, Annie didn't share her daughter's passion for local politics. Far from it.

'I'moffhometofeedthedogs. Getmorrresenseoutofthem.' She hacked into her sleeve once more, enjoying seeing her daughter wince, and then left the shop.

The two remaining women turned towards Christian and started discussing the various options open to them. In the background Jacques rested against the small fridge just inside the door, a broad smile splitting his face. He couldn't hear the details of the plan. He didn't need to. As long as Serge Papon and his obnoxious sidekick didn't get everything their own way there was hope for the commune yet.

After the upheaval of the Revolution, the one thousand-plus inhabitants of the three villages of Picarets, La Rivière and Fogas had seized their chance to break away from the

40

commune of Sarrat across the river and set up their own administration. For too many generations they'd grumbled about having to cross the river in all weathers to reach the town hall. Now they had the power to decide the location of their new seat of local government and remove the inconvenience forever more. And they chose the village of Fogas.

Not for the first time Christian cursed the stupidity of his ancestors as his car struggled up the steep incline that led to the village situated on the ridge of a mountain. His forefathers and their neighbours could have chosen La Rivière for the new town hall, the logical choice at the bottom of the valley and at that time already home to a small épicerie, a bar and a boulangerie. But no. Caught up by the heady power of their achievements, they'd opted for Fogas and so made obligatory for the majority of members of the commune the arduous journey along the narrow road which twisted and turned up the mountainside.

To make matters worse, there was nothing else to be gained by taking the Fogas road. Once the village had been reached, it meandered on for a couple of kilometres and then splintered off into various side roads serving hamlets, all of them dead ends and many of them unpaved. There was no shop, no bar and even La Poste had been sensible and placed the commune post office in La Rivière. So apart from the cluster of houses which formed the village and the old communal washbasin with its continually running tap, Fogas was simply the base for the town hall.

Although, as Christian rounded the last bend and saw the silhouettes of the Pyrenees in the darkening sky, he had to admit that the views were amazing.

'At last!' he said as he pulled the car up in front of the big stone building, the weather-beaten clock on its façade an hour out as was normal in the winter. On the decision of some council long before Christian's time, it had been agreed that changing the time every spring and autumn was potentially damaging to the clock and also to the aged *cantonnier* whose job it was to scale the ladder and turn the hands backwards or forwards. The decision had not been overturned on the appointment of fat Bernard Mirouze as the new *cantonnier* several years ago, much, Christian suspected, to Bernard's relief. The man could barely climb his house stairs without needing a rest, let alone a ladder up to the roof of the town hall. Therefore, the clock remained exact for only seven months of the year. For the winter it raced ahead by an hour as though pulling the inhabitants on through the darkest of months towards the promise of spring.

Christian hauled himself out of the car, trying to ignore the ominous quantities of steam issuing from under the bonnet as he went to help Josette with the passenger door which always needed coaxing. As she took his arm and they turned towards the town hall, he noticed her hand shaking, her face wan with tension.

'You look a bit pale. It wasn't my driving was it?'

Josette managed a smile and patted his arm.

'No. I'm just nervous. I know, I know . . .' She put up a hand to stop him answering, fully aware of what his response would be. 'I know. I have every right to be here. I was voted in demo-cratically after Jacques . . .' She faltered slightly before clearing her throat and continuing.

'But it still makes me nervous. And tonight we are really going to put the cat amongst the pigeons so I'm even more anxious.'

'Jacques would be proud. That's all you have to remember.'

Josette squeezed his arm in response and they headed up the steps towards the light and noise issuing out of the huge wooden doors.

'Did you remember to lock the car?'

Christian gave her a sly look.

'I never lock it. And the keys are in the ignition. One can only hope . . .'

She laughed, throwing her head back in a manner he hadn't seen for a long time. If for nothing else, thought Christian, all this palaver was worth it just to hear Josette's laugh once more.

'If I could begin by thanking you all for turning up at such short notice . . .'

'Humph! Not all of us *have* turned up.'

Pascal Souquet's lips twitched in irritation. Just once, he thought, just once it would be great to be able to get through a council meeting without the rabble interrupting. He whipped off his reading glasses so he could glare down his aristocratic nose at the source of his annoyance.

René Piquemal. He should have known.

'Unfortunately,' Pascal continued with a forced smile, 'two of our members will be voting by proxy this evening as they are unable to attend.'

But René was not going to let him off so lightly.

'Can we have it noted for the record that I left work two hours early so I could attend?' he barked. 'And just out of interest, how long does it take from Toulouse these days? An hour and a half?'

'It does seem a bit much,' interjected Monique Sentenac. 'I've had to close up the salon early so how come they couldn't make it?'

'Maybe they shouldn't be on the council if they can't get here for the meetings?' René suggested with gusto, eager to stoke things up.

'René has a point. They don't even live here . . .'

'That's ridiculous! They have every right to be on the

Conseil Municipal. Their families have lived here for generations . . .'

And suddenly, without Pascal understanding quite how it happened, the meeting was out of his control. Voices from all over the room were chipping in while Fatima simmered quietly in the background, her glowering countenance clearly displaying her fury at her husband's inadequacies.

'. . . lived here. Past tense Bernard. Past tense. They don't live here now . . .'

'But we've talked about this before. We should be thankful they want to be on the council at all . . .'

'*Thank*ful? For what? For the grace of their presence on high days and holy days?'

'Oh for goodness' sake René . . .'

Just as the meeting was on the verge of descending into utter chaos, Serge Papon pushed his robust frame up out of his chair and held up his hand for quiet.

'Settle down! Settle down! We don't want to be here all night, those of us who *could* make it.' He waited for the council members and the handful of spectators to fall silent and then turned to his deputy with a raised eyebrow and a sarcastic smile.

'Now, Pascal, if you *think* you are capable of getting on with it?'

A ripple of mirth ran through the room at Pascal's expense causing Fatima's face to turn even darker. Pink-cheeked, Pascal replaced his glasses and started to read out the motion that was being put to an emergency vote.

'Given the circumstances of the sale of the Auberge des Deux Vallées and the potential damage that said sale will effect on the commune of Fogas, I Pascal Souquet, Deputy Mayor of Fogas, hereby propose the compulsory purchase of the Auberge by the Commune of Fogas under the decree issued by the French Republic . . .'

Slowly the buzz of whispered voices filled the room and drowned out Pascal's recitation of the relevant laws and decrees as those present heard for the first time the full extent of the mayor's plotting.

He was going to buy the Auberge.

Using an extraordinary measure which allowed any commune first refusal on a property put up for sale within its boundaries, the mayor was planning to purchase the Auberge out from under the noses of the English couple and install his brother-in-law as manager. Something that had never been done before in the long history of Fogas. And all in the name of the commune.

It was ingenious, that much Christian could acknowledge as he listened to the excited chatter and tried to gauge whether the reactions were positive or negative. The mayor had even devised an argument to get around the clause stipulating that the commune had to act within two months of the property first being put up for sale. He'd stated that Monsieur Loubet had effectively withdrawn the property from the market in October when he'd agreed to sell it to the mayor's brother-in-law. By then accepting the offer made by the British couple, the mayor declared, Loubet was putting it back on the market and hence the commune had first right of refusal. And Serge Papon was determined to exercise that right.

'Is that normal?' Josette whispered in Christian's ear.

'What?'

'Pascal has put *his* name to the proposal.'

With a jolt Christian realised that she was right. Now why on earth would the mayor have let him do that when he clearly despised the man and his naked ambition?

Sensing that the meeting was escaping his control yet again, Pascal banged his glasses-case on the table and called for order, his voice shaking as he tried to exert his authority.

45

'If we could get voting under way please? I would hate to detain you any longer, René!'

He simpered at the squat plumber who muttered something which Christian couldn't catch but doubted was complimentary. Clearly Pascal was of the same opinion as he didn't ask René to repeat his comment for the sake of the minutes. Instead, he continued with the vote.

'All those in favour, raise your hand.'

Christian held his breath.

He knew without needing to look that both Serge and Pascal would have their hands raised. As would Bernard Mirouze, who was perpetually grateful for having secured the position as *cantonnier* in the commune, some suspected by dubious means, and would do anything the mayor asked of him. But what about the absentee voters?

Of course! Christian hit the heel of his palm into his thigh. That's why the mayor had let Pascal introduce the motion. To get the support he needed.

Both of the absentee voters, Lucien Biros and Geneviève Souquet, Pascal's cousin, lived permanently in Toulouse and were part of the second-home owners' faction that had got Pascal into power. So that gave them five votes. There were eleven council members and a majority was needed to carry any vote. They only needed one more to pass the proposal and as far as the mayor was concerned, Christian was it.

Christian felt the sweat start to trickle down his spine as he began to appreciate the magnitude of what he was about to do.

He was about to make an enemy of the most powerful man in the commune.

He folded his arms and swallowed nervously.

'Those for . . .' Pascal consulted the paper in his hand as

though reading it for the first time. 'In absentia, Lucien Biros and Geneviève Souquet.'

He lifted his eyes and started going around the room. 'Of those present, Pascal Souquet, Serge Papon, Bernard Mirouze and Christian Dup . . .'

Suddenly realising that Christian's huge hands remained tucked under his armpits, his arms folded across his broad chest as though preventing his body from betraying his conscience, Pascal came to an abrupt halt.

'*Christian?*' he squeaked.

Christian shook his head slowly, glad of Josette's support as her hand gripped his knee furiously under the table.

Perplexed by this unexpected turn of events, Pascal's gaze twitched frantically between Christian and the mayor, as though spectator to an invisible game of tennis.

'So . . . votes for . . . errmmm . . . I guess that's five. And errr . . . votes against?'

Christian released his hands from their confinement and extended an arm into the air.

'Tsssssssssssssssssss.'

The sound came from the mayor like the sudden release of pressurised gases before a volcanic eruption and Christian could feel the waves of hatred radiating across the table. In voting against the proposal, rather than simply abstaining, he was making it a lot harder for the motion to be passed.

'Me too. I'm against it.'

Josette's voice, soft but clear, cut through the growing tension and released the spellbound council members who were enthralled by the battle being played out before their eyes.

'Yes. Count me out too. Sounds dodgy,' Alain Rougé, the retired policeman, added.

Five for, three against. That left Monique Sentenac, Philippe

Galy, the newest member of the council who had taken Gerard Loubet's hastily vacated seat, and René Piquemal. All three had to vote against the proposal for it to be defeated. Abstaining wouldn't help.

Christian turned his gaze to Monique Sentenac who was fiddling with her pen and, no doubt, her principles. Véronique had persuaded Christian that, having been the subject of harsh village gossip twenty years before when her now-deceased husband had found her in a passionate embrace with a clergyman, Monique would vote against the measure because of its ruthlessness. As Monique carefully placed the pen back on the table and then slowly raised her hand, Christian had to acknowledge that Véronique was a good judge of character.

A very pale Pascal added another name to the growing list and moved to the next person at the table. Philippe Galy.

Philippe had never voted before and so Christian and his accomplices had had no evidence on which to base their speculation. He'd returned to the area a year ago on inheriting his grandfather's smallholding and on the strength of his family name alone, he'd been voted on to the Conseil Municipal when the former owner of the Auberge had decided to step down. He was the one unknown.

'Philippe?' Pascal said, his breaking voice reflecting his nerves.

'Against.'

Clear. Decisive. No hesitation.

Christian felt his spine relax and his shoulders drop. They'd done it. Josette patted his leg under the table.

'And . . . er . . . René?'

René cleared his throat.

'I'm not sure.'

And just like that, the tension was back in the room. René,

normally a dead cert to vote against Pascal and his faction, was undecided. The vote now hung by the slightest of threads.

'Not sure?' asked the mayor, pouncing on this unexpected opportunity with alacrity, his voice honeyed and coaxing, betraying none of the venom that had been directed at Christian just moments before.

'What is there to be unsure about? The purchase of the Auberge will benefit the commune. After all,' he added, his acute political skills coming to the fore, 'we don't want any more outsiders moving in. It's bad enough with the second-home owners, let alone foreigners taking our businesses.'

René nodded his head in agreement, seemingly unaware that his well-known dislike of the second-home owners was being manipulated.

'Yes, I agree . . .'

'You agree?' snapped Pascal. 'You support the proposal?'

But just as the hasty fisherman jerks the line too soon, so Pascal's eagerness to land the vote had alerted his prey to his presence.

'No. I *don't* support the proposal,' René replied with delibera-tion, causing a nervous tic to start playing under Pascal's left eye. And with due cause as the mayor, the consummate fisher of men, looked ready to strangle him for his hot-headedness.

'I agree that we ought to protect our business for locals. I just don't think this is the way to do it,' René concluded.

He shrugged, hands out, palms upwards, and addressed the room.

'If there was some other way perhaps?'

Christian let the breath he had been holding escape between his clenched teeth. It was now or never.

'Well, perhaps there is another solution . . .' he said and slowly got to his feet.

★　★　★

49

'Oh my goodness. We did it. We really did it!' Josette chortled the moment the car door was closed.

Christian laughed as he pulled out of the car park on to the steep road down to La Rivière.

'Yes, we did. But there's a long way to go yet.'

'Pouff!' She dismissed his note of caution with a flick of her hand. 'We still won. And against the mayor! Wait till I tell Jacques!' she declared, her excitement contagious in the small confines of the Panda.

Christian glanced at her sideways in the darkness of the car's interior, sure that her slip-up about Jacques was caused by the heat of the moment. But she was smiling broadly, no sign of tears as she clapped her hands together in glee.

'Ha!' she grinned. 'I wouldn't like to be in Pascal's shoes this evening.'

'Because of the mayor or Fatima?'

'Both!' she exclaimed and they burst out laughing.

By the time the meeting had ended the original motion had been voted out, René finally deciding to vote against it. Instead he'd been persuaded to support Christian's proposal which had been so hastily devised in the épicerie earlier that evening.

By a margin of six votes to four, with one abstention, the Conseil Municipal had agreed to order a full inspection of the Auberge and restaurant to take place within two weeks of the completed purchase. The Auberge was bound to fail as old Loubet had not kept up with new fire and safety regulations in the last decade. And once it had failed, the mayor had the right to close the business until it was brought up to standard. All just before Christmas.

Christian was confident that this loss of income combined with the cost of the necessary repairs would force the new owners to sell, with luck to a local or at least someone French who would be able to run the restaurant profitably. And he'd been able to convince enough of the council members to get the idea passed.

'Why do you think the mayor abstained?' Josette mused, slightly calmer now.

'No idea. Who knows what he's up to? All I know is that I'm a marked man!' Christian shuddered. 'And despite all our euphoria, it still feels a bit underhand.'

'It's better than the commune giving the mayor and his cronies free run of the Auberge! And without this alternative, that's what the council would have voted for. At least this way the new owners have a chance.'

'Not much of one.'

'No,' agreed Josette. 'But at least it's a chance.'

4

'Over there . . . no, over there please . . . Careful!'

Lorna rubbed a filthy hand through her tangled hair and wondered for the umpteenth time why she hadn't taken Paul up on his suggestion to sell everything and make the move to France unencumbered. She watched as the two delivery men, who'd obviously opted to take only half their IQ allocation at birth, placed, or rather dropped, the sofa in the exact opposite corner to the one she'd indicated.

'That do yer missus?' the brighter of the two asked.

'Perfect,' she muttered.

'I don't suppose there's much chance of a good ol' British cuppa then? Seeing as we're in Froggy land and all?'

Glad of the opportunity to escape the mayhem, even momentarily, Lorna headed for the kitchen to see if she could find the camping kettle, mentally preparing herself to find that the box, clearly labelled KITCHEN, had been deposited in one of the bedrooms.

She pushed open the kitchen door and smiled. In the week since they'd moved in, Paul and Lorna had worked non-stop and now the room that had made her shiver with revulsion a month ago was unrecognisable. The stainless steel worktops gleamed, the chip pan was devoid of dead reptiles and the fridge no longer resembled Alexander Fleming's laboratory.

They'd applied similar effort to the rest of the Auberge, removing the copious amounts of mouse shit, wiping down all the surfaces and piling up unwanted items of broken furniture in the garden ready for a bonfire. The one-eyed stag's head had been first to be culled, followed by most of the macabre paintings that had lined the stairs and already the hallway seemed a brighter place.

In the attic the catering tins, which had served their purpose as impromptu buckets, had been replaced with large plastic containers, tarpaulins spread out under them as extra precaution. With severe storms forecast for the area, Paul wasn't taking any chances, especially as they wouldn't be getting any work done until after Christmas. Even after much juggling of finances, the poor rate of exchange meant they'd barely managed to set aside enough to cover the urgent repairs to the roof; and that was at the expense of replacing the central heating system. Until they had earned enough to pay for a new boiler and oil tank, Paul would just have to make emergency repairs.

It was going to be a hard year, of that they were certain. But now they were here at last, they were feeling optimistic about their chances. And at least the infestation of mice seemed to be waning. Traps baited with dark chocolate had accounted for ten deaths already, Tomate had killed a further four, leaving their dismembered carcasses on the back step, and Paul had instinctively flattened one with a shovel when it had run across the cellar floor in front of him. Given that the mouse had become two dimensional it was unfair to say that Paul had been equally traumatised but it was a close call.

Fifteen mice in less than a week. That had to be a record of some sort, mused Lorna as she pulled one of the three boxes on the floor towards her. After a fruitless rummage in the only one marked KITCHEN, and having discounted the other two, both marked BEDROOM, Lorna resorted to reusing the saucepan that had been a surrogate kettle since their arrival. Her hand hovered over the unopened box of PG Tips she'd unearthed earlier but deciding they were too precious to waste on the removal men, she turned guiltily to the box of Lipton's from the supermarket in St Girons.

'Tea, Jim, but not as we know it,' she thought as she popped tea bags in the four cups, wondering if her obsession with good tea would be the last of her cultural barricades to be breached. She stirred the obligatory three spoons of sugar into the tea for the delivery men, picked up all four cups and took a deep breath before heading back into the dining room.

Sure enough, there was a bed propped in the corner, boxes piled up blocking the door to the hall and Paul standing in the middle of it all, his hair sticking up at funny angles.

'No, over there ... over ... OK ... whatever ...'

He caught sight of Lorna giggling in the kitchen doorway and gave a very Gallic shrug as the delivery men put the TV down on the bar.

'Cup of tea, lads?' he offered.

'Smashing. And a couple of biscuits if you have them? It's hungry work this.'

Damn. Biscuits. The only packet in the kitchen had been the victim of a mouse incursion the night before and bore the evidence in countless nibble marks. Lorna briefly contemplated just breaking off the crumbled corners but couldn't bring herself to do it and so reached for her coat and purse.

'I'll just nip to the shop.'

'I'll go, love. You take a rest,' urged Paul rather eagerly, having spotted that the delivery men were settling themselves at one of the tables and gesturing for him to join them.

'Did we tell you about when we moved Rod Stewart and all the football statues he had in his garden ...' one of them began.

'No it's fine, Paul. I'll go,' Lorna quickly replied.

'You sure?' he pleaded.

'And as for his chandeliers . . .'

'Very sure!'

Lorna headed out of the door, blowing Paul a cheeky kiss and getting a grimace in return. She pulled her coat tight against the cold wind and started walking up the road to the épicerie.

It had taken them three days to find the shop. Claude, the estate agent, had assured them there was one in La Rivière but after walking through the village several times they'd failed to locate it. The post office was easy to see, tucked in around the back, opposite the Romanesque church which jutted out into the corner of the Fogas road. But not the shop.

Finally they'd seen a car pull up outside the houses on the bend where the main road took a sharp left as it traced the river back up to its source towards the Col de Port. A man had gone into the house on the right and come out with a loaf of bread. There was no sign outside. It just looked like a normal house with a front door and a window. But once inside . . .

They'd pushed open the door to be greeted by a rude farting noise from the old bell above the entranceway and as their eyes adjusted to the poor lighting they'd realised they'd entered another age.

Immediately on the right was a basket full of fresh bread, a wooden cheese cabinet on the wall filled with semi-circles of mountain cheese, several plastic panniers with fruit and vegetables of varying quality and shelves straining under the weight of bottles of wine and beer, none of which sold very well judging by the dust. There was also a bizarre map of France which appeared to show where various types of knives originated from.

On the other side of the shop were more shelves stretching to the ceiling containing everything you could ever need – and a lot more that Lorna and Paul could never envisage needing. Zips of varying lengths and colours, mostly faded, boxes of matches, shoelaces, polish, toilet paper, washing powder, tins of cassoulet and confit de canard, UHT milk, firelighters, jam, local mountain honey, chocolate bars, biscuits, washing-up liquid, fishing flies, fishing line and, of course, an upright display case of knives.

They'd discovered that butter was kept inside the fridge by the door, even though the fridge was not plugged in, and that the eggs were not inside the cartons stacked neatly on top. Just as well as the dates on the boxes were over a year old. Instead you helped yourself to a carton and filled it with non-date-stamped eggs from a nearby pile. After years of sterile supermarket shopping, Lorna had had a slight twinge of worry and immediately felt like a townie. To compensate she'd chosen six eggs and a pack of butter but hadn't been able to bring herself to buy the unrefrigerated cheese. That would take time to get accustomed to.

As they'd stood marvelling at the contents of the épicerie, they'd spotted a woman behind the counter at the back, half-hidden by the lengths of *saucisson* hanging down from the ceiling. She was watching them intently as they chose their purchases.

Petite, with greying hair in a neat bob, she looked to be in her sixties. She'd smiled sweetly at them, her eyes sparkling behind her glasses as they carried their items over to the counter. But then Paul had put the bread down on a glass display cabinet next to the till and she had speedily removed it with a frown and handed it back to him, pointedly wiping the flour off the glass as she glanced towards the front of the shop muttering. Lorna turned to see who she was looking at but there was no one there.

'Sssorry,' Paul spluttered and her smile returned. Ignoring

the till, she wrote down the price of each item on a pad yellow with age, totted up the figures with a speed that suggested her mental arithmetic skills were razor sharp and then wrote down the total and turned the pad so they could read it.

Clearly she knew they were foreigners.

As Lorna passed the money across to her the woman leaned over the counter and whispered, 'Are you the new owners?'

She'd pointed towards the Auberge as she spoke, her French clear and easy to understand.

'Yes! The new owners,' Paul confirmed in a voice which sounded loud in the still interior of the shop.

'Ssshh!' the woman hissed, looking towards a doorway next to the counter which led into an adjacent room. But it was too late.

'Josette? Who's that?' bellowed a voice from the room beyond.

The woman rolled her eyes while Paul and Lorna looked at each other, not following what was going on. Then came the noise of a chair being pushed back as someone got heavily to their feet and Lorna was sure she heard the woman say '*Merde*' under her breath.

'Josette, did you hear me?'

The voice was louder and full of authority and then there he was, filling the doorway, a barrel-chested man with short, stocky legs and arms that suggested he'd been a manual worker before he retired. His head, seemingly too large for his body, culminated in a bulging forehead and the most calculating eyes that Lorna had ever encountered.

As he'd stood there assessing them, a slow smile spread across his face and Lorna thought she could smell power emanating from him. When he moved closer, she realised it was simply his aftershave.

'Welcome! Welcome!' he boomed, his hand outstretched to Paul. 'I am the mayor. The mayor of Fogas!'

Lorna grinned now at the memory. Their official welcome to the commune had included several glasses of pastis served in the bar next door to the épicerie. Some bar! It was basically a room with a very long table stretching down the middle, covered in an ancient plastic tablecloth littered with cigarette burns and dominated by the huge fireplace on the back wall. The lady from the shop had doubled as waitress while the mayor plied them with drink and held court. He'd phoned another man to come and join them, whose French had been easier to understand than the mayor's, even if he had seemed somewhat pretentious and less welcoming.

What was his name again?

Lorna stopped to think, leaning on the wall of the bridge where the road spanned a small stream which fed into the much larger river. To her left she could see the Auberge, balancing precariously on the water's edge as the river swept around it and over the weir with a roar.

Pascal! That was it.

Lorna had formed the distinct impression that Pascal had been looking down his nose at them the whole time; Paul had been less negative but had admitted that with a nose like that, it would be hard not to.

By the time they'd staggered back out into the daylight, the sunshine stabbing their now sensitive retinas like needles, the mayor had ascertained their plans for the Auberge and given them his blessing for their venture. He'd even escorted them out, his arm around Paul in an affectionate embrace as he welcomed his 'new son' to the commune.

Suddenly remembering that she'd left Paul at the mercy of the delivery men's tales, Lorna started towards the shop. She could see a small silver car parked outside the front. It looked like the mayor's car. She quickened her step. He'd be pleased to see her.

'And this too.' Serge Papon pointed a chubby finger at a length of dried sausage as Josette cut the string that held it suspended from the ceiling before catching it deftly in her hand and adding it to the bag of groceries on the floor.

'Shame Jacques never told me where you get it from,' Serge continued, studiously checking his shopping list compiled in his wife's neat handwriting. 'He was going to, you know, before . . .'

Josette raised an eyebrow. Sometimes it was hard not to admire the man's audacity. As if Jacques would have told him, of all people, the secret of their *saucisson*. It was the very fame of the spiced sausage that had given Jacques' family the idea to open the épicerie in the first place, all those generations ago. And she for one was not going to hand over that information to Serge Papon.

Over my dead body, she thought as she added up his bill. Or even better, his!

'Bonjour!'

Josette looked up from the pad she was writing on and saw Madame Webster had entered the shop and was now being engulfed in aftershave as she was kissed by Serge.

'Bonjour Madame WebSter,' he enthused, his pronunciation of her name emphasising its foreignness. 'How are you? Well? And Monsieur WebSter?'

The poor lady smiled back warmly, completely fooled by his bonhomie.

'He . . . is . . . well,' she replied with the measured speech that seemed to reflect her conscious mastering of the language. 'Everything is here. Beds. Tables. All our things.'

'Ah! Your furniture has arrived!' Serge continued as though he hadn't already seen the huge delivery van with the British number plates parked outside the Auberge.

'Yes. Furniture. We . . . are . . . very . . . busy!'

Madame Webster waved her hands in the air and then pulled a funny face to show how stressful it all was, making Josette laugh. Noticeably Serge didn't join in. He was watching Madame Webster intently, his eyes alight with cunning.

But Madame Webster was oblivious as she busied herself getting some bread and several packets of biscuits which she placed on the counter, well away from the glass cabinet.

Josette nodded to herself. Quick learner. Not like some around here.

'For the men who deliver,' Madame Webster explained. 'With a cup of tea!'

'Ha ha ha! How very Anglo-Saxon!' Serge was actually holding his belly and pretending to laugh heartily. '*A . . . COUP . . . OF . . . TAY!!!*' he mimicked in faux-English. '*A . . . COUP . . . OF . . . TAY!*'

Madame Webster was laughing with him, clearly tickled by his crass attempts to cross the cultural divide, and Josette had to stifle a snort of derision as she handed over the change.

'OK. Thanks. Goodbye.'

'*GODBYEE!*' Serge intoned after her, warming to his linguistic conversion.

The door closed in her wake and the smile immediately dropped from Serge's face. But he didn't pick up his shopping and go. Instead he strode purposefully into the bar, stuffing his shopping list in his back pocket as he went. Josette was left alone in the épicerie, lost in her thoughts as her eyes followed Madame Webster down the road.

It was such a shame. She seemed really nice.

★ ★ ★

Jacques was sitting in the inglenook half-asleep when he sensed something. It wasn't often that he got to sleep now, just one of the many things that seemed to have changed in the last six months. So it was with some irritation that he opened his eyes and his mood was made no better by seeing Serge Papon strut into the room.

The mayor crossed the floor in a couple of strides to stand in front of the window. He stood there, looking out for a few seconds, a crafty look on his face. Then he fumbled around in his back pocket and pulled out a mobile phone, dislodging a piece of paper in the process. With a grunt, he bent down to pick it up and thrust it roughly back into his pocket.

A mobile phone.

Pouff. Jacques rolled his eyes in despair. It wasn't true about old dogs and new tricks, he thought, as Serge stabbed out a number on the phone and then held it to his ear, his concentration still fully on the figure retreating down the road towards the Auberge.

'Pascal?' Serge asked, as the call connected, his voice unusually muted. 'It's me. The mayor. Is that letter for the Auberge finished?'

Jacques leaned forward and could just about make out some squawking at the other end. Sounded like that pipsqueak Pascal all right.

'Great. Good. Now listen, I want you to include Christian Dupuy's name . . .'

Christian? What about Christian? What was the old bugger up to now? Suddenly totally awake, Jacques turned from the fire so he could hear more clearly. Funny how his deafness still plagued him after everything.

'No, it's not normal. I know . . . LISTEN . . .'

Aware his voice had risen, Serge glanced around at the

doorway of the shop to ensure he was still alone. Happy that he was, he continued in a lower tone.

'Listen . . . Just do as I say, OK! Add a sentence that names Dupuy as the instigator of the inspection . . . Yes, that's fine. And one more thing Pascal. I want it delivered by mid-afternoon today. You hear me? No later. It has to be today.'

And with that he abruptly hung up and threw the phone on the table, a chilling smile playing on his lips.

'Think you know how to play politics, Christian?' he chuck-led to himself as he settled in his favourite chair, back to the fire as always. 'Now those incomers at the Auberge will know exactly where to place the blame.'

He threw back his head and laughed, a harsh sound devoid of humour.

Drawn by the noise, Josette poked her head into the room.

'Pastis!' the mayor demanded, making the most of an opportunity as always.

Josette, Jacques thought. He had to warn Josette about the letter which was clearly going to get Christian into trouble. But how? He tried to catch her eye as she prepared the drink at the counter at the far end of the room but she wasn't having any of it. She was studiously ignoring him again. He watched helplessly as she put the drink and jug of water down in front of the mayor and then stooped down right next to Jacques to stoke the fire.

But not once did she look at him.

She left the poker back on the hearth and walked out of the room, leaving Jacques in the company of the man he despised more than any other on the planet.

'Thinks he can get one over on me . . .' Serge muttered into his drink. 'I'll make him rue the day he chose to go up against Serge Papon . . . Jumped-up cow-hand.'

Jacques felt his blood start to boil. He had to do something. Anything. He looked longingly at the glowing tip of the poker and at the fat wedge of backside sticking through the back of the chair right in front of him. But he knew it was futile. He wouldn't be able to lift the poker, let alone shove it where it needed to be shoved.

He turned back in towards the fire and sighed in complete frustration.

And the fire ruffled in front of him.

Was that a coincidence?

He breathed out again and the fire flared accordingly.

Oh my God. He had power! He could move the flames.

OK, OK. Now what could he do with it?

Jacques' eyes wandered back to Serge's bottom where it pushed against the chair, the piece of paper dangling temptingly out of his back pocket.

That would do. Oh yes! That would do.

Barely able to contain himself, Jacques inched in towards the fire, the flames not bothering him in the least. He lined himself up opposite his target and took the biggest breath he had ever taken in his life. Or his death.

Then he blew.

Whooooofffffffffffffffffffffffffffffff.

The air exploded from his lips and scooped up a tongue of fire, dancing it across the hearth and landing it directly on to the piece of paper. A flicker. A splutter. And then the paper burst into flames.

Jacques sat back and started laughing so hard he thought he was going to die. Again.

It was the smell that first caught Josette's attention. She'd been deliberately avoiding the bar, not having the patience to tolerate any more of the mayor this morning nor the strength to put up with Jacques. Some days his presence just made her too sad.

63

But now, as she arranged the new delivery of bread, she could smell something odd coming from the room next door. It was like when Papa used to pour scalding water over a butchered pig: a mixture of charred bacon and burnt flesh.

She raised her nose and sniffed again. Definitely something burning.

'JOSEEEEEEEEEEEETTE!'

At the roar of distress from the bar, she dropped the last of the loaves and ran. She crossed the threshold and found herself in the middle of a scene worthy of Molière.

Jacques was rolling about on the floor in fits of silent laughter while the mayor was scampering around the table, screaming and slapping ineffectually at his backside. Which was on fire.

'Josette! Josette! Help!' Serge yelped as the flames got hotter and hotter and bigger and bigger.

Instinctively, Josette reached out and grabbed the water jug off the table with one hand, thrust the mayor face-down on to the table with the other and then poured the water liberally over his prostrate bottom.

The flames hissed and spat before they disappeared into wreaths of smoke leaving the mayor's flambéed rear end exposed.

Josette released her grip on him and stood back, not sure it was appropriate to be standing that close to the mayor when his bottom was still smoking. It didn't look too bad. Just a bit of smouldering flesh poking through the ragged ends of his burnt trouser pocket.

'I'll get some cream . . .' she began.

But the mayor had recovered his dignity and was in no mood to endure further embarrassments.

'Don't bother. It's fine,' he barked gruffly as he gingerly inspected the damage with his fingertips before pulling what was left of his wallet out of his back pocket.

So that explained the pig smell, thought Josette as she watched him chuck the charred lump of leather on the table. Maybe.

'How on earth . . . ?'

'Your fire!' muttered the mayor. 'It should have a fireguard by rights. Dangerous, that's what it is.'

Josette looked at the fire, burning quietly in the fireplace. And then she looked at Jacques sitting innocently next to it. He gave her a smile worthy of an angel but she wasn't fooled for a minute.

'Well perhaps you shouldn't sit so close to it,' she retorted, suddenly wanting the mayor and the smell he was giving off out of the bar, for his own safety. 'Now are you sure you don't want me to put some cream on it?'

The mayor glared at her, picked up his mobile and the ruins of his wallet and went into the shop to get his shopping. He left without another word, walking just like John Wayne as he made his way to his car. It was only when he opened the car door and gingerly sat down, a grimace flickering across his face, that Josette started laughing.

And laughing and laughing and laughing.

She paused to draw breath, holding her ribs, and Jacques was there beside her laughing too. It was just like the old times. She hadn't felt this good in ages.

5

In the late afternoon, when the commune school bus pulled into the lay-by opposite the Auberge, Chloé's heart soared. It was the same every day of the miserable school week. It wasn't that she was thick or couldn't handle the academic demands placed on her in the small school perched on the hillside across the river in Sarrat. Far from it. Much to the chagrin of Madame Soum, despite her penchant for staring out of the window and daydreaming incessantly, Chloé was consistently top of the class.

No it wasn't that she couldn't cope. It was simply that she wasn't built to be constrained inside four walls for prolonged periods of time.

The mornings always began with good intentions, Chloé determined to concentrate and elicit at least a smile from hatchet-faced Madame Soum. But somehow as the morning wore on and the pace of the lessons began to drag, Chloé would find her eyes drawn beyond the windows to the high mountains that marked the border with Spain. On a clear day they would stand majestic, often snow-covered, sharp outlines against the blue sky. On cloudy days they would be just about discernible, faint shadows hinting at their existence. And on the rare days when they weren't visible at all, Chloé would content herself with pretending that the grey cover of the sky was the canvas of the big top and in her mind she would be twisting and tumbling amongst the clouds, high above the valleys, while her body was tied to a desk and a classroom that was just too small to contain her.

Inevitably she would be brought back to earth and the sombre walls around her by a sharp rap of a ruler on her desk and an exasperated tut-tut from the teacher. And so Chloé would bury her head in her books and begin counting down the agonising hours to the end of the day.

Now, after a particularly dull day during which Chloé had accrued a record-breaking seven raps of the ruler, twelve tut-tuts and a verbal admonishment, she was finally free. Although she did have extra homework to do because she'd tried to explain that her inattention wasn't a reflection on Madame Soum's abilities as a teacher, but was instead related to the extraordinary beauty of Mont Valier in the winter sun. For some reason that had made Madame Soum even angrier.

Chloé shrugged off the memory and jumped off the bus behind the Rogalle twins and Gerard Lourde, feeling a flicker of pity for the handful of students who still had to endure the route up to Fogas before their day was finally over. She turned to wave goodbye to them and noticed a very large truck parked outside the Auberge. As she watched, its engines rumbled into life and it began to pull away, down the valley towards St Girons.

The truck seemed to have been the focus of attention for Maman too as she stood chatting to their neighbour, Annie Estaque. Spotting Chloé running towards them, Annie broke off the conversation to give her a kiss, her skin rough and dry against Chloé's cheek. Even though she adored Annie, Chloé tried not to breathe as she was enveloped in the ritual embrace as Annie always smelled of cows – and not the milky part either.

'Andhowarrrrrreyoulittleone?Wassschoolasssshdrrrrre adfulassssheverrrr?'

Chloé grimaced and nodded her head.

'I got extra homework!'

'Again?' asked Stephanie with a sharp tone. 'Were you daydreaming? You know we've talked about this.'

Chloé shuffled her feet and stared at the ground.

Annie snorted and put a wizened hand on Chloé's head, stroking the mass of black curls.

'NeverrrrryoumindChloé,' she cackled. 'Shhhe'sanoldb atthatMadameSoum!'

'Annie! Don't encourage her!' But Chloé could see that Maman was fighting a smile. 'Come on then, let's pop into the Auberge and then it's home and homework for you, missy.'

As she bent down and picked up the school bag Chloé had thrown on the ground, instinctively jettisoning the remnants of the school day, Stephanie gestured at the two bulging shopping bags at Annie's feet.

'Are you sure I can't take those up the hill for you, Annie?' she enquired.

Unable to drive and unwilling to learn, Annie made weekly trips to the épicerie for the bulk of her shopping and relied on mobile shops for the rest. But she was fiercely independent when it came to getting her groceries home so her reply was no surprise.

'Nothankyou.Hasn'tkilledmeyetanddon'texpectitwill.'

'If you're sure . . .'

'I'msurrrre.Butletmeknowhowthingshhhareovertherrrre.'

She gave a curt nod in the direction of the Auberge, gave Chloé's head one last pat like a favoured dog and then picked up her shopping and started her slow walk home up the hill to her small farm at Picarets.

'How do I look?' Stephanie asked Chloé as soon as Annie was out of earshot.

Chloé took in Maman's appearance for the first time.

Instead of her usual attire which included oversized jumpers and swirling, multi-hued skirts, she was wearing her best jeans, a white shirt and a smart jacket. And unless Chloé was mistaken, the jeans and the shirt had been ironed! Her hair had been tamed as much as possible, the red curls constrained in a ponytail, and her huge hoop earrings had been replaced with conservative gold studs, only two in each ear.

Chloé wasn't sure how to describe it.

'You look . . . tidy?'

'Like a waitress?'

'Yessss . . . I suppose. Why?'

Stephanie gestured towards the Auberge.

'No! Maman, you can't! You know what happened last time.'

Stephanie started walking and Chloé realised she was serious.

'But you said, Maman. You said,' she panted as she dashed after her mother, trying to argue her point and keep up with the longer stride. 'After Monsieur Loubet sacked you, you said no more waitressing. You hated it!'

Stephanie stopped suddenly and turned towards her daughter whose features were strained with a level of concern normally reserved for adults. She placed her hands either side of Chloé's face and stroked her cheeks gently.

'I have to, love. We need the money.'

'But I could quit school and work . . .'

Stephanie laughed softly. 'You're nine, Chloé. Nice try but you have to go to school. Now come on,' she said as she tilted Chloé's downturned face up to hers. 'It won't be that bad. And they seem to be really nice people.'

'They won't be that nice . . . not if you lose your temper again.'

'It was a one off,' Stephanie retorted. 'He shouldn't have

69

pinched my bottom! Especially not when I was carrying a plate of cassoulet.'

Chloé giggled despite her worries, delighted by the idea of the lecherous customer and the look of surprise on his face when the waitress tipped the plate of beans and sausages on his head.

'And besides, I can't have been that out of line,' concluded Stephanie with a laugh. 'His wife left me a huge tip!' She winked at her daughter, linked their arms and together they crossed the road towards the Auberge.

'God am I glad to see the back of them!' Paul announced as he closed the front door on the departing removals van.

Lorna didn't reply. She was standing in the middle of the huge dining room, surrounded by boxes, looking completely exhausted.

'Where do we start?' she asked in a small voice. 'We're supposed to be opening in just over a week's time!'

'We start with a cup of tea and then we open the post. The rest can wait.' Paul slipped an arm around her shoulders and guided her towards the only table that was still visible, the rest submerged beneath sofa cushions, computer equipment, duvets, pillows and of course, boxes and boxes and boxes.

Lorna collapsed gratefully on to a chair and reached for the pile of letters strewn on top of Paul's laptop. By the time Paul returned with the tea the cat was chasing a balled-up envelope around the room while Lorna had already opened three cards from friends wishing them well in their new venture, an electricity bill for Monsieur Loubet which he'd sneakily forgotten to pay and a catalogue full of restaurant furniture. But it was the last item she'd opened that held her attention, her forehead creased in concentration.

Lacking a stamp, the letter had seemed innocuous but one

of the sheets of paper inside carried the insignia of the town hall.

'What's that?' Paul asked as he sat down next to her.

'I'm not sure, but it looks official.' She placed the first page on the table so they could both see it. 'It's something about . . . a visit of some sort?'

Paul skimmed the letter but apart from picking out what looked like a date and a time, and a few names, he was none the wiser.

'Babel Fish!' he declared, pulling his laptop towards him and starting to type in the French text. He hit the button to translate and they both leaned in closer to the screen:

> *Mister*
>
> *I have the esteemed honour to inform you, proprietor of Inn of the Two Valleys, that the Group of Visit of the Commission of Safety will proceed to the visit of safety controls at your establishment on* **15 December** *at* **10h00**.
>
> *The visit is to be carried out on the request of Mister the Deputy Mayor* **Christian Dupuy** *of the commune and the reason for the request being the changing of owner.*
>
> *The person in charge, convened by Mister the Deputy Mayor* **Christian Dupuy** *of the commune, will take all the necessary measures to allow the control of his establishment and in particular of technical installations.*
>
> *You will find a copy herewith of the letter from Departmental Service Set Fire To and Help of Ariège.*
>
> *We ask you to believe dear Sir in the assurance of our devoted feelings*
>
> *Mister the Mayor of Fogas*

'Well that makes it a *lot* clearer,' Paul said with a touch of sarcasm as they reread the dodgy translation. 'What on earth is a *visit of safety controls*?'

'I don't know but it involves a lot of people!' Lorna showed him the second page which basically reiterated the first but with an additional list of names at the bottom, all prefaced by a title.

'Does that say *police*?'

'I think so.'

'The *police* are coming?' Paul's voice rose to a squeak. 'Don't they have guns in France?'

'The police, the mayor, someone from the Department Service Set Fire to and Help of Ariège, someone from the Veterinary Department and someone else. I don't know what the letters DDE stand for.'

Paul's shoulders slumped and he rubbed a hand over his weary face.

'So a policeman, a fireman, the mayor, an unknown and a vet! That's a hell of a visit. We could do with a bit of help understanding this.'

'Yes but who?' Lorna threw the letter back on the table and felt the beginning of a migraine flicker behind her left eye.

'Bonjour! 'Ello! Am I disturbing you? I bring cake!'

Like an angel sent from above, Stephanie stood at the back door, a plate in her hands and Chloé at her elbow.

'Stephanie!' exclaimed Lorna. 'Just the person!'

'So . . . zat is it.' Stephanie leaned back from the table and shrugged. 'You 'ave an inspection the Monday next.' She pulled the band from her hair, curls instantly exploding from their confinement, and started to massage her scalp. God but speaking English was hard work. All those 'ing' endings and the weird pronunciation that sounded like Annie Estaque hacking her guts up.

'An inspection. On Monday. And it's Friday today!' Paul shook his head in disbelief. 'It seems like awfully short notice.'

'And we still don't know what they're going to inspect,' added Lorna.

'Per'aps it is 'ow you said. Routine?'

'Maybe. It just seems . . . I don't know, a bit more serious. And who is this guy anyway? This Monsieur Dupuy?'

Stephanie looked at the name written in bold and felt her chest tighten as it had when she'd first read the letter a few minutes ago. She shrugged again, hoping to give off an air of nonchalance that she wasn't feeling.

'Christian? 'E is just an *adjoint*, a, 'ow you say, deputy?'

'But why has he demanded the inspection?'

'I don't know.' It was the only answer Stephanie could give. She had no idea why an inspection had been called. In all her time working at the Auberge she'd never heard old Loubet refer to any official visits so she couldn't help thinking that it was going to be more than just routine.

But what was even more perplexing was Christian's role. The letter clearly named him as the instigator of the inspection and that worried Stephanie. A lot. Something wasn't right. But until she knew more, she wasn't about to share those concerns.

'Maybe Stephanie is spot on, Lorna. Maybe it is just routine and we have nothing to worry about.'

'Hmmm.' Even to Stephanie's non-English ears, Lorna didn't sound convinced. 'It would have been nice if he could have popped in with the letter himself and explained it. I'd like to have met the man before he started throwing his weight around. And he could have chosen a better time!' She waved her hand at the chaos of belongings surrounding them. 'It'll take us all weekend just to get this lot cleared away, never mind prepare for an inspection.'

Stephanie couldn't follow everything that was being said but she got the gist and had to bite hard on her tongue to stop herself leaping to Christian's defence.

'Well, it's too late now to do anything. The town hall will be closed. But,' Paul said, turning to the coffee machine gently hissing behind the bar, 'seeing as we have cake, anyone fancy a coffee? If I can get the machine to work that is.' He tugged at the filter to release it, filled it with the freshly ground coffee and then twisted it back on to the machine.

'Fingers crossed,' he muttered as he pressed the espresso button. Nothing happened. 'Bloody machine.'

'You need a slap!' advised Stephanie.

'Sorry?'

'A slap. You need a slap. Just there.' She leaned across the bar and Paul jerked backwards, not sure of her intentions. But she ignored him and instead gave the coffee machine a resounding thump on its side. It gurgled and bubbled and then dark coffee started streaming into the cup.

'Oh, I see. A slap. On the machine. Of course. What else?' Paul tried to ignore Lorna who was giggling as she headed into the kitchen to get plates and a knife. 'How did you know that, Stephanie?'

'I use to work 'ere.'

'You worked here? For Monsieur Loubet?'

Stephanie nodded and then decided the time might be right to make her pitch.

'To be 'onest, zat's why I am 'ere. I 'ave my CV. Per'aps you will need a waitress?' She handed over the page of A4 which had taken her an age to produce on Christian's computer. She really wasn't the technological type. And now she felt anxious as she watched Paul skim down the meagre page, Lorna reading it over his shoulder. It was amazing how trite a life seemed when it was reduced to mere work.

Stephanie stared out of the window, glad to see Chloé bounding up the back steps with Tomate hot on her heels. The silence in the room was getting hard to bear.

'You've done a lot of different things,' Lorna remarked as Chloé and the cat came in.

Knowing this was about the point where her interviews always went wrong, Stephanie started twisting her hair band nervously.

'Grape-picking, cheese-making, teaching yoga, singing in a band. Wow.' Lorna looked over with a genuine smile. 'You've had an interesting life!'

'Yeah!' enthused Paul. 'Fascinating! But what made you quit the Auberge? You were here for what, two years in all?'

Quick as lightning a lie popped into Stephanie's head. And then she looked down at Chloé who was resting lightly against her side, her face turned up, watching her mother.

She just couldn't do it. Even in a language her daughter wouldn't understand.

'Well . . .' she began. 'I was put at ze door.'

'Put at the door?' queried Paul.

'I think she means she got the sack.'

'You got the SACK? How?'

'Zere was a customer who tweaked my bottom. So I showed 'im I wasn't 'appy.'

'Good for you,' retorted Lorna. 'What did you do?'

Stephanie took a deep breath and ploughed on with the truth. 'I put a plate of cassoulet on 'is 'ead!'

Lorna let out a shriek of laughter, startling both mother and daughter, while Paul was just grinning from ear to ear.

'Excellent!' he pronounced. 'That's brilliant.'

'It's not bad?' Stephanie enquired, a bit perplexed.

Paul shook his head and glanced at Lorna, who was wiping away tears of mirth.

'I think she's exactly what we need? Don't you think?'

'Definitely. Can you start after Christmas?'

Stephanie was dumbfounded. It had been that simple. She was going to get a job. And with lovely employers, not old goat Loubet who, if not doing her on her wages, was always trying to do her in the laundry. OK, these English might be slightly mad. Employing her for starters. But they were good people.

'Yes,' she finally squeaked and then quickly gave an outburst of French for Chloé's benefit.

Chloé's eyes widened.

'*You got a job? And you TOLD them about the cassoulet?*'

'*Yep.*'

Chloé looked at the couple behind the bar who were busy making coffee and cutting up the cake. Amazing. They actually wanted to employ Maman. But then, they hadn't tried the spice cake yet. And knowing Maman's cooking, it was bound to be interesting.

'So let's get this straight,' Lorna began as they all sat down at the table. 'Monsieur Loubet sacked you because you upset a customer.'

'No, not because of zat. Monsieur Loubet, 'e doesn't care about ze customer.'

Paul frowned. 'Well, why then?'

'Why? Because I wasted ze cassoulet, of course!'

Paul and Lorna burst out laughing again while Stephanie smiled indulgently at them. It was true what they said about *les Anglais* after all. They just didn't understand about the French and their food.

'*Ugh Maman! That's disgusting!*' Chloé spat the lump of cake back on to her plate and reached for her Orangina, gulping it down to wash away the taste.

'*What on earth is the matter?*' Stephanie bit into her own slice of cake just in time to see Lorna and Paul start to silently choke on theirs. She chewed it and it was OK. Light, moist, with a slight hint of . . . CHILLI.

'Aghhhh . . .' She grabbed her coffee and drank noisily, Paul and Lorna doing the same.

'I am so sorry,' she finally managed when her tongue had stopped burning. 'I think I 'ave made an error! I 'ave used ze chilli not ze cinnamon.'

'Now that,' said Paul, pushing his plate and his remaining cake away from him, 'is what I call a spice cake!'

Stephanie grinned. 'But you are not wanting me to work in ze kitchen, no?'

'No!' Paul and Lorna replied in unison as all four of them broke into laughter once more.

'Thanks for coming round,' Lorna said as she opened the door half an hour later for Stephanie and her daughter. 'You've been a great help.'

'It was nothing. Really.'

'And thanks for the cake,' added Paul with quintessential politeness, a smile dancing in his eyes.

'Any time! Let me know what 'appens Monday next.'

'We will,' Paul promised. 'But it probably is just routine. Nothing to worry about.'

'And anyway,' added Lorna, 'what's the worst that could happen? There's no way the mayor will allow us to be shut down no matter what this Monsieur Dupuy is up to. He's too nice.'

Stephanie turned away. She could feel that tension in her chest again. Something was about to go badly wrong, she could sense it. And as for Lorna's faith in the mayor, knowing him of old, Stephanie didn't share it.

With an effort she hoped didn't show, she smiled and turned back to face them.

'I'm sure you are right Lorna,' she said as she kissed first Lorna and then Paul on each cheek. She walked away with Chloé clutching her hand, her heart heavy despite her new job. She had a strange feeling of empathy with Judas Iscariot.

6

Monday 15 December arrived with the thickest frost of the winter so far, leaving the trees white and brittle against the sharpness of the blue sky. Up in Fogas the mountains sparkled in the morning sunshine, their size magnified in the clear air.

But whatever beauty the frost bestowed on the village, it also brought drawbacks. Outside the town hall, the road was treacherous despite the gritting of the night before, a thin patina of ice turning the steep incline into a death trap and making the road impassable to all but the very foolhardy.

Serge Papon pulled back the fussy net curtains that his wife insisted on hanging at every window and looked out on the road. Despite the early hour he could see Pascal Souquet inching up the hill towards the office, his ambition driving him to work even though his handmade Italian leather shoes provided no grip on the slippery surface.

A twisted smile of anticipation briefly flickered across Serge's fleshy features as he followed the progress of his deputy mayor, arms flailing and legs faltering as he tried to keep his balance. With one final lunge, he made it to the gate of the town hall, grabbing on to the stone pillars and hauling himself into the car park relatively unscathed.

'Prat!' Serge let the curtain fall with a twinge of disappointment. Seeing Pascal fall flat on his arse would have been a brilliant start to what was going to be a momentous day in the history of Fogas.

Hearing a muted cough from the room above, Serge moved away from the window towards the kitchen and started making a cup of herbal tea. He pulled a face at the smell as he placed the cup on a tray next to a plate of croissants and tried not to notice that the croissants were misshapen and stodgy.

He grunted in annoyance.

Why didn't Fogas have a bakery? The thriving boulangerie of his youth located next to the épicerie in La Rivière had closed down in the early sixties along with the petrol station and the butcher's. And now the commune had to rely on the bread delivered to the épicerie at midday from the bakery up towards the Col de Port. No fresh croissants for breakfast. No *chausson pomme*. Instead, they had to content themselves with supermarket, mass-produced rubbish that was barely fit to feed pigs.

With great control, Serge suppressed his irritation. He added a small vase filled with garden pansies to the tray, picked up the lot and gingerly began the walk upstairs to the bedroom, his twisted hands not as stable as they used to be. He crossed the room, trying to avoid the worst of the squeaking floorboards, and placed the tray on the small table next to the bed.

Glancing down at the huddled mass of bedclothes, he could barely see his wife's face, pinched and grey in the shaft of sunlight filtering through the half-open shutters. Careful not to wake her, Serge reached out and gently smoothed back a strand of hair that was lying across her eyes.

She'd had another disturbed night. It seemed to be a recurring thing, almost as though the diagnosis earlier that month had unleashed the full force of the disease.

Serge turned from the bed and from the thoughts that threatened to suffocate him. They'd cope. They always did. And right now he had work to do.

In Picarets the frost was just as hard. Stephanie stood at the kitchen window looking out at the large back garden which she was secretly hoping was the beginning of an organic garden centre. The polytunnel was etched with white lines like a multitude of cracks and the manure on the rhubarb was now a solid lump of ice. She clutched the steaming mug of coffee in her hands and wondered if the harsh weather would have spared some of the less hardy plants that she was bringing on.

Two more years and she would be ready to open. Until then she needed the job at the Auberge to stay afloat so today's inspection could have a huge impact on her plans. Annoyingly, she wasn't going to be around to hear how it went.

A frantic phone call on Saturday from the yoga centre in Toulouse that she occasionally worked for had led to her agreeing to teach a five-day course starting today, standing in for someone who'd succumbed to the flu. She'd debated whether to accept the offer but she desperately needed the cash. Plus, if things went badly at the Auberge today, she might be glad of any future work the yoga centre could offer her.

Stephanie watched as a robin landed on the bird table in the garden, skidding slightly on the icy surface. It picked futilely at the frozen seeds and the solid lumps of bread and she felt its frustration.

That was how she felt about this mess at the Auberge. Frustrated; and still confused as to Christian's part in it all. He'd been away all weekend, having taken his mother to visit his sister over in Perpignan, so Stephanie hadn't had a chance to talk to him.

Maybe she was worrying over nothing. After all, it wasn't like Christian to be involved in something underhand. Even so, some sort of instinct to protect him had prevented her from telling Annie about his name being in the official letter when she'd dropped in on Friday night. She didn't think Annie would approve of that and he'd been nothing but good to herself and Chloé since they'd arrived in the area.

Realising he was wasting his time, the robin gave up trying to get his breakfast and flew off. Stephanie followed his flight and then turned from the window and hollered up the stairs for Chloé to hurry up, suddenly fired by a desire to get the day under way. There was nothing more she could do about the Auberge until she got back anyway.

She gave her mug a quick rinse and left it on the draining board, double-checked to make sure she had everything she needed for the week and then called Chloé again. The response was a barrage of heavy footfalls as Chloé tore down the stairs, school bag trailing from one hand while she tried to tie back her hair with the other.

For someone who spent so long daydreaming about being a trapeze artist, she was awfully heavy on her feet, mused Stephanie as she reached for her car keys and ushered Chloé out of the door ahead of her.

By the time Stephanie's van trundled past Annie Estaque's farmhouse, Annie had already milked the cows and left the milk-container out on the road for Christian to drop down to the lay-by. Not that milking took very long now with the small herd she had. But God it was cold on a morning like this, fingers sticking to the metal of the milking machine, breath collecting in clouds in front of her, hers and the cows'.

She chucked the scraps from last night's meal in two bowls and opened up the back door where her two Pyrenean sheepdogs were waiting patiently for their breakfast in the yard. She put the bowls on the ground and patted the dogs fondly, her mind elsewhere as she followed the progress of the blue van as it twisted and turned down the valley.

After Stephanie had called in Friday night with the news from the Auberge, Annie had made up her mind to do something she'd stopped doing a long time ago. To get involved. For the last thirty-five years she'd kept her head down and just got on with running the family farm, shunning the summer fêtes, the weekly market in St Girons, anywhere that crowds of her neighbours might gather and gossip. Because thirty-five years ago, she'd been the subject of that gossip. She knew well what it was like to have people whispering behind your back or, even worse, in front of you.

But now she'd decided that she would help the new people at the Auberge in any way she could. She knew nothing whatsoever about them but what was happening to them was wrong. And that bastard Papon was behind it. That alone was enough to galvanise Annie into action. That and the fact that Stephanie and Chloé were going to be directly affected whatever the outcome of today's inspection.

The van disappeared around a bend and Annie walked purposefully back into the house, hacking into her sleeve as she went. She smiled as she imagined Véronique chastising her for being vulgar. What Véronique didn't understand was that Annie had deliberately cultivated this coarse exterior years before as a deterrent to anyone tempted to get close. Now it was purely habit.

Upstairs in her bedroom Annie changed out of her tatty old cardigan that she used for milking, choosing instead to wear a fleece sweater that Véronique had given her last Christmas and which she'd never worn. She swapped her cow-stained trousers for a clean pair of cords and then pulled her thick winter coat out of the wardrobe and gave it a quick brush. She got a rag from the kitchen and cleaned the worst of the farm muck off her boots and placed them by the back door. Then she laid a fire in preparation for her return.

Finally, satisfied that she was ready to go, Annie sat down at the large wooden table that dominated the kitchen, pitted and scarred through generations of use by the Estaque family, and started to make a shopping list. She didn't need a lot. Just a few things for Chloé who would be staying for four nights, something Annie was really looking forward to.

She finished her list and checked the time. It was too early to head off right now. The inspection wasn't until ten o'clock. If she timed it right, she could be in the shop while it was going on and be passing the Auberge just as it finished. And then she would decide on her next step.

She sat there watching the ancient long-case clock in the corner tick away the minutes, her mind drifting back to when things had been different, before she'd got pregnant with Véronique. Automatically her hands clenched in defiance.

This commune had made her life miserable simply because she'd made one mistake. She was damned if she was going to stand by and let them do it to someone else.

Down in the valley, La Rivière was still shrouded in mist, the sun a vague promise behind a dense veil of vapour. Frost had settled on everything, outlining every branch with thick white crystals, scratching patterns across the windows and rendering the river indistinct through the swirling clouds of moisture rising off its surface.

Paul turned on the coffee machine, giving it a pre-emptive thump on the side for good measure, and unlocked the front door. Across the road he could see Stephanie's old blue van gingerly making its way down from Picarets, the rear end fish-tailing slightly as she turned on to the main road.

Black ice. That might hold up their visitors a bit, he thought.

'Cup of tea?'

Lorna had sneaked up behind him and wrapped her arms around his chest, her head nestled between his shoulder blades. He turned within her embrace and kissed the top of her head.

'That'd be lovely. Did you sleep OK?'

She gave him a wry glance, one look at the black shadows smudging her eyes enough of an answer.

'Me neither. I'll be glad when this inspection is over.'

'So will I,' agreed Lorna, hugging him fiercely. 'Then we can just get on with running the Auberge.'

As it turned out, the only person who seemed to be adversely affected by the difficult driving conditions was the mayor. At least that was the only reason Paul could think of for his tardy appearance.

By ten thirty, Paul and Lorna were starting to flag, having spent half an hour doing their best to entertain Major Gaillard of the Fire Department, Monsieur Chevalier of the Veterinary Department, Monsieur Peloffi from the mysterious DDE and two policemen whose names Paul had missed as he'd been too busy staring at their guns. Although he had managed to use the time to clarify why the inspection party included a vet which had been puzzling him all weekend. Monsieur Chevalier had happily explained that of course his remit not only covered animal welfare but also food hygiene. Paul was still trying to make sense of that when the front door finally swung open.

'Good morning! Good morning to all!' At last the mayor breezed into the Auberge, no apologies for not being on time, his arms out ready to greet Lorna. His presence immediately electrified the room and where there'd been muted conversations between the assembled men over their espressos, now there was raucous noise as they all vied to acknowledge him.

Once released from his pungent embrace, Lorna watched the mayor circulate, backslapping and handshaking, clearly revelling in the inherent power of his position. When he'd greeted everyone and there was a general move to begin, she took her chance to ask him where Deputy Mayor Dupuy was.

'Ah, yes. Monsieur Dupuy.' The mayor turned to Lorna with an apologetic smile. 'Unfortunately Madame WebSter, he is too busy today to attend.'

'Too busy? But he . . . calls . . . this inspection,' Lorna replied, getting annoyed that the very man who'd imposed this disruption on them wasn't even going to show his face. She gestured at the letter with the deputy's name highlighted in bold. 'He must being here, no?'

The mayor simply patted her hand. 'Don't worry about it,' he said and abruptly turned to Major Gaillard. 'Shall we start?'

He walked away, leaving Lorna feeling sure, language barrier or not, that she'd just been condescended to from a great height. She watched the group of men head into the kitchen, sensing that the majority of them wouldn't notice if she, a mere woman, didn't join them at all.

Sod that! She picked up her notebook and followed them. It helped her resolve that Paul was gesturing frantically for her to catch up, looking terrified at the prospect that she might leave him to it.

Once in the kitchen, Monsieur Chevalier took control. Under his direction, cupboards were opened, cleaning products examined, the chip pan was checked for oil quality and the temperatures of the fridges and freezers were recorded, Monsieur Chevalier making copious notes on a clipboard all the time. While the group prodded and poked and peered and probed, Lorna and Paul stood to one side feeling like their very lives were being dissected.

'God it's a bit full on!' whispered Paul as Monsieur Chevalier held the oil sample up to the light and then wrote something down, the Mayor watching over his shoulder like a hawk, his face impassive.

'And what are *they* looking for?' Lorna nodded her head in the direction of the two policemen who were having a heated discussion about her bread-maker, one of them lifting out the bread pan to peer at the element within. Paul followed her glance and a look of bemusement crossed his face.

'God knows,' he whispered. 'But I'm not about to tell them to stop. They have guns you know!'

Lorna tried in vain to smother a giggle but the policemen heard the sound and looked up, the younger one blushing slightly at their scrutiny. He hastily reassembled the appliance and gave a nonchalant shrug of the shoulders.

'It's for my wife,' he offered. 'She wants one and I was wondering if the bread was any good?'

'Pah!' interjected his colleague, not waiting for Lorna or Paul to respond. 'How can it be as good as fresh bread from the bakery? Newfangled American rubbish!'

'But it's more convenient . . .'

'Convenient? How convenient will it be when the bakery closes down?'

'We don't buy our bread at the bakery. We use the supermarket.'

'The *SUPERMARKET*? You buy that crap? That's the trouble with you youngsters . . .'

The argument resumed with even more intensity, Paul and Lorna only following bits and pieces but mesmerised by the gestures, the raised voices and the passion. Just as Paul was convinced that the two men were going to draw their guns to settle the matter, Monsieur Chevalier indicated that he was finished and everyone moved back to the big room, the argument and the bread-maker instantly forgotten.

After the kitchen, the group worked methodically through the rest of the Auberge from top to bottom. Fire extinguishers were taken off the walls and checked, the rooms and occupancy numbers noted, the fire alarm tested and the electrics given a superficial examination. All the while Lorna couldn't help suspecting that some of the men had come along simply out of curiosity as it seemed to be Major Gaillard and Monsieur Chevalier who were really in charge.

Finally they went outside to access the cellar, the last room on the visit. Paul flung open the double doors and there before them were the old boiler and the leaking oil tank. Major Gaillard's sharp intake of breath was audible and for the first time since the inspection had commenced, Lorna felt truly worried. She turned to catch Paul's eye and witnessed the tail end of a smile disappearing from the mayor's face, his eyes bright even in the gloom of the windowless space.

It was clear there were problems. Paul had to answer a multitude of questions about the heating system which taxed his language skills and Major Gaillard's patience but his replies didn't seem to alleviate the deepening frown on the fireman's face. After what felt like a lifetime, Major Gaillard finally snapped his pen back in the holder on his clipboard and declared he was finished.

With a universal sense of relief, everyone trooped outside, the mist having burnt away leaving a blue sky which was almost blinding after the half-light of the cellar. The inspection party started making their farewells and within moments, they'd all gone, leaving Paul and Lorna standing in the drive, slightly bewildered and none the wiser as to how they'd fared.

87

'Is that it?' Lorna asked as the police van drove off, the two officers still arguing inside.

'I guess so.'

From the gate they could see the mayor shaking hands with Monsieur Peloffi from the DDE who hadn't said a word throughout and whose role Paul and Lorna still didn't know. He pulled away in his car as Major Gaillard, Monsieur Chevalier and the mayor started walking towards the bar.

'Going for a pastis no doubt!' remarked Paul as the three men crossed the bridge in the distance.

'You'd think they could have told us.'

'What? That they were going for a drink?'

'No!' retorted Lorna. 'Whether we've passed or not!'

'Oh, right. Yes, you'd think the mayor could have given us some idea. Well, at least it's over and you know what they say.' Paul threw his arms around Lorna and gave her a huge hug, his relief obvious. 'No news is good news.'

Lorna wished she could share his optimism. Somehow, she suspected their problems were only just beginning. And she mentally damned the absent Monsieur Dupuy for causing them.

'So let me get this straight.' Serge Papon put his glass of pastis down on the table and looked directly at Monsieur Chevalier. 'You're saying there was nothing out of order in the kitchen whatsoever? Not even the oil?'

'Exactly!'

Serge stared at him a little longer, sensing the other man's unease at such scrutiny.

'Humph. And what about you?' He turned his attention to Major Gaillard.

'The boiler and the oil tank. I'm not happy with them at all.'

Serge's face became wreathed in smiles.

88

'Go on.'

'Well, for a start the oil tank has a leak. And for another, it's too close to the boiler, which is very old.'

'So what do you suggest?'

'A new oil tank, preferably situated on the outside of the Auberge, not in the cellar, and a new boiler. Then fireproof walls erected all around the boiler, an emergency stop button installed on the outside of the firewall and an emergency fuel stop fitted to the feed from the oil tank.' Major Gaillard looked up from the notes he had been reading and reached for his drink.

'Sounds very serious,' Serge noted gravely. 'Enough to close the place.'

Major Gaillard scrunched up his face and shrugged his shoulders. 'It doesn't have to be. Obviously I can't pass them until those works have been completed and I'd also like to have a certificate for the electrics from a certified electrician. But they can continue to operate with your blessing and we could set a deadline for everything to be sorted. Say a year perhaps?'

Serge leaned back in his chair, one facing the fire after his last experience at the bar, and rubbed his chin.

'So is it a potential danger to clients?' he asked.

'Well yes, I suppose so but . . .'

'And isn't the point of this inspection to certify that establishments like this are safe?'

'Yes but . . .'

'So really we should recommend that it's closed down pending the improvements.'

Major Gaillard slowly lowered his drink to the table and turned to look at Monsieur Chevalier whose eyes were nearly popping out of his head in surprise. In all their years inspecting premises in the Ariège Department, many far worse than the Auberge des Deux Vallées, not once had a mayor suggested that an establishment should be closed. Normally they fought tooth and nail using all their powers to keep the places open. What Mayor Papon was proposing just didn't make sense. Not for the commune. Not for the owners.

'I don't understand,' Major Gaillard managed at last. 'Why would you want to close it?'

Serge smiled, a cold twist of lips that left his eyes untouched. 'I'm simply doing what's in the best interest of the commune.'

Major Gaillard suppressed a shudder, downing the last of his drink to hide it. 'Ultimately, closing the Auberge is not my decision as you know,' he stated as he wiped his moustache. 'That's up to the commune. I'm willing to sign off on the inspection as a fail. What you choose to do with that is entirely up to you.'

And with that he stood up and left the bar. He wanted no part of whatever was going on in the commune of Fogas. But he couldn't help feeling sorry for the new owners of the Auberge.

Annie Estaque had timed her visit to perfection. From the sanctuary of the épicerie, she watched as the fireman stomped out of the bar and down the road to his car, clearly displeased with the discussion that had taken place; the one on which Annie and Josette had been eavesdropping.

'He'll have to put it to the Conseil Municipal,' Josette declared. 'He can't just close it.'

Annie snorted and shook her head. 'He'llcloseit. Marrrkmyworrrds.' She gathered the handles of her shopping bag which was a lot lighter than normal as she'd done most of her shopping on Friday.

'Sure you don't need anything else, Annie?' Josette asked, her twinkling eyes letting Annie know that her real reason for visiting the épicerie had been rumbled.

Annie cackled in reply and let herself out of the shop just as Serge Papon exited the bar. He strode past her, not registering her presence, his face contorted in thought as he marched towards his car. She watched him go, not realising that she had been holding her breath until she was inhaling deeply, as though to cleanse her lungs after a bad smell. She started walking down the road, not really sure what her next step should be, but definite that there should be one.

As Annie came level with the front of the Auberge, she heard a door slam in the distance and out of the corner of her eye she saw a young woman come round from the back, her head down as she approached the gates. Annie continued past and turned up the road to Picarets, her ears pricked to hear which way the woman went. Sure enough she was following Annie, her steps rapid, no doubt from years of city living. Véronique had been like that when she came back from college in Toulouse. All fast movements and haste. Fogas had soon knocked it out of her. What on earth was there to hurry about around here? Unless you entered a field with Sarko the bull by mistake. Annie chuckled.

'Bonjour!' The woman had drawn alongside Annie and was about to overtake her when she seemed to hesitate. 'I can helping you?' She gestured at the shopping bag which Annie had more or less forgotten, it was so light.

Annie was on the verge of giving her customary refusal when she realised this might be the perfect opportunity. God given, Véronique would say. Not that Annie subscribed to that nonsense. Not any more.

'Thankyou. Thatwouldbeagrrreat help.' Annie held out the bag to make her meaning clear as she could see the woman didn't have a clue what she'd just said and, in doing so, broke a long-standing habit. She let someone help her.

*   *   *

The sun was high in the sky and the frost a distant memory by the time Lorna left Annie's house, her walk to let off steam having turned into a social visit. Annie stood at the back door watching her make her way down the track, the dogs accompanying her as far as the road as if they too had taken to her. Lorna turned and waved one last time and then set off down the valley to the Auberge.

Annie was surprised to be still smiling as she closed the door and started clearing away the cups and plates off the table. A cup of tea indeed! she thought, laughing at the idea that her new British friend lived up to the stereotype. Luckily Annie had remembered a gift-box of Twining's tea that Véronique had given her some years ago and which Annie had duly thanked her for, before promptly shoving it to the back of a cupboard. Turned out to be just the thing. Annie had even had a cup herself to complement the locally made biscuits that she'd picked up as a treat for Chloé at the shop this morning. All very sophisticated. Véronique would have been proud.

An hour or more they'd been chatting. And Annie had been on her best behaviour throughout. She hadn't entertained anyone like that for years. Decades even. And perversely the language difficulties on both sides had made things easier. They'd talked about the Auberge, the farm, the commune and the mayor, although Annie hadn't ventured her views on that one. It seemed that young Lorna had been swayed by his charm and Annie wasn't about to dissuade her of her opinion. Not yet anyway. Time enough for that. After all, Annie herself knew all too well just how charming the man could be.

She straightened up from wiping the table and looked at the clock. Christian would be home for lunch by now. She would give him a call and get things started before she got Chloé's bed ready. If they were going to outmanoeuvre Serge Papon they would have to be quick.

She crossed to the large dresser and picked up the phone, her eyes resting briefly on the photo next to it. Annie and her parents standing outside the farm, Papa's arm resting on her shoulders, Maman laughing at something happening out of sight. It was the week before Annie had discovered she was pregnant. She touched the photo like a talisman and then started dialling, her lips set in a thin line of determination.

Thirty-five years was a long time to wait to get even.

7

Serge Papon sat at the window of the Café Galopin and stared at the River Salat as it tumbled over the weir, oblivious to the beauty of the sun shimmering across the top of the water. An espresso lay nestled between the twisted fingers of his left hand while his right drummed a staccato rhythm of impatience on the metal table top.

He looked at his watch and felt a surge of irritation in his chest.

Where was the buffoon? He should have been here by now. They didn't have long. A couple of hours at most.

A couple of hours. That was all that stood between him and sweet revenge. Two days on from the inspection and the Auberge was that bit nearer his grasp, the two foreigners that bit nearer to having to go home. And as for Christian, he'd reacted exactly as Serge had anticipated. Beneath that ponderous, peasant-like demeanour was a mind almost as fine as his own. But with one major weakness. Christian liked to play fair.

Serge chuckled as he drained the last of his coffee. Playing fair was not something that constrained him in the politics of life; quite the opposite. And it was for that very reason that he was sitting in this half-empty café in the early afternoon watching the river.

As he lowered his cup, a movement across the Pont Vieux caught his eye. Something fleeting and furtive and . . . orange?

Serge narrowed his eyes and focused on the bustle of people crossing the bridge in the heart of St Girons. Sure enough, there was Bernard Mirouze, darting from shop doorway to pillar and then shadowing an old lady with a poodle, doing his best to be discreet as Serge had instructed. All the while wearing his orange hunting beret.

Serge groaned. The man was an idiot. How on earth did he think he would be able to hide his bulk in the middle of St Girons? The *cantonnier* moved with the grace of a wounded elephant and even now people were pointing and laughing as he zigzagged his way across the bridge in his camouflage trousers, his beret vibrant in the slanting rays of the winter sun.

Finally Bernard made the door of the café and slipped inside, whipping round to check no one was following him and sending the table nearest to him crashing as his generous arse caught it side on. Startled, he leaped back and knocked over the coat stand on the other side of the entrance. As the owner moved across to prevent any more chaos, shooing Bernard away from the door and muttering loudly about imbeciles, Bernard noticed Serge sitting at the table at the back of the room and crossed towards him.

'I don't think anyone saw me,' he asserted with a smile of achievement.

Serge swallowed his instinctive reply and signalled for two espressos, as much compensation for the damage caused as to give himself time to calm down.

'You're late,' he finally managed between gritted teeth.

Bernard's smile disappeared to be replaced by a frown of concern. 'Sorry, sorry, Monsieur Mayor. It's just that I had to go home to get my beret as I forgot to bring it with me this morning and you said I should be cautious so I thought I should wear a disguise and it being Wednesday, hunting day, I thought, well it's perfect, nobody will ever suspect a thing and so—'

Serge held up his hand to stop the torrent of language issuing from the nervous *cantonnier*. Perhaps the coffee hadn't been a good idea. The man was highly strung enough as it was.

'Enough,' he said. 'We don't have time for this. The council meeting is in two hours and I need you to do something for me. Something that no one else must know about.'

Eager to be of assistance Bernard leaned forward to hear more, sloshing coffee on to the saucers as his belly jarred the table. He started to mop ineffectually at the mess with a napkin, knocking the table even more in the process.

Serge clenched his jaw and reached across to place a hand on Bernard's arm, his gnarled fingers digging into the soft flesh. Bernard froze, his eyes locked with the mayor's and he was stared into stillness.

'I need you to listen carefully. Very carefully. Do you think you can do that?'

Bernard swallowed loudly and then nodded.

'Good,' continued Serge, his eyes still fixing the *cantonnier* in place. 'Now here's what I want you to do . . .'

Christian was running late, which wasn't like him. He understood why the council meetings were brought forward in the winter, no one wanting to be travelling the mountain roads at night once the frosts arrived. But the earlier start meant that he got a lot less done and he hadn't even managed to fit in a shave today!

He took a quick glance in the ancient mirror in the hall which was fogged with age, producing a sporadic reflection that was more glass than image. He'd do. Not as if there was anyone going that he needed to impress. Even so, he ran a

96

hand through his still-damp hair in a vain hope that it would quell the curls once it was dry.

'Are you off?'

He turned in the hallway as his mother spoke to him, nodding in reply.

'Do you want me to keep some dinner for you?'

Christian tried to ignore his father vigorously shaking his head in the background behind his wife's back.

'No, it's fine,' he said, smothering a smile. 'I'll get something while I'm out.'

He wasn't sure where, with the restaurant at the Auberge being closed, but his mother's cooking was bad enough straight out of the oven without the added benefit of reheating. Clearly his father was of the same opinion as he responded with an exaggerated wink of conspiracy.

'I saw that!'

'What?'

'That wink!'

'What wink? I had something in my eye . . .'

Laughing at his parents' banter, Christian pulled on his coat and stepped out into the late afternoon. To the west, the sun was starting to dip behind the mountains, leaving behind a sky streaked with colour and a sharp edge to the air. There was snow forecast for the next few days and with the drop in temperature and the gathering clouds, Christian was sure it would come. He hoped it wasn't going to be another harsh winter. After the cost of the bluetongue vaccinations he could do without having to buy in feed for months on end. A short burst of winter, an early spring and a long summer. That would be perfect.

Despite the cold, the Panda started first time. Christian turned up the heating full blast and set off down the hill towards Picarets. To his left lay fields of sloping pasture, gently

dropping down the mountainside; his land, farmed by generations of Dupuys before him. But as for after him . . .

Christian pushed the thought from his mind, concentrating
instead on Sarko, his prize Limousin bull, who stood in the
middle of one of the fields, pawing the ground and snorting.
If Christian hadn't been late already, he might have been
tempted to stop to make sure nothing was up but he drove on,
having learnt this was everyday behaviour for one of the most
contrary animals he'd ever had the misfortune to own. He
glanced quickly in the rear-view mirror as he passed and was
pleased to see the bull had gone quiet. A flash of orange in the
corner of the mirror caught his eye but when he tried to make
out what it was he could only see the small copse that encircled the edge of Sarko's field.

Christian turned his attention back to the road and soon the
small cottage that marked the start of the village was in sight
with its immaculate front garden and its midnight-blue shutters which were covered in huge suns when open and tiny
stars when closed like now. They always made him smile.
Trust Stephanie to stamp her personality on something as
functional as shutters.

Automatically Christian cast an eye over the house as he
went past and noticed that one of the hinges on the shutters
had worked loose and needed fixing. He'd drop in tomorrow
and sort it out before she got back on Friday.

The house actually belonged to Christian's mother, inherited from her mother, and had lain empty for a long time
before Stephanie had arrived in the area seven years ago,
desperately needing somewhere to stay. Christian had been
unsure about taking her on as a tenant, a single mother with
no job in a region with no employment prospects, but his
mother had insisted and she'd been right. Stephanie kept the
cottage pristine, always paid on time and had become a vital

member of the community, with even Annie Estaque eating out of her hand. More importantly, she'd become a close friend.

He wondered what she'd wanted to talk to him about last weekend, his father having volunteered nothing more than that she'd called in, much to his delight. Christian's parents adored their tenant and were constantly dropping hints, none of them subtle, that she would be an ideal daughter-in-law. And when you added Chloé to the mix, a ready made granddaughter . . .

Poor Stephanie. She'd had to endure countless meals at his mother's invitation and not once had she refused, despite the quality of the cooking. She'd even put up with his mother's vague concept of vegetarian food which included ham and bacon. Sometimes Christian felt guilty that they were just friends but try as he might, he couldn't imagine anything more. He shuffled uncomfortably in his seat, feeling the parental pressure even though he was alone.

Hoping its incessant adverts and musical nostalgia might drive him to distraction, Christian switched the radio on to Radio Couserans, the local station, and drove on through Picarets. Most of the houses, which formed two tiers set into the mountain on either side of the road, were already shuttered against the coming dark, quite a few of them, as second homes, permanently closed up until the next school holiday. There wasn't a soul in sight. It was like a ghost town. So much quieter than the village Christian remembered from his youth when there were always kids hanging around outside and adults gathered in the shade of the old lime tree in the summer.

But most of the kids he was at school with had had to move away to find work, to Toulouse, Marseille, Paris; even the US for a few. Not many made it back apart from for holidays and it meant that the village was suffocating, slowly but surely, falling in on itself with no new blood to sustain it. It was the same in Fogas and La Rivière and that was the main reason why Christian had joined the Conseil Municipal. But solving the problem was far from easy.

Although not according to Annie Estaque.

Christian left the village behind and turned into the tree-lined road down to La Rivière. Ahead the valley widened slightly, producing a broad stretch of good pasture which broke up the woodland. Sitting proudly above it was the Estaque farmhouse, one of the oldest buildings in the area built in the mid-nineteenth century by a relative who'd made his money bringing blocks of ice down from the peak of Trois Seigneurs in the summer to sell in the towns and villages of the Couserans and even as far away as Toulouse.

A hard life that had bred hard people. The same man was rumoured to have carried the huge long-case clock in the kitchen all the way out from St Girons on his back as he didn't trust using a horse and cart. Determined, stubborn, and very outspoken. Annie was a chip off the old ice block all right!

As he came closer to the farm, Christian could see her out feeding the dogs at the back of the house and so beeped the horn. She stood up, sheltering her eyes against the low sun to see the car, and then threw up an arm in response. Christian took the gesture to be one of greeting although, knowing Annie, it could just as well mean *bugger off*.

He grinned at the thought of her phone call. She'd always been forthright in her views but in all the time he'd known her, he'd never heard those views expressed about anything other than farming. The right way to milk a cow. The right time to bring in the hay. The right place to buy your feed. Never once had he heard her pass opinion on things in the commune. She kept herself to herself and was respected for it.

Now that had changed. First she'd questioned the mayor's

plans to buy the Auberge which had led to Christian opposing him. Then on Monday she'd called at lunchtime, furious about the inspection at the Auberge and determined that the mayor shouldn't be allowed to close it.

And she'd persuaded Christian she was right and eased his conscience into the bargain.

The very thing that worried Christian most about the commune was its long-term viability. It needed incomers to settle in the area and bring with them children to keep the schools open and taxes to keep the economy going.

But even more importantly, there had to be work to keep them there or before long they too would leave, the way that Christian's generation had had to leave in the past and the generation after him would have to in the future. And Fogas, La Rivière and Picarets would become an empty collection of uninhabited houses like the summer pasture villages in the high mountains.

As Annie pointed out, the new owners of the Auberge were not only willing to take on a failing business and turn it around, but had also employed a local person into the bargain. It was exactly what the commune needed. So what if their culinary skills weren't quite those of a French person, it hardly mattered in the long term. What mattered was that the commune made these people welcome and did everything in its power to keep them here. And that meant getting behind their business.

So Christian was on a mission. It wouldn't be easy. After all, it was he who'd suggested the inspection in the first place, even if it was just to thwart the mayor's more extreme proposal. But he was confident he could persuade the more rational members of the Conseil Municipal that it was in the best interest of the commune to give the new owners time to make the recommended repairs while keeping the Auberge open and earning money. Not surprisingly, since he'd come to that opinion, Christian had slept a lot easier.

Rounding the last bend, Christian could see the Auberge below him, the sunlight already gone from its front, leaving it deep in winter shadow, and he wondered if the owners had any idea of the machinations that had surrounded their arrival. He drove on, relieved to be playing the part of peacemaker at last, a role in which he was much more comfortable.

Without knowing it, Christian had already played the part of peacemaker that day. At the precise moment that he looked in his rear-view mirror to check on Sarko the bull, Lorna and Paul were in the middle of a disagreement about how to end their afternoon stroll. They'd walked up the road to Picarets, intending to complete a circuit of the commune via a path that led across the mountains to Fogas and then back down the road to La Rivière. But they hadn't allowed for the steepness of the hills nor the shortness of the days. They'd made good time to Picarets and had picked up the footpath that led out of it but now, as they stood on the track above the road in the lengthening shadows of the trees, they were having a heated discussion.

'Look.' Paul pointed at the collection of buildings in the distance. 'That farm over there is here on the map. We have to go past that and then we're almost there.'

'Almost there?' Lorna's voice rose on the last word. 'You're forgetting the climb beyond it, the drop into the valley and then the climb up to Fogas. And that's before we even start the walk down to the Auberge.'

'It's nothing,' Paul scoffed. 'Twenty minutes max to Fogas and thirty minutes down. We'll easily do it before dark.'

Lorna looked to the west at the sun drooping low on the horizon and shook her head. 'No way, Paul. Not today.'

Before Paul could protest, a small blue car passed by on the road below them catching Lorna's attention as the driver craned his neck to look at something in his mirror.

'That's the man who waved at us!' she exclaimed. 'You know, in November, the day we came to look over the Auberge.'

'Hmm?' Paul looked up from the map. 'Him? He looks too fat.'

'Too fat?' Puzzled, Lorna turned to see Paul looking at another man wearing a bright orange beret and camouflage trousers emerging from the trees in the field across the road. 'Not him, the man in the car!'

But the car had already disappeared and the man in the field was far more interesting.

Intrigued, they watched as he proceeded to weave and dodge across the open space below them like someone who'd had one pastis too many. Then he threw himself to the ground and covered the last few yards on his belly, like a beached whale inching towards the sea, his head constantly moving from side to side as though on the lookout for danger.

'What on earth . . .?' Paul whispered.

'It's Wednesday. He must be hunting!'

'Hunting what? And where's his gun?'

The man cautiously raised his head at the edge of the field and surveyed the road. There was no traffic, nobody around. Satisfied he was unobserved, he started to crawl under the single strand of wire that barred his route, his immense bulk barely clearing it.

'Isn't that an electric . . .' Lorna began as the man's rear end dipped under the wire but not quite enough. They heard the muffled yelp across the road as two thousand volts surged through the layers of fat covering his behind.

'. . . fence. Oh my God, that had to hurt,' Lorna muttered but Paul wasn't listening. He was too busy trying to stifle a giggling fit, tears running down his face.

Unperturbed by the shock, the man hustled down the road, rubbing his bottom as he waddled towards the gate of the neighbouring enclosure. With one last furtive look, he lifted the latch and then swung the gate open.

'Isn't that the field with the . . .'

'*BULL!*' hissed Paul as a tonne of snorting beast came charging towards freedom, eyes wild and flecks of foam spraying as he tossed his head to get a better look at the object of his attack, the bright orange of the beret taunting him.

With open mouths Paul and Lorna watched as the man abandoned all covert movements and hurtled towards the sanctuary of the first field, his fat legs trembling as he covered the short distance, the ground shaking beneath him as the bull thundered out of the gate and after him. Sensing his chance, the bull lowered his massive head and lunged at the huge target that the man's fleeing arse presented, horns primed to gouge the flesh and tip the man into infinity. Then, just as it seemed the inevitable was going to happen, in a moment of sheer genius inspired by terror the man ripped off his orange beret and frisbeed it along the road ahead of him while simultaneously hurling himself once more under the electric fence and into safety, oblivious of the pain.

For a split second the bull broke stride, confused as to which target to follow, the fat mound of flesh or the orange disc which was still sailing ahead of him, caught on the breeze. But at that moment the last rays of the sun caught the beret, making it vibrate with light, and the bull charged after it once more. As it descended, the edge of the beret hooked over the tip of the bull's horn and no matter how much the bull shook his head, the beret dangled in front of him, enraging him further. He stormed off up the road, roaring and bellowing, the object of his rage tantalisingly out of reach no matter how fast he went.

Satisfied that the road was clear of danger, the man crawled under the wire once more, this time managing to clear it without mishap, and hustled across to a small path which joined the track Paul and Lorna were on further up in the trees. They watched him labour his way, panting and wheezing, up the steep incline towards Fogas.

For a few minutes they remained in silence, awed by the drama they had just witnessed.

'So I guess that decides it then,' Paul finally ventured.

'Yup. Back the way we came?'

Paul nodded and they cautiously picked their way back down to the village, careful to keep an eye out behind in case the bull returned.

8

Josette wasn't behind the counter in the épicerie when Christian pulled up. Instead, Véronique was sitting on the stool, completely immersed in a book lying on the glass display case. Her hair was released from its usual constraints, the silver clip that normally pulled it from her face discarded next to her, as though torn from her head in frustration as she clearly struggled with the text. A sudden frown creased her brow as her finger traced the words across the page, trying to make them stick. She sighed and started the passage again.

Watching furtively from outside, Christian was struck by the thought that she looked different somehow. She looked . . . young! And almost pretty. He shook his head, reminding himself that this was Véronique Estaque, and entered the shop.

Véronique jumped up guiltily when she heard the door open, turning pink as she swept the book off the case and on to her lap, the cover hidden from sight.

'Not another *Lives of the Saints*?' Christian teased with a smile as he greeted her.

Véronique didn't rise to the bait but merely pushed the book further out of sight.

'Who is it this time? Bernadette? Francis of Assisi? Or the devout shepherdess St Germaine, patron of our beloved parish church?' At this Christian cocked his head to one side, pressed his hands together in supplication and pursed his lips in what he believed was a pious pose. Véronique couldn't help but burst out laughing.

'You'll rot in hell, Monsieur Dupuy!' she exclaimed, only half joking.

Christian tossed his head in dismissal, the scorn on his face far removed from the beatific demeanour of moments before. 'Well, there'll be plenty from this commune to keep me company. Now, where is the saintly Josette? We're going to be late.'

'Didn't Fatima call you?'

'Fatima Souquet? Why on earth would she call?'

Véronique looked puzzled. 'She dropped down fifteen minutes ago to pick up Josette. She said your mother had called to say you were going to be late and asked her to take Josette up to the meeting.'

Now it was Christian's turn to look confused.

'Maman phoned Fatima? She loathes the woman.' He scratched his head, pulled out his mobile and cursed. As was often the case, he'd forgotten to turn it on so it was possible he'd missed some calls.

'How odd,' he muttered as he turned the phone on and then thrust it back in his coat pocket. 'It's not like Fatima to do someone a favour.'

'It's not a problem is it?'

'Well, I was hoping to talk to Josette on the way up. You know, about the vote.' Christian checked his watch and started towards the door. 'Damn! I'll just have to try and catch her before the meeting starts. See you later.'

The door rattled in his wake and the Panda spun off at speed leaving Véronique alone on her stool once more. Alone except for Jacques who was sitting on the fridge having watched the entire exchange. He slipped stealthily to the floor as Véronique pulled out her book and put it back on the glass counter, causing Jacques to wince as if in pain. She opened it at the passage that had been troubling her, propped her head on her hands and started to read again.

Unobserved, Jacques glided across the room and crouched down in front of the counter, trying to read the title of the thick tome through the glass. He could see a man with a bushy white beard on the front looking every inch the saint, but he couldn't make out the title. Not from this distance and without his reading glasses on.

Just as he was straightening up, his joints creaking faintly, Véronique finally lost patience with the book and slammed it shut, startling the life out of Jacques and causing him to grab hold of the glass case. Hastily pulling his hand away from his precious knife cabinet before it left a mark, Jacques caught his breath and then craned over to get a better view of what was causing Véronique such distress.

He read the title once. He frowned and read it again. And then he started to laugh. Silently of course.

'*The Thought of Karl Marx*!' Véronique snorted with derision. 'It would be a lot easier to read if he'd actually had only *one* thought!'

She sighed and opened up the book again, resigned to her fate, her finger working laboriously down the page. Jacques watched her, face serious with concentration while her left hand constantly touched the silver cross around her neck as though for reassurance.

Véronique Estaque, the pillar of the church in the commune of Fogas, was reading communist philosophy. Whatever next? He wandered to the front of the shop and hopped back up on to the fridge, his mind returning to the much bigger question he had been puzzling over since Josette had left for the meeting.

What was Fatima up to?

★   ★   ★

Josette was feeling really uncomfortable. For some reason, Fatima Souquet was being over-attentive to her and it just wasn't normal. Bad enough that she'd had to put up with the woman's nervous driving up the snaking road from La Rivière to Fogas, Fatima panicking every time they'd met a car coming down and nearly plunging off the edge. But having to listen to her prattle on about her wonderful family and her perfect husband was really starting to grate on Josette's nerves. It was with some relief that she heard the mayor starting to call everyone to order. But where was Christian?

'Bonsoir! Sorry I'm late.' Christian rushed into the meeting room as people took their chairs, and caught Josette's eye over the mass of heads, gesturing for her to save him a seat. Before he could get to her, however, the mayor pulled him aside in a private conversation and the empty chair next to Josette was suddenly filled. By Geneviève Souquet.

'Bonsoir, Josette. How are things?' she enquired, looking down her Toulousain nose.

'Fine, fine,' Josette answered automatically, her attention on Christian and the mayor. Several times it appeared that Christian had started to move away, only for the mayor to ask another question or raise another topic, keeping him by his side.

'I wish we could get this underway,' exclaimed Geneviève with a note of irritation, pointedly glancing at her watch as though having to actually attend the council meeting was interfering with her short break in the mountains.

Her wish was granted as René Piquemal called out: 'Are we doing this tonight or what? Some of us want to get home to a hot dinner!'

'Not Christian!' quipped Alain Rougé to much laughter.

Christian acknowledged the joke with a fatalistic grin, using the levity to break away from the mayor and head towards

Josette. Just as he realised that the seat next to her was taken his mobile phone started to sound in his pocket. He raised his hand in apology and made his way to the exit. He pulled open the door and Bernard Mirouze collapsed into the room, out of breath and covered in mud, the odd bit of bramble still sticking to his trousers. But Christian didn't register the unusual appearance of the *cantonnier*. He was too busy trying to hear the person on the other end of the phone.

As the door closed behind Christian, the rest of the council members noticed Bernard for the first time.

'What on earth happened to you?' Monique Sentenac asked as Bernard staggered towards the nearest available chair, the legs squeaking under the sudden slump of his weight.

'Did you get into a fight with a wild boar?' joked Alain.

'You should see the boar!'

'Why, is it wearing his beret?'

'Yeah Bernard, where's your beret?'

The hilarity continued, even Pascal allowing a sneer to cross his normally supercilious features. But the mayor wasn't laughing. He was staring intently at his *cantonnier* and Josette thought she saw something pass between them, more of a nod than a wink. Whatever it was, it seemed to galvanise the mayor, who clapped his hands and called the meeting to order. He was reading out the agenda for the evening when the door opened and an ashen-faced Christian stuck his head into the room.

'Sorry. I have to go. Sarko's got loose again and Papa can't find him. He thinks he might have gone over the edge of the old quarry.' He threw a glance at Josette. 'You know how I want to vote, Josette.'

And with that he was gone, leaving a low murmur of disquiet in the room which was filled with people who understood Christian's anxiety. The bull falling into the quarry and breaking a leg was only one potential danger. Of equal concern was the possibility of the huge animal wandering on to a road and causing an accident. That was a scenario no farmer wanted to confront as it could mean financial ruin.

The mayor stood up and the room fell into silence.

'Considering Christian's predicament,' he began, his face grave, 'I propose that we abandon all but the major issue on tonight's agenda and reschedule another meeting for the New Year. That way we can finish early tonight and assist Christian in his efforts to locate his bull.'

'Excellent idea!' Alain called out, everyone else present nodding in agreement and applauding the mayor's sense of camaraderie. All except for Geneviève Souquet who could be heard muttering that she didn't see why she should have to make a second trip from Toulouse just because some imbecilic farmer couldn't control his bull. Luckily for her, only Josette could hear her complaints and they fell on deaf ears. Josette was too busy worrying about having to address the meeting now that Christian wasn't there.

'So,' continued the mayor, 'we turn to what was Item Four: the proposed enforced closure of the Auberge des Deux Vallées following its failure of the safety and hygiene inspection on Monday the fifteenth of December.'

Josette gripped her hands together underneath the table, feeling the weight of responsibility like a lead collar on her shoulders. She took a deep breath and thought of Jacques. She could do this.

The journey down from Fogas with Fatima was, if possible, worse than the journey up as it was truly dark by the time the meeting concluded, making the winding road even more difficult to negotiate. The only benefit as far as Josette was concerned was that the arduous driving conditions kept

Fatima quiet. Which was just as well as Josette was in no mood to talk.

It turned out she couldn't do it after all. She couldn't persuade the Conseil Municipal that the Auberge needed to be kept open for the sake of the commune. She couldn't counter their arguments about health and safety. And more importantly, she couldn't stop the mayor from twisting and turning her words until she seemed to be arguing his point for him.

She had failed. Miserably. And as a result, the Auberge was to be closed and God knew what would become of Monsieur and Madame Webster.

If only she had the mayor's glib tongue or Christian's quiet confidence that made people sit up and listen. Instead she'd got flustered when confronted with the report detailing the problems in the Auberge, the leaking oil tank and the age and proximity of the boiler. She'd had to agree that they were serious safety issues, which gave the mayor even more ammunition.

But the thing that had really swayed the council had been the fact that Christian had proposed the inspection in the first place. No matter how much she protested that he didn't support the closure of the Auberge, that he had changed his mind about the newcomers, this fact was unassailable.

As René had remarked before he cast his vote, Christian had persuaded him to support the inspection and now he, René, felt duty bound to abide by its findings. The Auberge didn't conform to standards and so it was the council's responsibility to close it down. Alain had expressed a similar notion and finally the proposal had been passed with a large majority of seven to four with only Philippe Galy and Monique Sentenac supporting Josette and Christian.

'Here we are,' Fatima announced brightly, as glad to be at the end of the journey as Josette was.

'Thanks for the lift,' Josette managed as she got out of the car.

'Let me know if you hear from Christian about the bull. Pascal was desperate to help with the search but with his allergies . . . you know how it is.' Fatima simpered and waved and then started to reverse.

Josette stood outside the shop watching Fatima execute a thirty-three-point turn and thinking uncharitable thoughts about Pascal and his allergies. The only thing he was allergic to was getting cow shit on his leather shoes and dirt under his fingernails. Jacques used to despise the man as much for his soft hands, untouched by physical labour, as for his airs and graces.

The rear lights of Fatima's car disappeared into the distance and Josette let herself into the shop. Véronique had closed it up for the night, the windows all shuttered and the lights off except for a small light in the back of the building and suddenly Josette was glad of the dark. Glad that she didn't have to see herself reflected in the glass counter as she sank on to the stool. Glad that she was away from the sneering condescension of Pascal and Geneviève, belittling her at every turn until she lost all confidence. And glad that no one else could see the tears that were streaming down her face.

It was all her fault. She'd tried her best but it clearly wasn't good enough and she'd let everyone down. Because of her, the English couple were going to lose their business.

A sob rose in her chest and caught in her throat, restricting her breathing until it escaped and she was left gasping and sobbing, her heart aching as the stress of the night released the emotions she had been trying so hard to control for the last six months. She laid her head down on the display cabinet and cried until she thought she would dissolve, her frail body shaking as the tears left tracks across the pristine glass. She cried for her failure, for the Websters, for letting Christian down.

But most of all she cried for the best friend she'd lost when she lost Jacques.

Jacques couldn't do a thing. He could only stand and watch as his wife cried her heart out, his hand on her head, stroking her hair as she used to like him to do.

But she was oblivious.

He felt a pain in his chest as she lay there beyond his help. A sharp pain like when his heart had given its final beat and the world had faded away from him, the light receding further and further until it disappeared altogether only for him to return to this black and white existence.

Gradually, he felt Josette go still under his hand, the tears subsiding and her breathing becoming slower and slower. She'd fallen asleep. Just like she used to do when he stroked her hair. Perhaps he'd calmed her after all. He ran his fingers through her hair one last time and then eased away, careful not to make any noise even though he knew it was impossible.

He tiptoed across the shop to the door which was still unshuttered and looked down the road at the Auberge. Judging by Josette's tears, the meeting tonight had not gone well and the mayor would get his way. That was bad enough. What was worse was that he'd hurt both Christian and Josette in the process. That was enough to make Jacques' blood boil. If he had any blood left that was.

He sighed and the 'closed' sign on the door fluttered in response. He had never felt so impotent in all his life.

'Over here. I think I've . . . MERDE!'

René's disembodied scream came clearly across the dark space of mountain and Christian knew immediately what it meant. He scrambled round to the back of the van and lowered the tailgate, straightening up just in time to see a light bobbing towards him along the moonlit road.

'He's . . . he's . . .' René panted from beyond the torchlight, unable to complete the sentence. But Christian was ready, the side door of the van already opened.

'Faster, René, faster,' he shouted as the darkness behind the plumber separated, giving shape to a mass of muscle and horn gaining on the man before it.

'Oh my God . . . oh my God . . .' René sprinted past Christian, up the ramp and into the van, the bull thundering after him. As Christian threw up the tailgate and bolted it shut, trapping the beast within, he had a single moment of panic that René might not realise there was an escape route. He poked his head around the side of the vehicle and was glad to see René collapsed on the tarmac beneath the side door, his lungs working overtime as he gasped for air.

'That's it!' he wheezed. 'I'm giving up cigarettes!'

Christian laughed and extended his arm to drag the plumber up from the road which was already glistening with frost. In the distance he could see the lights of the other members of the search party converging as they came down from the woods and the hillsides. If they hadn't heard René's scream, they would be able to hear Sarko thrashing around in the van and would know the bull had been found.

'You got him then?' Alain called out and when Christian answered there was a cheer from the group. He saw Papa give Philippe Galy a big hug of relief and even the mayor was smiling.

Christian surveyed the hastily assembled band of men and felt a surge of pride. This was what the commune was about. In times of crisis, they all put their differences aside and pulled together. That was how it should be.

'So, who wants to come back for a quick bite to eat?' Papa asked, only to be met by a resounding silence. He grinned, acknowledging the reason for their reluctance, and changed the offer. 'Well, maybe a drink then?'

'That's more like it!' shouted René, his breath finally recovered. 'Think I'm at least owed a glass of something. Nearly lost my manhood back there to Sarko's horns.'

'Of course, that would imply you had one to lose!' came a reply and the men trooped wearily back towards the farm, laughing and joking, glad that the evening's adventure had come to a happy ending.

Christian double-checked the bolts on the tailgate and then grabbed hold of the side door which was still standing open and pulled himself up to look into the back at the now quiet beast. He shone his torch over every inch of the bull, reassuring himself that he was really there, no broken bones, no wounds. It could have been so much worse. Christian started to sweat at the thought. The quarry with its deadly embankments, the road with its infrequent but fast traffic.

He gulped and swung the torch back to Sarko's head, the bull's eyes catching the light as he stared mournfully back.

'Silly old sod!' Christian muttered affectionately. It had taken nearly losing the bull to make him realise how much he was attached to the animal despite his repeated attempts to escape. 'First time you managed to get the gate open though!'

The bull snorted in response.

'Yeah, I know. You might not be responsible this time. But when I find out who is . . .'

At first it had puzzled Christian that the electric fence had still been in place and the gate undamaged after the departure of the bull. Normally when Sarko escaped he took the fence with him. But this time it looked like he was innocent.

Several people in Picarets had told Christian they'd seen a

couple carrying a map and backpacks walking down the road from Sarko's field about the time he'd gone missing. Obviously they'd been hiking in the area and left the gate open behind them. Christian growled just thinking about it. Careless idiot townies.

Sensing that he was unsettling the bull, Christian prepared to step down but as he did so, something reflected the light of his torch, something on one of Sarko's horns.

'What have you been up to?' Christian queried as he stretched his arm into the enclosure and gingerly ran his hand down the sharp point of horn. He felt the object under his fingers, soft and furry. Carefully he eased it off and brought it into the bright circle of light.

It was a ragged square of orange fabric, no more than five centimetres across. Christian stared at it, his thoughts percolating slowly, recognising what it was on some deeper level. He tried to clear his mind and finally it came to him.

A hunting beret.

That was what it looked like. A piece of hunting beret.

Christian rubbed it between his fingers and looked out into the night, aware that some other memory was being triggered in the far corners of his consciousness. Someone he'd seen. Something he'd seen.

Sarko bellowed and kicked the side of the van, startling Christian back into the cold night. He put the fabric in his jacket pocket, closed the side door and clambered up into the cab.

It would come to him. Time enough. Right now he needed a drink and some dinner. He was even hungry enough to eat something cooked by Maman.

The van rumbled off into the distance, leaving the woods where Sarko had been hiding to lapse back into darkness as the first flakes of snow started to fall. They drifted softly earthwards through the bare branches of the trees, sticking to boulders and coating the fallen logs and dead leaves until the forest floor became a vast expanse of white punctuated only by a splash of orange where shreds of material lay scattered beneath a badly gouged ash tree. Eventually, they too would be covered.

9

Forty-eight hours of solid snowfall later the commune was in a state of emergency. The higher mountain roads were impassable, electricity lines were down in all three villages, most of the phones were out and the silence of the snow-covered forest was periodically broken by the crack of yet more falling trees. It was the worst snowstorm that Serge Papon had ever witnessed. He was convinced that for his wife it might be the last.

He stared out of his office window in the town hall at the swirling flakes, trying to follow them as they danced and jived before his eyes, pulling him deeper and deeper into their monochrome world until he felt his head spin and he had to hold on to the windowsill for support.

The crisp sound of metal chinking on metal broke the spell and Serge dragged his eyes away from the storm and glanced down into the car park where a young woman was crouched down at the front wheel of a small yellow car.

The new postwoman.

Serge grunted as he watched her lay out a set of snow chains on the ground next to the wheel and then consult the instructions.

Typical! She didn't have a clue how to fit the chains. What on earth was La Poste thinking in assigning a slip of a thing like that to do a man's job?

Since Yves Rogalle had retired two years ago the commune

had suffered a succession of postmen and women, none of whom stayed very long as the route was arduous and the pay meagre. It was irritating in the extreme but despite firing off multiple letters in his official capacity, Serge had been unable to get the situation rectified.

Pah! Progress. It was eroding the very heart of the place.

Monsieur Mené, the postman from his childhood, had walked the route up and down the mountains every day without fail. No car. No snow chains. Snowshoes only in exceptional circumstances. There wasn't a thing happened in the commune but he'd known about it. Then La Poste had introduced the motorbike and then the car and finally the relationship between the postman and his customers had disintegrated, leaving behind a speedier service which lacked the human touch of its predecessor.

Now, instead of a chat over a coffee or something stronger while the local gossip was relayed, the elderly people who lived alone in the hills were more likely to catch only a glimpse of a yellow car disappearing at speed when their post was delivered. Apart from at the end of the year when the postmen and women were trying to sell their precious calendars! Serge had never objected to buying an unneeded calendar from Yves in return for his hard work. But lately, he didn't even recognise the faces above the uniforms when they came asking for their Christmas bonus.

The postwoman was still reading the instruction booklet when Pascal strode into the car park, his snow boots crunching new tracks across the yard and his vibrant purple and lime-green ski jacket looking out of place alongside his leather briefcase. He gave a curt reply to the woman's cheery greeting and walked straight past her into the entrance hall, completely ignoring her plight.

Serge shook his head in disbelief. He could cope with his

deputy's narcissistic tendencies and even his shallow nature. But the apathy he displayed towards his neighbours incensed the mayor. The other night had been a prime example with everyone pulling together to find the missing bull while Pascal Souquet sat at home and manicured his nails. As if he was above them all rather than a debt-ridden bankrupt who'd managed to lose everything on some stupid speculative investments. Some kind of pyramid scheme Serge didn't fully understand. All he knew was that if it hadn't been for the family home Fatima had inherited in the village, Pascal would be living in a box on the Champs-Elysées. There was no excuse for the man's hubris and Serge clenched the windowsill even tighter at the thought of it, silently vowing that he would do everything in his power to stop that man from becoming the next mayor of Fogas.

That's if the bastard didn't cause him to have a heart attack first!

With a sigh Serge reached for his coat, resigned to the fact that he would have to help out the woman with the chains if the post was ever going to get delivered. He slipped his arms through the sleeves and as his hands emerged, twisted and swollen, he was struck by the unavoidable reality of his age. He probably wouldn't be able to manipulate the cold metal links or be able to pull them tight enough to get a proper purchase.

He stood contemplating his useless hands, despising Pascal even more, confronted as he suddenly was by his own frailties.

What a waste it was giving health to a man like that. Like putting testicles on a ewe.

A shout in the yard below pulled him back to the window.

Bernard. Complete with new beret and a swagger that was

meant to entice the ladies but merely made his backside wobble. Serge watched as he crossed the car park to the young woman and knelt down next to her, shooing her aside with well-intentioned condescension.

The woman shrugged her shoulders, picked up the second set of chains and walked round to the other side of the car. A few minutes later she re-emerged looking pleased with herself as Bernard tried for the fourteenth time to close the cable hook, only for the metal to slip from his hands, leaving the chains in a tangled heap at the bottom of the wheel. The woman grinned at him and made some comment which Serge couldn't catch but which caused Bernard to redden and pull the chains up once more. As he did so, she glanced at the booklet and pointed at the links of metal strung across the front of the wheel halfway up.

Serge chuckled as Bernard cursed loudly, realising his mistake. He quickly unhooked the front clasp which had been causing the problem and the job was finished in minutes. As the postwoman pulled out she waved back at him and then disappeared into the blizzard, leaving Bernard staring after her, a bemused look on his face as though he had just encountered an alien species.

Fools and eunuchs, Serge muttered to himself as he shook off his coat and settled down to work, pulling the kerosene heater closer to the desk. That was what he was surrounded by. Fools and eunuchs. What were things coming to when a young girl like that couldn't rely on the men around her to even fit her snow chains? Not that she'd seemed bothered. But that only made it worse.

He scratched his legs in frustration as his eczema started to burn. The doctor had said this latest health problem was purely a result of old age but Serge was convinced it was a physical manifestation of the itch of irritation that seemed to be permanently beneath his skin these days. Always just out of reach.

With great restraint, he stopped scratching and reached for the pile of papers in front of him. He skimmed through the first, a request from Philippe Galy for permission to convert an outbuilding into a *gîte*, and put it to one side. The next two were letters from the Conseil Général in the departmental capital, Foix, requesting his presence at yet more useless meetings. But the last one held his attention long enough to soothe his irascible mood.

It was the official inspection report from Major Gaillard.

Serge scanned the text, running his eyes down the page until they came to rest on the word that mattered:

DEFAVORABLE

He murmured the word like an incantation, savouring the way the vowels and consonants wrapped around his tongue like a hearty Bordeaux. *Défavorable*. He leaned back in his chair and folded his arms across his chest, taking a deep breath of satisfaction as his senses reeled on the intoxicating power inherent in the paper in front of him.

He'd done it. The Auberge was as good as his. Well, his brother-in-law's. Same thing really. And none of it had been done in his name. The over-ambitious Pascal had jumped at the chance to propose the motion to buy out the Auberge and, as Serge had predicted, Christian, unable to countenance something so unscrupulous, had put forward a counter-proposal.

Serge laughed softly. He'd taken a huge gamble on Christian but it had paid off. The man had exceeded his expectations. Coming up with the idea of the inspection on his own had saved Serge from intervening and Christian's natural powers of persuasion had even afforded Serge the luxury of abstaining from the vote.

His name wasn't on a thing.

So when Jean-Louis bought the Auberge for a drastically reduced price some months from now, no one would be able to point the finger and accuse the mayor of corruption.

Apart from Bernard of course.

The sudden roar of an engine from the yard below sundered the snow-packed silence and Serge rushed to the window to watch Bernard reverse the tractor, now fitted with the snow-plough attachment, out of the shed. Two days he'd been driving the commune snow plough and in two days the town hall had had more claims on the insurance than over the last decade. He'd managed to destroy a fence on the tight corner at La Rivière, smash the wing mirrors on four cars, have a near miss with Monique Sentenac's yappy poodle and finally, the most spectacular of all, he'd reversed at speed into Pascal's brand new 4×4.

The man was a liability.

Although people had offered him free drinks in the bar when the news about Pascal's Range Rover got round. Served Pascal right for buying foreign rubbish.

With the reversing successfully completed, the tractor jerked forward and the snow plough scraped along the gate-post as Bernard negotiated his way out on to the road and down the hill. Not too bad. He'd missed the parked cars oppo-site and the gatepost was only superficially damaged. Maybe the man was just a slow learner!

Although the incident with the bull had been a close thing. Too close!

Serge moved across to the heater for warmth as a shiver ran along his spine.

Bloody Bernard! All Serge had needed was a diversion to

124

get Christian away from the council meeting. He'd suspected his deputy might have a change of heart about closing the Auberge and he'd been right too, given the way Josette voted. Just as well he'd used that viper Fatima to keep them apart the night of the meeting or Josette might have made a more persuasive argument.

So he'd spoken to Bernard. A simple task. Something to remove Christian and his ability to talk people round to his way of thinking. But the stupid *cantonnier* couldn't just open the gate and let the bull saunter off as Sarko was apt to do. No, not Bernard. He had to become a human target, so enraging the beast that it ran berserk into the forest halfway up the mountain.

Perhaps, Serge conceded, he should have known better than to send an idiot to do the deed. After all, he was well aware, from years of close association with Bernard thanks to some tenuous connection on his wife's side of the family, that the man could drive a saint to distraction, let alone a short-tempered bull. God knows, he felt like gouging a few trees himself after half an hour in the imbecile's presence.

He scratched absently at his legs as he sat back down. The damage could have been catastrophic. A tonne of prime stock rampaging loose in the mountains, frothing at the mouth. It didn't bear thinking about. Christian could have been ruined.

And to his surprise Serge felt something quiver in the dusty recesses of his conscience. Like the flame of a candle trying to pierce the suffocating darkness of a mine shaft, it flickered slightly and then went out.

Before it could reignite, the mayor of Fogas got out his pen and started to draft a letter. He would deliver it today with a copy of the report. There was no turning back now.

The Conseil Municipal had voted on it and their word was final. And it was the best option for the commune after all.

He signed it with a flourish, dropped it into the office next door and then grabbed his coat and started down the stairs. While Céline, the secretary, was typing up the letter he just had time to pop in and see his wife. Shrugging on his coat as he went, he wondered how long they had left before she was confined to hospital. Not long now, he imagined. The doctor had refused to speculate, telling them to take each day as it came. Easy enough for him to say.

Facing a future as bleak as the weather, Serge stepped out into the falling snow, instinctively hunching his shoulders, as much against the bitter wind as against the cold fingers of grief which had begun to wrap themselves around his heart.

'*Vous voulez une chambre? . . . Quelle date? . . . Allo? . . . Allo?* Bugger it!' Paul sighed in exasperation and slammed the phone down, causing Lorna to look up from the laptop.

'They hung up on you?'

Paul nodded.

'Another marketing call?'

'I think so. Typical. We go the whole morning with no phone or power and the minute they're restored, the first caller is trying to sell me something!'

'What was it this time?'

'Faxes I think. Trouble is, they spoke so fast I couldn't catch it. If I don't hear the words *chambre* or *restaurant* I'm lost!'

Lorna laughed sympathetically. Since moving to France, answering the phone had turned from an everyday activity into Russian roulette. Either it was a potential client or a marketing call and telling them apart while listening to a barrage of language with limited French was proving very difficult, not to mention potentially damaging to the business.

Paul had quickly adopted the strategy of firing questions at the caller in the hopes of pre-empting their needs and to some extent it was successful. So far they had managed to secure several reservations for the opening of the fishing season in March but even more importantly, they were almost fully booked for the New Year's Eve party in two weeks' time.

However, his technique only served to infuriate any sales-people who called. Lorna could just imagine the frustration of some poor lad in Paris trying to sell a fax to some foreigner who just kept asking if he wanted a room in a very thick accent. She didn't blame the guy for hanging up.

'It can only get easier,' she said reassuringly as Paul sat back down next to her at the table in the dining room where they were doing the accounts.

'Unlike this lot!' Paul pushed the bank statements and bills away from him. They'd been working on their finances all afternoon and it hadn't got any clearer. Or rather, it was all too clear.

They were living perilously close to the edge.

As new owners, they'd registered the Auberge at the Chambre de Commerce and were now being asked to pay the astronomical social security charges levied on all small busi-nesses in France. To cover the first quarter they had to find nearly a thousand euros by the end of January, before the business had even started earning properly.

Added to that were bills for the accountant, insurance and heating oil and for the food that they'd ordered in for the restaurant for New Year. Based on the bookings they'd picked up they would just about make it to February without having

127

to touch the money they'd left in their bank in the UK. Which was just as well as the way the pound was plummeting against the euro, their cushion of eight thousand pounds was no longer as plump as it had been when they'd arrived.

They'd suffered an even greater setback when they'd called in builders to get quotes for the roof. The cheapest was thirty thousand euros, way more than they'd anticipated. Who said France was cheap?

Paul gathered up the papers strewn around the table and thrust them back into the folder. The new roof would have to wait until they'd earned enough to either pay for it outright or get a loan. As for the boiler and the oil tank, they were a long way off. Things were just too tight. Especially with all the talk of a recession.

'Was that the post?' Lorna asked, hearing a car outside.

'I thought she'd been?' Paul stood up in time to see a small silver car pull off, snow chains churning, leaving a criss-cross pattern in the deep snow. He pulled open the front door and waded over to the postbox, his fingers shaking with the cold as he inserted the key. Sure enough there was a letter inside. A letter without a stamp.

Shaking off the worst of the snow, he headed back into the Auberge and started tearing open the envelope while Lorna cleared away the rest of the accounts.

It was from the town hall. Again. But this time it was more than just a letter. It looked like an official document of some sort was attached.

'I think it's the inspection report.'

Lorna smiled over at him. 'Well? Good news I hope?'

But Paul was too busy scanning the letter to reply. As he reached the bottom, the blood drained from his face.

'What is it?' Lorna's voice was sharp with fear. 'Do you need the French dictionary?'

'No . . . No need for that. It's perfectly clear,' Paul said as he dropped the letter on to the table and grabbed the back of the chair for support. 'We're closed,' he whispered. 'The mayor has closed us down.'

10

Stephanie didn't care if she never had to teach another yoga class in her life. Five days of elderly women in Lycra farting as they contorted themselves into various unnatural positions was more than enough for her. Plus she'd been away from Chloé and the mountains for what seemed like a year.

She pulled hard one more time, applying tension to the snow chains and feeling the muscles in her back stretching as they fought the effort and the cold. Satisfied that the slack had been taken up she moved around to the other tyre and repeated the process before getting back into the van.

She knew she was being overcautious but she wasn't willing to take a risk on the road up the mountain with just snow tyres. She'd already passed several abandoned cars coming out from St Girons, one dangling precariously over the steep river bank, deep skid marks leading up to it and even deeper footprints leading hastily away.

Stephanie stared out the windscreen, past the wipers flapping ineffectually at the incessant flakes, into a wall of white.

Snow. More of it than she could remember in her time here and still falling, already covering the tracks that she'd made only minutes earlier. Chloé was going to be ecstatic, especially as it had fallen just in time for the weekend.

The thought made Stephanie smile as she eased the van out of the lay-by on to the roundabout at Kerkabanac where the road out of St Girons split into two. Not long now. She felt the usual flutter of anticipation as she started the drive up the valley to home.

Home! The very idea made her laugh out loud.

Her, the woman with gypsy blood whose feet her ex-husband had once threatened to nail to the kitchen floor in order to tame her wanderlust, finally finding somewhere she wanted to stay for more than a week. And in sleepy Picarets of all places. That was something she hadn't seen coming when circumstances had forced her to flee with a two-year-old daughter in tow. They'd been looking for a bolt hole and had found a haven.

But finding work in the area wasn't easy. They'd arrived with a small suitcase and a car boot full of garden tools and since then Stephanie had been trying to eke out a living, getting seasonal work in the summer and relying on child benefit and the odd yoga class in the winter. But it wasn't enough. Soon Chloé would be at school in Seix and before long, perhaps, university, all of which Stephanie was determined to provide for her.

But that took money.

So, all the way back from Toulouse she'd been calculating and planning. With the job at the Auberge she could start putting a bit of money aside and in her free time she would concentrate on her organic garden centre. She'd start small with a few trips to local markets in the spring and the autumn, building up a client base over the next few years until she was ready to open.

She even knew where she wanted to locate it. Just past the épicerie in La Rivière there was a piece of waste land right on the river bank. It was badly overgrown with several trees that would need cutting down but it was the right size and next to the communal car park which could provide parking for her clients. She'd contacted the Bureau du Cadastre and had been over the moon to find out it was owned by Josette. Stephanie was sure she'd rent her the land for a reasonable fee.

It was the start of something big, Stephanie was convinced, and she couldn't wait to tell Chloé of her plans. But first she had to negotiate the rest of this journey in one piece.

Keeping the van in a low gear, Stephanie inched up the road which was down to one lane in places where passing locals had cut fallen trees enough to allow traffic through and no more. No one liked to linger outside when the weather was like this and more trees could fall at any minute. She regretted not throwing her own chainsaw in the back before leaving for Toulouse. It would have given her a bit more comfort.

Tense now as conditions deteriorated, all thoughts of the future forgotten, she twisted in her seat so she could scan the forest along the roadside as she drove, hoping that at least would give her the warning she needed.

She wound down her window so she could hear better although there was nothing she could do if a tree did fall. No point flooring the pedal in response. It would more likely result in a cold dip in the river than anything else.

A loud crack made her flinch, her hands clenching on the steering wheel as the van trundled on. Another crack and then the slow screeching of wood tearing. She tried not to panic, eyes glued to the road ahead. There was no movement. And then she saw it, in her rear-view mirror, a huge ash tree crashing to the ground some distance behind her and sending tremors through the van.

She swallowed hard.

Close. Maybe if she'd been a few minutes later leaving Toulouse or taken slightly longer fitting the chains . . .

She shook her head to clear her mind. No point thinking

like that. Two more corners and she would be at the lay-by opposite the Auberge. She focused on the road ahead and hoped to God the school had had enough sense not to open today and that the school bus would be spared this run.

As she turned the last corner, the devastation was the worst she'd seen. Swathes of trees had fallen, leaving a chicane of branches and broken trunks littering the road and if she wasn't mistaken an electricity line lying right across her path. She pursed her lips and drove over it, praying as she did so that someone at EDF had turned off the power.

When the Auberge finally came in sight, Stephanie felt sick with relief. She pulled into an area of the lay-by that had been cleared by the snow plough and turned off the engine. She'd walk home from here. She just couldn't face the road up. Not after that journey. Judging by the other cars abandoned around her she wouldn't be the only one to go home on foot. But first she needed to know whether to wait for the school bus or not.

She grabbed her bag off the back seat and switched on her mobile.

Damn. Out of battery.

The lights of the Auberge shone across at her, warm and inviting. She'd use their phone and maybe get a coffee before heading off. And besides, it was a good chance to find out about the inspection at the same time. That way she could treat Chloé and herself to a celebration pizza from the pizza van in Seix tomorrow night. If the snow cleared up that was.

Taking just her handbag, she followed the snow plough's tracks up the road to the front door of the Auberge. She stomped her boots to clear them and turned the handle and stepped inside.

'*Bonjour!*'

Paul and Lorna were sitting at the nearest table with their backs to her, Paul's arm around Lorna's shoulders.

'*Bonjour . . . Ça va?*' Stephanie raised her voice and Paul turned and stood up.

'Stephanie . . . hi. Sorry, it's not a good time . . .'

'Something is ze matter?' Now that she was inside with the door closed, Stephanie could feel the tension, like all the air had been sucked out of the room.

'No . . . yes . . . shit.' Paul's arms rose and fell like a marionette in the hands of a small child. He looked over at Lorna and Stephanie followed his gaze.

'*Merde!* What 'as 'appened?'

Lorna dabbed at her eyes which were puffed up and sore from crying, the tears still fresh on her pale cheeks.

'We failed the inspection.'

Stephanie's eyebrows shot into her hairline and she swung her focus back on to Paul.

'It's true? Zey failed you?'

Paul nodded.

'But you can still to do business, no?'

Lorna handed her the letter and silently left the room, unable to talk about it any more. The door hadn't even closed behind her when Stephanie exploded.

'Ze sons of breeches! Zey can't to close you. It is not legal! We must to protest!' She read the letter again, getting even more incensed. ' 'Ave you called zem? At ze *mairie*? Did you speak to ze mayor?'

Paul nodded again, this time with weary resignation. 'The town hall is closed until after New Year. I got the answering machine.' He gave a sardonic smile. 'Someone knew how to time this.'

Stephanie whistled softly. Someone meant business all right.

'So, what does zis mean? For you and Lorna?'

134

'We have to cancel all our reservations for New Year's Eve at least. And somehow we have to find the money for a new oil tank and boiler.'

'You can to do zis?'

'I honestly don't know.' He gently took the letter from her, refolded it and slid it back into its envelope. 'I'm sorry Stephanie, but this affects you too.'

Stephanie bit her lip, knowing what he was about to say.

'I'm really sorry, but we won't be able to take you on. Not for the foreseeable future.'

Stephanie didn't notice the blinding white snow, the wind whipping at her skirt, the cold seeping into her bones. She was too bloody mad. All she saw was a mist of red as she stormed down the steps of the Auberge and out on to the road. And beyond that, just about visible, a blue Panda parked at the épicerie. Without even being conscious of the decision, she started striding towards it.

The bastards. Playing around with people's lives like that. And for what? A political squabble of the tawdriest nature. It was enough to make her commit violence.

She needed that job. The commune needed people like Paul and Lorna. But the old farts on the Conseil Municipal couldn't see that. All they saw were outsiders and that set them running in panic, planning and conniving until the newcomers were ousted or got fed up with the lack of support and moved on of their own accord.

She knew what it was like. Sure there were people who'd been good to her and Chloé since they arrived. But there were just as many who would be happier to see them gone. And if they got away with this kind of crap with the Websters, who was to say what problems she would face when she tried to open her garden centre.

She swore again, her temper really flaring as she marched towards the shop, head down, oblivious to the tractor coming towards her, clearing the snow as it went. When she finally realised her predicament it was too late: she had nowhere to go. She only had time to catch a glimpse of a fat face and an orange beret before it was upon her.

Whoooooooooooooossssssssssssssssssssshhhhhhhhhh.

A wall of wet snow arched into the air from the blades of the plough as it sped past and covered Stephanie from head to toe, taking her breath for a split second as her body registered its sudden immersion in icy temperatures.

'You BASTARD!' she finally screamed in its wake, her rage robbing her of her eloquence. But the snow plough was gone, leaving her to stomp towards the shop like a snowman who'd spent a bit too long in the sun.

'Did you see that?' Christian laughed, pointing at the figure walking towards the shop through the blizzard. 'They just got covered by the snow plough. They look like the abominable snowman!'

Véronique chuckled but Josette only managed a half-smile and it didn't stay long, slipping from her face as quickly as it had arrived, leaving her looking pensive and old.

Christian and Véronique were worried about her. She hadn't been herself since the night of the council meeting and nothing they said could dissuade her of the opinion that the whole mess with the Auberge was all her fault.

'Not that funny?' he ventured.

She sighed and continued wiping the glass of the knife case, the cloth sweeping across the already immaculate surface in a desultory fashion while her thoughts were clearly miles away.

Christian glanced at Véronique but before he could say

anything the épicerie door crashed open and the snowman stormed in. Three strides and it was across the room giving Christian time to register the movements as vaguely familiar before it stretched out a snow-covered arm and brought the flat of its hand across his cheek in a resounding slap.

'YOU BASTARD!'

Christian staggered back in surprise and also an instinctive desire to get out of range of any repeat performances. He peered at the figure before him as the lump of snow masking its face fell to the ground, dislodged by the ferocity of the attack, revealing flashing green eyes and damp red curls.

'*Stephanie*? What on earth . . .?'

But she had already turned and left the shop, slamming the door behind her.

'What have you done to upset her?' Josette demanded, showing signs of an interest in life for the first time in days.

'Nothing . . . not a single thing,' spluttered Christian, rubbing his jaw where long fingers had blazed a crimson trail. 'Apart from laughing at her just now. It couldn't be that could it?'

Véronique glared at him. 'Of course it's not that! You must have done something to hurt her,' she stated, her voice laden with suspicion and disapproval and . . . disappointment. She sounded disappointed.

Christian shook his head, protesting his innocence while the two women eyed him warily.

'Well if you haven't done anything you'd best go after her and sort this out!' commanded Josette. 'And tell her to come back in here and we'll get her some dry clothes. Go on! What are you waiting for?'

'He's scared she'll slap him again!'

Blushing at the accuracy of Véronique's remark, Christian hurried out of the shop.

Stephanie was already halfway down the road when he caught up with her, her shoulders still hunched in fury and the snow still dripping off her.

'Stephanie? Are you OK?'

The look she gave him made his insides go cold and he flinched as her hand swung out again. But this time it was to merely brush the remaining snow from her face.

'OK? You're asking if I'm OK?' She took a deep breath to steady herself before turning from him, ready to walk away.

'Wait.' Christian put a hand on her shoulder, which was sopping wet. 'Stephanie, please? At least come back to the shop and get a change of clothes. You'll catch your death in this.'

Stephanie felt her anger collapse beneath his visible concern and suddenly she was aware of just how cold she was, shivers running up and down the length of her body.

'Seriously. Let's get in the warmth and then I promise, you can slap me all you like!'

He slipped off his coat and wrapped it around her.

'Come on. No point lingering out here. That bastard Bernard and his bloody snow plough will be back through any minute and I don't want to end up like you!'

A giggle rose in her throat despite herself as she leaned into him, his arm warm across her shoulders as they headed back to the épicerie.

'So your name was on the inspection letter and now she's lost her job! No wonder she slapped you!'

'I should have known it had to be something to do with the Auberge. Why else would she be so upset with me?'

Véronique's face flushed revealing exactly what she'd thought was the cause.

'You thought I'd . . . with Stephanie?' Christian looked at her in shock. 'Is that what everyone thinks?'

Véronique squirmed.

'Jesus! This place is unbearable!' Christian knocked back the last of his coffee and slammed the cup down on the saucer. 'It's bad enough with my parents without you starting.'

'What's the problem with your parents?' Josette asked as she came into the shop, closing the door to the bar softly behind her.

'Nothing,' muttered Christian, running a hand through his hair. 'How is she?'

'Asleep. We'll let her have half an hour and then you could drop her home. She's worn out, poor thing.'

'Right. What about Chloé?'

'She's with Maman,' said Véronique. 'I managed to get through on the phone and they have power back on as well so she's fine there for now.'

Christian nodded, still unable to look Véronique in the eye. Funny how it mattered what she thought of him.

'So, what are we going to do?' demanded Josette, folding up her glass-cleaning cloth and putting it in a drawer.

Christian sighed. 'Not much we can do. The mayor has made fools of us all and got us at each other's throats. And there's bugger all we can do about it.'

'Nonsense!'

There was something in the tone of Josette's voice that made Véronique and Christian stand up straight.

'So he's made idiots of us. So what. Are you telling me we can't sort this out between us?'

Christian stared out of the window where the Auberge was visible once more after the snowstorm.

'I'm not sure I still want to help them,' he admitted, turning back to Josette. 'Not after Sarko.'

139

'You don't know for sure it was them,' she protested.

'No but several people saw them walking down from Picarets straight after he escaped and now we know they had a reason. According to Stephanie, they thought I was to blame for the inspection.'

Josette dipped her head in acknowledgement. 'OK. Maybe they do blame you for this mess. But that doesn't mean to say they opened Sarko's gate.'

'Well who did then?'

Josette made a noise of exasperation. 'I don't know. All I know is that this situation is in danger of ripping the commune apart. And as far as I can see, the only way to stop it is to try and help each other.'

'But even if we did want to help, Josette,' Véronique answered, 'where would we get the money they need to reopen the Auberge?'

As if faced with an insurmountable hurdle, Josette deflated and the energy she'd felt buzzing around her bloodstream for the first time in days fizzled and died.

Dejected, she walked through to the bar and checked on Stephanie who was fast asleep, her head resting on her arms on the table. Jacques was standing behind her, stroking her hair like he used to do to Josette when they were first married. He smiled at her and held a finger to his lips which almost made her laugh.

A ghost telling her to be quiet.

She shook her head at the absurdity of it and wandered over to the window.

The Auberge stood there, covered in snow, no lights visible from the interior.

Josette leaned against the cold glass, her breath misting the window and blurring her view.

She'd think of something. She had to.

Right now, that was the only thing keeping her going.

She stared blindly out of the épicerie until the snow began to fall again like a heavy curtain draped across the commune, cutting it in half and rendering the Auberge invisible behind its folds once more.

I I

By the time the snow finally stopped, the citizens of Fogas had forgotten all about Christmas. So concerned had they been with the intermittent electricity supply, the poor state of the roads, their rapidly dwindling wood stocks and the dangers of meeting Bernard in the snow plough that the special day had passed them by before festivities had even begun.

The communal Christmas tree had gone up in the car park opposite the épicerie a week before as usual, decorated with a few straggling bows and a string of lights which the mayor was too tight to plug in. But this year weather conditions had been so bad that Bernard had cut down the first tree he'd found in the forests above Fogas and so the end result was even more wretched than usual, with pathetically thin branches drooping sparsely from an emaciated trunk.

The overall effect was more grotty than grotto.

Paul eyed the tree with malevolence as he walked back to the Auberge, trying to alleviate his bad mood by inhaling the scent of the freshly baked bread he was carrying. It didn't work as he was no more in the festive spirit when he reached the front door than when he'd left.

Christmas Day had been spent in misery. They'd gone for a walk but bad weather had forced them back early, so they'd cooked their Christmas dinner and tried to pretend that they weren't looking down into the abyss of insolvency. Hard to do when the Auberge was closed by order of the commune, they were turning down bookings daily and until New Year was out of the way there was very little they could do to resolve the problem.

Paul had made countless phone calls to tradesmen and builders, trying to get estimates for the work that needed doing but either there was no answer, or the answer was that there was no one available. Not until after New Year's Eve. Likewise with the town hall and the Chambre de Commerce in Foix.

It seemed like everyone was on holiday and having a good time.

Everyone except them.

The only person he'd managed to get a straight answer from was the bank manager and it had been a firm no. Given the current economic crisis, there was no chance of financial help from the bank until the notice of closure had been lifted and they were able to trade. No income, no loan.

Paul slammed the door shut behind him and immediately locked and bolted it.

If the commune was going to order them closed then they would bloody well be closed and sod anyone wanting to use the phone or leave parcels for others to collect on their way past as some people had been doing. Like the Auberge was the hub of the community or something.

Paul sighed and leaned against the door, his anger dissipating as quickly as it had formed. He knew it wasn't the entire commune that was to blame.

From behind the post office came the clear call of the village bells as they began to ring the Angelus. Seven o'clock already. New Year's Eve. Normally they would be getting ready to go out in Manchester with friends. Tonight they were facing the prospect of another night in with the accounts.

They'd turned down an invitation from Stephanie to join her and Chloé for a meal simply because they weren't good company right now and didn't want to inflict their bad moods on anyone else. Plus there were bad storms forecast and if the roof was going to fall in on the Auberge, Paul felt he should be there.

He turned from the door and headed towards the kitchen where he could hear Lorna busy cooking the dinner. Sausages and mash. Not very traditional but still his favourite. His nose twitched at the smell. And then twitched again.

What on earth was that stench? It smelt like rotting meat.

He pushed open the kitchen door to see Lorna frantically thumbing through the French dictionary, her glasses halfway down her nose.

'What's—'

She raised a hand for him to be quiet as she skimmed down the relevant page, glancing now and then at the label on the empty packet of sausages in her hand. Finally her finger came to rest and she swore loudly.

'What's the matter?'

Lorna took off her glasses and glared at the sausages sizzling away in the pan.

'Offal!'

'What's awful?'

'OFFAL! Those lovely Cumberland-esque sausages we bought? They're offal.'

'WHAT?'

'As soon as they hit the frying pan I knew there was something wrong.' She switched off the heat under the pan in disgust. 'Damn it! Why can't something go right for once!'

Paul took hold of her hands, which had curled into tight fists of temper, and pulled her towards him.

'We've still got the mash,' he suggested, trying not to

144

inhale the rank smell emanating from the stove. Lorna snorted into his shoulder, whether in rage or amusement he couldn't tell.

It was New Year's Eve and as far as Paul was concerned, the next year could only get better.

Stephanie threw the dress back down on her bed and stared into the depths of her wardrobe once more. Therein lay the problem. Her wardrobe had a lot of depth and very little by way of clothes.

A few pairs of jeans, a couple of skirts, some tops, a dress and a jacket. That was it. It never normally bothered her but she wanted to make an effort tonight, as much by way of an apology as anything else.

It was almost two weeks since she'd lost her temper with Christian and she still couldn't think about it without cringing. Slapping him like that in front of everyone was extreme even by her fiery standards. But especially so when she thought about all he'd done for her and Chloé since they'd arrived. And to make it worse she'd got home that night to find a fire lit, milk in the fridge, bread on the table and the broken shutter fixed.

She felt awful. To the point where she'd almost refused the annual invitation to join the Dupuys for the New Year's Eve celebrations. It was agony enough suffering a nine-hour meal of foie gras, oysters, and various platters of cold meat with a hostess who didn't quite grasp the concept of vegetarianism. Normally the only upside was that Madame Dupuy bought in all the food and so what there was that could pass as vegetable was at least edible and not burnt to a cinder.

But this year she would have to sit across from Christian all night knowing how dreadfully she'd behaved and she really didn't know how she was going to cope.

'Oh for God's sake!'

Finally impatient with her own dithering, Stephanie reached into the wardrobe and jerked out a dark green floral top she'd bought at the market in St Girons two years ago. With a pair of jeans it would be just fine.

She quickly dressed before she could change her mind, berating herself the whole time for being so pathetic. It wasn't as if Christian was interested in her or anything. She didn't need her gypsy intuition to tell her that. And if she hadn't already sussed it out, overhearing his reaction to Véronique in the shop when they thought she was sleeping would have been enough to put her right.

He'd sounded horrified at the mere suggestion of Stephanie being more than just a friend.

She smiled wryly at the memory. A year ago she would have been upset by his response. She'd heard the rumours flying around the commune about the pair of them and part of her still wished they were true. But over the last twelve months she'd come to accept that Christian Dupuy's heart lay elsewhere. And he didn't have a clue as to where exactly that was.

But she did.

She grinned at herself in the mirror and ran her fingers through her hair which was even more wayward than usual.

Yes, he was in for one hell of a shock when he finally woke up and realised where his future lay. That was one of the benefits of inheriting gypsy blood. Knowing things without being told. Feeling things no one else could sense. Like the old hand stroking her head, soothing away her stress as she lay on the table in the bar, the smell of the fire and the aged scent of drinks long drunk mixing with the unmistakable sharpness of an aftershave she hadn't smelt in six months.

The sound of the bamboo wind-chimes in the back garden rattling in the strengthening breeze brought her back to the present. Sometimes it was cool being one step ahead, she admitted to herself as she gathered her car keys off the dressing table and prepared to go.

'You look great, Maman!' Chloé grinned at her in appreciation from the doorway, her voice suddenly full of faux-innocence. 'Isn't that the top Christian likes?'

Stephanie glanced at her daughter whose eyes were full of devilment.

'Is it?' she replied with equal innocence. 'I had no idea!'

Chloé's clear laugh rang out around the room and suddenly, in comparison, Stephanie felt as wise as a newborn baby. Clearly the Romany influence hadn't skipped a generation.

Annie Estaque didn't need any exotic heritage to sense the trouble that was coming. She only had to look at the sky. She'd climbed the ridge at the back of the house and now stood astride it, her head tipped back to watch the frantic pace of the clouds as the wind whipped them across the heavens. Normally she'd have been entranced by the appearance and disappearance of the stars as they winked on and off above her but she was too busy reading the coming weather.

And it wasn't good news.

She'd known last night when she'd seen the moon peeking out through a high haze of cloud that the storm was coming. Been even more sure when the cloud level had dropped dramatically during the day. She didn't need the radio to tell her what to expect or the glamorous young weather woman on the TV with her Code Orange Alert to warn of the trouble looming. Papa had taught her well, standing alongside her on this very ridge, pointing out the various cloud formations as he assessed the weather for the coming harvest or the timing of the transhumance.

One summer, years ago when she was very young, a professor from the University of Toulouse, on holiday in the Pyrenees, had tried teaching Papa the Latin names for the clouds he knew so well.

Cirrostratus, altocumulus, stratocumulus, nimbostratus, cumulonimbus . . .

Papa had listened to the man with the bafflement of someone being offered a complicated tool for a simple task, mystified as to why anyone would want to turn something so straightforward into an academic puzzle. Much easier to classify the clouds by portent: fair weather clouds, rain clouds, clouds that heralded a change in pressure.

He'd been right. But still the Latin names had stayed with Annie and sometimes when she couldn't sleep she would find herself reciting them like a rosary for believers in the power of Nature.

Looking now at the dark mass in the distance rolling ever closer, she'd no doubt be reciting them again tonight as the storm kept her awake. This was a big one. This one was going to cause damage.

With a last worried glance at the horizon, Annie turned away from the storm and felt the strengthening wind buffet her back before she dropped down from the ridge and descended to the farmhouse. Her cattle were already safely housed in the barn; as safe as anything could be with what was coming.

She let herself in the back door and with a cursory pat for the two waiting dogs, she started getting things ready for the night to come. Candles, torches, wood for the fire, blankets and cushions on the old armchair in the corner. No point going to bed. She wouldn't be getting any sleep anyway.

She settled herself on a kitchen chair and reached for the

phone. Time enough to give Véronique a quick call and make sure she was OK.

As Annie dialled the first few numbers the light bulb flickered ominously overhead. It was going to be a long night.

In the small apartment above the post office the phone rang and rang, echoing in the emptiness. As though in reply, an unlatched shutter banged noisily against a window and the doors rattled but no one reached for the phone.

Down below, a door slammed shut and Véronique cast a huddled shadow in the street light as she darted across the road, fighting the weather to reach the church. With growing strength, the wind fought back, tearing at her clothing and whipping her hair around her face before thrusting her roughly into the shelter of the walled graveyard.

Never her favourite place on the sunniest of days, tonight the dancing shadows and shrieking wind had Véronique on edge, her nerves jangling as she hurried between the gravestones, trying not to think about the dead and buried beneath her feet. A final gust on her back propelled her into the church porch where there was just about enough light to see the lock on the huge wooden door. She turned the key and slipped gratefully into the dark tranquillity of the old building.

Tranquil except for the banging noise that had brought her out into the worsening storm. Sure enough, there was the source. One of the side windows was open and it was snapping back and forth in the tempest, the stained glass close to breaking.

It was just as well she'd decided to investigate as already the wind had wreaked havoc inside the confines of the small church. The altar cloth had been lifted off and discarded in a heap across the aisle, the ceremonial candlesticks had been knocked over and most of the devotional candles had been blown out, leaving the air heavy with the scent of spent prayers. Those few that remained alight were sputtering in the strengthening gusts.

Feeling justified at venturing out in such awful weather, Véronique swiftly crossed the church, slipped off her shoes and clambered up on to a table piled high with religious literature to close the window. She could just about reach it, straining up on tiptoes as the table wobbled beneath her on the uneven floor. But just as her fingers curled around the latch, the force of the wind tore the window out of her hands before abruptly slamming it shut in her face.

Momentarily thrown off balance, Véronique staggered backwards, the table seesawing violently in response, and her stockinged feet slipped on a stack of glossy pamphlets entitled *What Happens to Me When I Die?* Suddenly aware she was about to get first-hand experience, she toppled off the table, arms flailing futilely in an attempt to save herself as she fell through the cold air and landed heavily beneath the statue of St Germaine, patron saint of the little church. Her head impacted hard on the stone floor and the snap of her right leg ricocheted round the now-silent interior.

She lay there for a second, pain and nausea washing over her, vaguely aware of something rocking, the noise of something unsettled, unbalanced, teetering on the edge. Then suddenly there was a burst of light, an explosion of sound and Véronique saw St Germaine descend from heaven towards her, borne on the rushing wings of a thousand angels.

So, she thought as the face of the pious shepherdess loomed ever closer, *this* is what happens to me when I die.

Then everything was plunged into darkness.

★   ★   ★

The stray bolt of lightning had hit the electricity cable running between the post office and the church. The resultant flames were small at first, a smouldering half-hearted fire which wasn't going to do any harm. But then a spark was caught by a draught and carried on to a piece of material and soon the fire had grown beyond control, its heat cracking glass and tearing at the doors, warping the structural timbers and peeling the paint off the walls.

By the time the neighbours noticed and called the fire brigade, the flames were licking at the roof tiles and smoke was belching out of the windows.

But Véronique was oblivious. She was at peace, held fast in the arms of St Germaine.

Serge Papon was at the window when the lights went out. *Fzutt.* Just like that. The whole of Fogas snuffed out like a candle. The dark was so total, he could barely make out the lace curtain in his hand.

He let the curtain fall and groped his way back towards the bed, gently feeling along the bedcovers for the cold hand of his wife. Her fingers fluttered briefly in response and she uttered a low groan.

'Not long now my love. The ambulance is on its way.'

He patted her hand, not really knowing what else to do. He'd called the doctor when it had become apparent that his wife's condition had taken a turn for the worse and the doctor had immediately called the ambulance. But beyond that, Serge felt inadequate, his position in the community counting for nothing in the face of his wife's illness.

Outside the storm was raging up the valley, showing no signs of easing and somehow even more menacing in the pitch-black conditions. Suddenly, thunder crashed overhead and the room was briefly vivid, the curtains, the bedside table, the still form of his wife below the bedclothes and above them all, the outlines of the crucifix on the wall.

As his eyes struggled to readjust to the following dark, much to his own surprise, Serge started reciting the rosary. The dusty words of his youth came back to him slowly at first, stumbling and hesitant and then with more and more conviction as he felt his wife drawing comfort from his prayers, her whispered responses barely audible above the howling wind.

He was on his second decade when the lights of the ambulance split the night as it rounded the bend into the village. He didn't stop while the medics lifted his wife on to a stretcher and into the back of the vehicle. He barely skipped a beat when the ambulance slowed up in La Rivière to get round the fire engine and the crowd of people gathered in the road by the church. In fact the whole way into St Girons, while the wind roared outside and the medics tried to make his wife as comfortable as possible, he kept praying, as much for his sake as hers.

The lack of electricity didn't bother Pascal Souquet, deputy mayor of Fogas. He'd been prepared for it and had rigged up the generator which was now chugging away outside the ramshackle annexe jutting off the town hall which served as a community hall. No, what bothered him was the company he was having to keep.

As he strutted around the packed room, offering a smile here and a brief handshake there to the New Year's revellers, he tried not to think about the friends and acquaintances he'd left behind in Paris. Doctors, lawyers, artists . . . So much more refined than the people here tonight. So much more cultured. And as for the food . . .

'Darling,' Fatima cooed in his ear while encircling his arm

with a vicious grip. 'You're letting it show dear. Remember, these people are your future!'

She released him and disappeared into the crowd, leaving the air behind her heady with perfume and disappointment.

Pascal rubbed his arm, impressed and scared by his wife in equal measures. Of course, this had all been her idea. A soirée. A small gathering to celebrate the New Year targeted at the second-home owners who descended on the village every festive season and had no one to celebrate it with.

It was ingenious. They'd hired the community hall, put up a few party lights, rigged up a disco and the second-home owners had fallen over themselves to attend. Even with the price. Fatima had suggested thirty euros a ticket and when Pascal had objected, pointing out that it would be too expensive for most of the locals, she had merely raised an eyebrow and smiled.

She'd been right. The locals had stayed home, refusing to pay out to sit in a prefab building in freezing temperatures, whereas the second-home owners hadn't batted an eyelid. So now he had a captive audience, his power base all in one place, and all desperately grateful for the party he'd organised for them.

If only they weren't all so provincial . . .

He glanced at his watch. Ten to midnight. Was that all? God, he had *hours* left to bear. His life wouldn't be worth living if he left before the traditional onion soup was served at five a.m.

'Have you tried the foie gras? It's excellent!'

A large woman in a billowing black dress, skin greasy with make-up, was thrusting a plate under his nose. Pascal had no choice but to accept.

'Thank you,' he murmured with a smile, taking a slice of toast and biting off a small end. As the lumpy meat paste hit his palette, he felt his throat close in reflex, bile rising into his mouth. It was all he could do not to retch in front of her.

153

'Isn't it delicious?' the woman gushed.

'Mmmm . . .' Pascal managed, not trusting himself to open his lips.

As she moved away with the plate to tempt other party-goers, Pascal discreetly spat the remaining morsel into his napkin and dropped it into the pot of a fake fern. He'd told Fatima it was a mistake to entrust the catering to a group of women from the village and he'd been right. The oysters had been gritty, the champagne of poor quality and now the foie gras was barely fit to grace a cat's bowl. No doubt they'd done their shopping at Aldi!

A roar from the far side of the room caught his attention and he turned just in time to see Lucien Biros knee-sliding across the space set aside for dancing, strumming the life out of an improvised guitar in the shape of a broom while others began jiving around him.

Oh good God. Someone had put Johnny Hallyday on already. *Five* more hours of France's answer to Elvis. It was worse than torture.

Pascal looked up to the heavens, obscured by the asbestos tiles on the annexe roof, and prayed for salvation. Before long, his prayers would be answered.

By the time Christian and Stephanie got down to La Rivière in response to Josette's call, there was a large crowd gathered in the road between the church and the post office, their faces lit by the dancing flames as they watched the firemen battle the blaze. Christian made his way to the front where the small figure of Josette was visible, her hands clasped to her face as she stared at the burning building.

'Where's Véronique?' Christian shouted to her above the roar of the wind. 'Is she OK?'

Josette turned to him and that's when he noticed the tears

glinting on her cheeks. She shook her head, unable to say anything, simply pointing at the fire in response, and Christian felt fear strike his soul.

'No!' He looked back at the building, the roof alight, flames at the windows, dense plumes of smoke spiralling into the night. Véronique. She was in there.

When Christian started running towards the fire there was little anyone could do to stop him. René Piquemal would be overheard to comment later on in the bar that it was like watching Christian in his heyday for the local rugby team, lumbering towards the building like his hero Chabal. Stephanie grabbed one of his arms but he shrugged her off with ease and when one of the volunteer firefighters from Massat tried to stand in his way, arms out wide to bar Christian's approach, the man was shoved aside by a simple hand to his chest. No one was a match for the huge farmer, not once he was up to speed.

But a stray fireman's hose was a different matter.

Just as he reached the door to the burning building, running at full pelt, Christian's left foot caught in the coils of hose snaking across the road and he was sent sprawling, his chin hitting the doorstep as he crashed to the ground mere feet from the flames.

Stephanie was the first to react. She raced over to his motionless body and grabbed hold of one of his legs, tugging at it in an effort to pull him away from the fire. Quickly joined by René and two other men, together they managed to drag him back to the other side of the road where they sat his still lifeless form up against a wall.

'Christian?' Stephanie leaned over him and gently slapped his face. 'You OK?'

Christian's eyelids flickered and he mumbled something and then he shook his head and his eyes flew open.

'Véronique!' he shouted, struggling to get up off the ground as René and Josette tried to hold him down.

'Stop it, Christian,' pleaded Stephanie as he writhed around. 'Please, stop. It's no use.'

And suddenly Christian went still. Whether it was the sight of the flames in the background or the rare tears welling up in Stephanie's eyes, something caused him to collapse and his head fell on to his chest, huge hands covering his face as the enormity of the evening's events settled in. He let out a low moan.

Véronique was dead.

How on earth was he going to break the news to Annie?

The fight gone out of him, he staggered to his feet and leaned against the graveyard wall, his mind numb with shock, his eyes not really seeing. And his ears playing tricks on him.

What was that?

As he twisted to face the wind which was now whistling from the other direction, down the valley from Fogas, he heard it again.

He noticed Stephanie turning too, her head cocked to one side as though listening for something.

There it was again, faint but sure.

'Christiannnnnn. Help meeeeee!'

Véronique's voice, carried to him from beyond the grave.

'Did you hear that?' he whispered to Stephanie, goose bumps on his arms. 'It's Véronique! She's calling me from . . . from . . .'

'From the church! It's coming from the church!'

'What . . . you mean . . .'

'Véronique!' Stephanie shouted. 'She's not in her apartment! She's in the church!' and she took off running across the graveyard, Christian and René close behind. They reached the huge door and burst inside where, by the light of the fire

156

at the post office opposite, they could just about discern two figures lying entangled on the ground on the far side of the church. And unless Christian was mistaken, the smaller of the two was missing a head.

'You took your time!' murmured the figure on the bottom, the one that still had its head intact.

'Véronique!' Christian exclaimed in relief.

Not knowing whether to laugh or cry, he dropped to his knees and carefully lifted the decapitated statue of St Germaine off Véronique and set it to one side.

'My leg,' Véronique mumbled, clearly in pain. 'I think it's broken.'

'I'll call an ambulance,' René said, pulling out his mobile and heading out of the church to get better reception just as Josette and several others rushed in.

'You had us worried there,' Christian joked, his voice not quite steady as he removed his coat and gently laid it over Véronique.

She managed a snort in response.

'You mean . . . you're not going to tell me off . . . for being in the church . . . when I should have been safe at home?' she gasped. Her head lolled back and her voice became weaker. 'That's not like you. Are you losing . . . your socialist principles?'

'Something like that,' he muttered as she passed out. Stephanie and Josette caught his eye and he shook his head ever so slightly. They all knew Véronique's dedication to her church had saved her life. But there was no need for her to know that her apartment had burnt down completely and she'd lost everything. Time enough for that later, when the storm had passed and things had calmed down.

For now it felt good just knowing she was alive.

★　★　★

When the flashing blue lights of the ambulance finally pulled away from the church, the storm had almost finished with the commune of Fogas. Almost.

High up above the valleys that wound through the mountains the wind was building to its finale, the clouds roiling and churning in the sky and the force of the gale increasing, preparing to unleash its wrath like a rampaging beast on the villages below.

First it bore down on to Picarets, tossing aside garden furniture and plant pots and tearing up a polytunnel, making light of the metal struts and laying waste to the plants inside. It roared over the houses, twisting satellite dishes and snapping TV aerials, before following the valley through the forest to pounce on the solitary farmhouse, flicking the ridge tiles from the slate roof, dislodging stones in the gable wall and buckling sheets of metal on the side of the barn as it passed.

From there it swooped down into La Rivière, howling along the river and rattling across the roof tiles, severing unlatched shutters from their hinges, cleaving huge boughs off the trees and dismembering the commune Christmas tree. It skipped over the last few houses, the smoke from the now-smouldering fire sucked into the vortex as the tempest surged up the hill, gathering in strength to hurricane force as it went.

Higher and higher it climbed, uprooting trees and razing telegraph poles, electric cables snapping and crackling as their supports gave way. Finally it crested the ridge and swept into Fogas, skimming slates off houses on to cars below, smashing windscreens and lacerating metal. It screamed up the road towards the town hall, destroying chimneys and demolishing wooden sheds, leaving behind a trail of devastation, until at last it reached the annexe where the noise of the generator and the throbbing rock and roll music had deafened the revellers to the storm's approach. There, just as the old clock started to chime, in its last gasp the wind reached down and ripped all the asbestos tiles off the roof, exposing the figures below who were left running for safety like ants scurrying from an overturned nest.

With that, the storm passed. And the New Year began.

12

'You mean you 'ad no damage? None at all?'

Paul shook his head and gestured out of the dining-room window to the back yard, where in the long shadows of the winter sun Chloé was chasing Tomate through the fallen branches that covered the ground.

'Just a few limbs off the old ash and of course more rain damage through the holes in the roof. And we now get Al Jazeera TV! But nothing major.'

'You were lucky!' Stephanie exclaimed.

Paul said nothing, not wanting to admit that things would have been a lot easier if the roof had been ripped off in the hurricane. At least that way the insurance would have covered the cost of a new one. But it felt churlish to joke about it when everyone else in the commune had suffered far worse and many were still without power. From all accounts the post-mistress had only just escaped with her life after a fire gutted her apartment. A stained ceiling and a twisted satellite dish were nothing in comparison.

'And you?' he asked.

Stephanie pulled a face. 'Ze plastic 'ouse for my plants? It was destroyed. Totally. And all ze plants too.' She gave a shrug, trying to make light of it. 'It is not so serious.'

And it wasn't. Not in light of what had happened to Véronique, losing all of her possessions and her home. Nor had Stephanie been injured like some of the people who'd gone to the New Year's party where the roof had been blown off. And she hadn't lost her barn or had major damage to her house like Annie Estaque.

But even so, it felt like the end of the world.

First the job at the Auberge had been taken away and now her attempts to create a new life for herself and Chloé had been set back by at least two years with the destruction of her polytunnel and the plants inside it.

She'd felt sick when she'd finally got home on New Year's Day, having picked up Chloé from the Dupuys'. After a night of high drama culminating in a trip to the hospital with Véronique, the sight of the twisted hoops of metal and the torn plastic scattered around the back garden in the weak morning sunlight had been enough to make her burst into tears. Even more upsetting were the plants which, deprived of their protection, had been battered by the rain and shredded by the wind.

All of her work had been in vain. She was back to square one, teaching yoga to flatulent old ladies and praying that something else would turn up.

Which was why she was here at the Auberge. Trying to make something turn up.

'*Bonjour* Stephanie,' Lorna called out as she entered the room. '*Ça va?*'

Stephanie embraced her and grinned in reply. 'Your French! It is getting more good. Soon I won't 'ave to speak English!'

Lorna laughed at the exaggerated praise. 'Well I wouldn't go that far but we have been studying hard. Even though we're not sure about the future . . .' She cast a glance at Paul as she said it.

'We spent most of Christmas and New Year trying to work out our finances,' Paul explained with a grimace. 'And it doesn't look good! It seems like the new boiler and oil tank are

going to cost a lot more than we thought and as for the roof . . .'
He tailed off and reached for a pile of letters on the table next
to an open laptop.

'Here. Look at these,' he said, passing them over to
Stephanie.

She flicked through them, her eyebrows arching higher and
higher as she did so.

'It's a joke, no? Zey are for real?'

Lorna nodded and Stephanie let out a low whistle as she
glanced at the estimates which had arrived in the post over the
past few days.

'*TEN* thousand for a boiler and oil tank? *THIRTY* thousand
for a roof? We should to change jobs!'

'Well, short of robbing a bank,' Paul continued, 'we can't
see any way we can afford to do this work. And if we can't do
the work, then we can't pass the inspection and we can't open.'

'So we're seriously considering selling the Auberge,' Lorna
concluded, her face downcast as she voiced the difficult decision they'd reached.

'No! No need to sell!' exclaimed Stephanie, making them
both jump. 'Zat's why I am 'ere. To get you some money!'

An hour later Paul sat back from the computer, his head
aching and his mind spinning. But for the first time in ages
there was hope in his heart. It seemed like Stephanie was on
to something.

'So let me get this straight. We can apply to the Chambre de
Commerce for grants which will give us a third of the money
we need?'

Stephanie nodded.

'So in that case, the work we need to do to pass the inspection and reopen the Auberge would cost just under seven
thousand euros.'

'Yes.'

'Well that seems a bit more palatable.' He did a few more calculations on the computer and whistled softly.

'We can just about do it. If we take into account the other bills we have to pay by the end of the month. But in order to be eligible for the grants, we have to become an Hôtel de Tourisme, is that right?'

Stephanie nodded again.

'Which means yet another inspection!' groaned Lorna.

'Yes, but it is not so . . . 'ow you say, rigid?' Stephanie said. 'Not like ze last one.'

'Well what's the worst they can do if we fail?' remarked Paul with a smile. 'We're already closed by order of the commune.'

Lorna's laugh had more than a touch of derision but Stephanie gave the question serious thought. This was France after all and she suspected her Anglo-Saxon friends didn't quite get the idiosyncratic nature of French bureaucracy. Anything was possible when civil servants were involved.

'Nothing,' she finally concluded to Paul and Lorna's relief. 'I think zey can to do nothing more.'

'In that case then,' continued Paul, 'how soon can we get an inspection organised?'

Stephanie stood up from the table and crossed the room to pick up the phone.

'Beat ze iron while it is 'ot!' she announced and started dialling. Within seconds she was talking away in rapid French.

'Wow! She doesn't hang around does she!' Paul exclaimed as he reached across the table and took Lorna's hand, his voice suddenly brimming with excitement. 'Do you realise this could change everything? If we get a grant, we could afford to replace the oil tank and boiler and have the Auberge reopened in time for the start of the season! And then we can begin saving for the roof.'

Lorna smiled at his renewed enthusiasm but said nothing.

'You don't seem sure?'

She rubbed her forehead as though erasing her worries.

'It's just, I don't know. I'm afraid to get my hopes up in case . . .'

Paul squeezed her hand, not needing her to finish the sentence. They'd just spent a miserable few weeks trying to deal with the consequences of the last inspection. It seemed ironic to be pinning their hopes on yet another one.

'Ze thirteenth?' interrupted Stephanie, her hand over the mouthpiece of the phone. 'For ze inspection. It is OK?'

'The thirteenth? Of January?'

'Yes. I told zem it is urgent!'

Paul and Lorna exchanged startled glances. It was only a week away. Lorna shrugged her shoulders and nodded.

'OK,' Paul replied as Stephanie reverted back into French and concluded her call.

'Christ!' Lorna let out a shaky breath. 'This is all happening a bit fast.'

'Better than sitting around doing nothing.'

'Yes! Better zan doing nothing,' Stephanie agreed, catching the end of their exchange as she hung up the phone. She moved over to where Lorna was sitting and put a hand on her shoulder, her eyes wiser than her years.

'Not to worry, Lorna,' she said, looking down into her face with an uncharacteristic intensity. 'You will to get ze money.'

And for a split second, Lorna believed her.

Stephanie clapped her hands and shook back her hair as though preparing to dance.

'And now,' she declared theatrically, her arms raised like a preacher, 'today is ze Epiphany so we must to eat *galette des rois*!'

Paul visibly blanched as Stephanie reached into the bag she

164

had brought with her and pulled out a cake just as Chloé and Tomate burst into the room on a blast of fresh air.

'Is it time for the cake, Maman?' Chloé demanded, clearly excited. Discarding her hat and coat, her curls springing out in all directions, she hurried over to the table and sat next to Lorna, the cat jumping straight up on to her lap.

'Have you had kings' cake before?' she asked Lorna and when Lorna shook her head, Chloé started to explain the tradition in her best simple French. But Paul wasn't paying any heed. He was too busy trying to work out how to get out of this without being rude.

Stephanie cut the first slice and passed it across to Lorna, who was still listening to Chloé. Then she cut a second piece.

'And for you Paul . . .' she said, using French for Chloé's benefit as she held out the plate. But Paul put up his hand and shook his head.

'But you must try it! It's tradition,' she insisted.

Paul grinned weakly and patted his stomach.

'I eat a big lunch. Not hungry.'

Lorna gave Paul a quizzical glance but said nothing while Chloé was regarding him with incredulity.

'OK. Your loss!' Stephanie replied with a shrug before handing the plate to Chloé instead who took it with murmured thanks, still puzzling over Paul's behaviour.

Why would anyone refuse to eat kings' cake? Was he mad? Then suddenly she remembered the last time they'd eaten cake together.

Of course! He thought Maman had made the cake!

She waited until Lorna and Stephanie were busy chatting and then beckoned frantically for Paul to lean over to her until she could whisper in his ear.

'Don't worry,' she hissed at him. 'Maman didn't make the cake! We bought it in the bakery in Seix.'

Paul looked at Chloé and then at the cake and then back to Chloé.

'Really?'

Chloé nodded, her eyes dancing with laughter as she sat back in her seat. Paul grinned in response. That changed everything.

'Err . . . Stephanie. I make a mistake,' Paul said, pointing at the remainder of the cake as Chloé stifled a fit of the giggles. 'Can I having some?'

Stephanie reached for the knife, a knowing smile flickering across her face.

'I thought you were full?' Lorna queried as Paul took the plate eagerly.

'I was,' he answered before taking a big bite of the cake and winking at Chloé. 'But I suddenly got my appetite backkkag hhhhhhhhh!'

Paul stopped eating, his face white with shock as he carefully reached into his mouth and pulled out a small, hard object that had nearly broken one of his teeth.

'You found it!' Chloé squealed, dislodging the cat unceremoniously from her lap before running over to Stephanie's bag to look for something. 'I can't believe you weren't even going to have any and now you've found it!'

'Found what?' Paul asked, nonplussed as he stared at the tiny ceramic figure of Mickey Mouse in his hand.

'The *fève*. You 'ave found ze *fève*. It is always 'idden in the *galette des rois*,' Stephanie explained with a large smile. 'Chloé told you zat I didn't make ze cake, yes? But she didn't tell you about ze *fève*, no?'

'Hang on a minute,' Lorna interjected, her voice incredulous. 'You mean you didn't want the cake because you thought Stephanie had made it?'

Stephanie burst into laughter as Paul had the grace to blush.

'It's OK!' She waved away his apologies. 'I don't to blame you. My cooking is *merde*!'

Paul grinned sheepishly while Chloé placed a cardboard crown on his head with great ceremony.

'You're king for the day!' she announced. 'It's supposed to bring you luck.'

'Well, let's drink to that,' said Paul, adjusting his lopsided crown and lifting up his cup of tea in a mock toast. 'God knows we're due a bit of luck.'

Véronique was in a rotten mood. Six days in hospital with a broken leg, cracked ribs and suspected hypothermia had left her feeling worn out and irritable. It was impossible to get any peace and quiet with people coming and going on the ward all the time. And her frayed temper wasn't helped by the incessant *click click clickety click* of the grandmother in the next bed who seemed to be knitting the world's largest sweater.

But what was making her even more miserable was the unbearable itchiness of her leg under its thick casing of plaster. It was driving her to distraction. Worse than the pain in her ribs. She'd tried wriggling her toes to alleviate the discomfort and even twisting the cast, which had hurt. A lot. But the itching had continued, prickling her skin like an army of ants creeping over her flesh, until she was ready to tear her own leg off just to stop it.

Finally she'd had a brainwave. She'd borrow a knitting needle off the old dear next to her and kill two irritants with one stone.

Now she was staring morosely at her thigh where the top of the needle was just about visible, wedged tight between her leg and the cast.

It was stuck.

She'd pushed it further and further trying to satisfy her

craving to scratch until the head had gone so far in that she couldn't get her fingers around it to pull it out. No doubt it was going to cut off the blood supply to her leg any time soon and then she might have to have the leg amputated. All because of an itch she couldn't reach, tormenting her like a bad case of hives.

To make matters worse, her neighbour was still clicking away with her knitting, oblivious, using her spare needles which she apparently always had with her. Just in case some stupid cow in the next bed decided to lose one down her plaster cast.

Véronique pulled her pyjama bottoms back up and threw herself against the pillows, the searing pain in her side reminding her that she wasn't supposed to make any sudden movements. Feeling utterly wretched, she screwed her eyes shut to stop the tears of frustration from spilling on to her cheeks.

As if an itchy leg was the worst of her problems. The doctor had told her she could go home today and she'd had to bite back a laugh of derision.

Home? She had no home. Not any more. Everything she owned had been burnt in the fire apart from the clothes she'd had on when she'd left her apartment; a jumper, a T-shirt and some underwear. They'd had to cut off her trousers to treat her leg so she didn't even have a complete outfit. She'd just have to leave the hospital in the extra-large pyjamas her mother had bought for her to fit over the cast.

As to where she was going to stay, that was another matter. Maman's house was out of the question as the storm had rendered it uninhabitable with part of the roof torn off and structural damage to a gable wall. Of course, Maman was still living there, too stubborn to move while the repairs were being carried out. But for Véronique and her broken leg . . .

So instead, while the full impact of the fire at her commune-owned apartment was assessed and the necessary work undertaken, she was being parcelled off to Josette's like a refugee. Only she had no possessions to take with her.

She tried to give herself a mental shake, knowing that she ought to be more grateful for Josette's gracious offer of accommodation. But it was difficult not to be despondent and despite her best efforts, a tear seeped from under her clenched eyelids.

'Vérrronique? Itshhhokaylove. We'llshhhortit.'

A calloused hand slipped over her own where it lay gripping the bedspread and the unusual show of affection threatened to break what little reserve she had left.

She wiped away the remaining tears and opened her eyes with a lopsided smile.

'Bonjour Maman.'

Annie smiled back and patted her on the head.

'That'shhhbetterrr. Nopointincrrryinggirrrl. It'shhhjus tabrrrokenlegishhhall. Everrythingelshhhe . . .'

She waved her hand dismissively, showing her opinion of material possessions.

'I know, Maman. I should be glad I'm alive. And I am . . .'

Véronique went quiet, contemplating not for the first time what might have happened if she hadn't gone over to the church. Her heart went cold every time she thought about it. Instinctively, her left hand moved to the small cross at her neck.

'Shhho. Youaboutrrreadytogo?' Annie continued, her voice brusque as though she too didn't want to think about the awful alternatives.

Véronique nodded, gesturing at her neighbour and lowering her voice.

'I'll be glad to get away from her infernal knitting!' she muttered.

And then she remembered.

'Maman, I don't suppose you've got your hunting knife with you?'

Annie slipped her hand in her pocket and pulled out a small but lethal-looking bone-handled knife with a wicked blade. She raised her eyebrows, looking over at the old lady and back at her daughter.

'No, not for that!' Véronique said, laughing for the first time that day as she struggled to get out of bed without too much pain. She stood up, balancing on her good leg. 'It's for this,' she said and started to pull her pyjama bottoms down.

Bloody hospital parking! Having dropped Annie off at the entrance, Christian had driven round and round the car park trying in vain to find a space and in the end he'd had to leave the Panda on a grassy bank the far side of the main building. If the brakes failed the car would roll down the steep slope that the hospital was perched on and end up in the middle of St Girons.

Not that that would be a bad thing. It was insured.

Christian shifted the brightly wrapped present in his arms and made his way through the main doors, past reception and down the hall towards Véronique's ward. It was so good knowing she was getting out of this place. He never felt at ease in hospitals, his awkward frame always in danger of knocking over some machine or tripping over some piece of equipment. Plus he hated the smell and the unnatural quiet. No birdsong, no cattle bells and no wind on his face.

His head filled with images of the mountains, Christian nonchalantly turned the corner and swung through the door into Véronique's room where she was standing with her back to him.

With her pyjama bottoms pushed down and her backside completely bared.

The sight of her naked, rounded buttocks was too much for him. His mind fused, his mouth dropped open and his hands let go of the present which fell to the floor with an almighty crash.

Véronique whirled round at the noise and screamed in surprise.

'Get out!' she shrieked, whipping her pyjamas up in haste as Christian staggered backwards, the door closing in his face.

Mortified, she turned on Annie who was standing with her knife at the ready, looking vaguely nonplussed at the fuss.

'You could have said he was coming!' she spat.

'Youneverrrashhhked,' Annie retorted. 'Nowdoyouwantth atneedleoutorrrnot?'

Minutes later, when Annie opened the door, retrieved knitting needle in her hand, Christian hadn't moved. Not an inch. Not an eyelid.

'Thinkherrrladyshhhiphashhhcalmeddown. It'shhhshh hafetocomeinnow.'

'Ugh? What?' Christian blinked slowly, like someone coming out of a coma, and rubbed his eyes which were slightly out of focus, multiple naked bottoms still vivid like sunspots on his retinas.

He shuffled into the ward, his gaze firmly fixed on the floor, and began to address Véronique who was sitting on the bed, studiously looking out of the window, her cheeks pink.

'Sorry about—'

'DON'T mention it. EVER!'

At her waspish tone, Christian nodded meekly and hung his head some more. Taking pity on him, Annie tried to change the topic.

'Shhhowhat'shhhinthat?' she demanded, gesturing at the large present lying abandoned on the floor as she put her knife back in her pocket.

'Oh, that.' Christian regarded the package ruefully. He carefully picked it up, the faint jingle of ceramic on ceramic confirming his suspicions.

'It's a present,' he said, placing it on the bed next to Véronique, his face averted, still unable to look directly at her. 'But I think I've broken it.'

Already regretting snapping at him, Véronique murmured her thanks and began to undo the ribbon, glad of the distraction. She pulled back the wrapping paper and gasped, whether with shock or pleasure, Christian couldn't tell.

'Shit!' he moaned, regarding the shattered statue of St Germaine which lay nestled in the vibrant paper. 'I'm such an idiot! I glued the head back on and it looked OK but now it looks like . . . like . . .'

'LikethebrrrideofFrrrankenshhhtein?' Annie cackled.

Annie was right. Poor St Germaine did look more hideous than holy.

Christian had spent ages trying to repair the statue but even his best efforts had left a vivid scar around her neck and her skin was patchy where he hadn't been able to match the exact shade of paint. The overall Gothic appearance had been exacerbated by her most recent mishap. Her pet lamb which lay at her feet had been severed in half by the impact with the hospital floor and her shepherd's crook and most of her right arm now lay at an odd angle to the rest of her body.

'Sorry. I just thought . . .' he faltered. 'It . . . she . . . sort of saved your life and the priest was going to throw her out so I . . . mended her. But just now . . .'

He gestured helplessly at the floor, not daring to mention the cause of the accident.

'I can try and fix her again. If you want me to that is?'

Véronique looked up at him and smiled, her hand squeezing his arm.

'Thanks. I'd like that,' she said, her throat working as she held back the tears she'd been fighting all morning. 'It's a lovely gesture. Especially for someone who doesn't believe in saints. And I'm sorry I made you drop her.'

She reached over and tenderly wrapped the broken saint back up in the paper.

'And right now,' she continued, her light tone belying her emotions, 'she's the only thing I own. So thank you, Christian.'

She struggled to her feet and kissed him on the cheek, making him cough with embarrassment.

'Goodgrrrief!' Annie interjected. 'Getamoveonandlet'sh hhgetoutofherrrebeforrrethishhholddearrrhashhhahearr rtattack!'

She tipped her head at the old lady in the next bed who was staring in astonishment at the three of them, her needles poised in mid-air as she tried to take it all in.

The woman had finally stopped knitting.

As though a load had dropped from her shoulders, Véronique suddenly started giggling, trying to ignore her protesting ribs and holding on to Christian's arm for support as he settled her into the wheelchair. Caught up in the euphoria, Annie and Christian joined in, until they were all weak with laughter, Christian barely able to push the wheelchair as they made their way out of the ward with Annie chortling as she followed behind, clutching the dismembered saint.

It was some time before the grandmother got back to her knitting. And five whole days before she realised she'd dropped several stitches.

13

Véronique and Christian were still giggling like teenagers when Annie left them at the car. They'd managed to get Véronique on to the back seat with her leg outstretched but it had taken a lot of manoeuvring given the small interior of the Panda, which had caused even more mirth. No doubt it was a release of tension, relief at the fact that Véronique was alive and well.

Annie gripped the handles of the empty wheelchair tighter, her normally impassive face awash with emotions as she headed towards the hospital.

She hadn't allowed herself to think about what might have been. She wasn't one for such foolish pursuits. But since the fire she'd been tormented by nightmares, waking up abruptly in the middle of the night, scared and alone and afraid to go back to sleep. The dreams had varied but the outcome had always been the same: losing Véronique. For the first time since her daughter was a defenceless baby, Annie felt terror deep in her soul.

And it had changed her relationship with Véronique, which was why she'd volunteered to take the wheelchair back to reception. She wanted to make an appointment.

Annie wheeled the chair up to the desk where a young lady took it off her with a smile.

'Canyoutellmehowtogettothedentalhoshhhpital?' Annie asked her.

'Pardon?' The girl's smile slipped a little as she struggled to understand.

'Thedentalhoshhhpital? Whichway?'

'I'm sorry?' No longer smiling, the girl shook her head and lifted her shoulders. She had no idea what Annie was saying.

'Buggerrrit!' Annie growled, embarrassed. 'I'llfinditmysh hhelf.'

And she stomped off down the corridor leaving the young woman watching her with a bemused expression, contemplating whether she ought to call the psych ward and see if they'd lost a patient.

Annie was mad all right. Just not that kind of mad. She was cross with herself more than anything. How had she let it go this far? Why hadn't she sorted out her teeth before? They'd never fitted right from the first day she'd had them but she hadn't cared. In fact, if they made her more difficult to understand, all the better. But suddenly, since the fire, she'd started minding.

With a tut of annoyance at herself, she took the first turning she came to, thinking that eventually she'd come upon a sign or another desk where she might fare better. It couldn't be that hard to find.

She was turning into her third corridor, indistinguishable from any of the others with bland linoleum, beige walls and the sharp smell of disinfectant, when she saw him. Some sort of sixth sense made her look up and there he was, at the far end. His solid physique was unmistakable, oozing authority as he strode towards her, a huge bunch of flowers in his arms, his broad face just visible above them.

Serge Papon.

'Oh shit,' Annie cursed, whipping around so her back was to him, pretending to read the poster about visitor hygiene to give herself time. Véronique had said he'd popped in to see her the other day. She'd been touched by his concern. Of all things. But Annie hadn't expected him to be quite so concerned that he'd be back a few days later.

She heard his measured tread coming towards her and then slowing. She braced herself for the ritual embrace, the forced conversation, the pungent smell of his aftershave already enveloping her.

A heartbeat passed. Then another. And then nothing.

Slowly she turned her head but the corridor was empty apart from a nurse walking away from her, the squeak of her shoes on the floor the only sound.

He must have gone into one of the wards.

Who was he visiting? And with such a big bunch of flowers? Annie eased away from the wall and began inching her way towards the nearest door, which was open. She peeked inside but he wasn't there. Just a couple of beds with human forms under the bedclothes, both hooked up to drips, tubes all over the place. Depressing.

And then she heard the deep timbre of his voice coming from the room opposite where the door was slightly ajar. She quickly crossed the hallway and stood with her back to the wall, wondering if she dare risk a glance in. As she debated whether to chance it, she could hear the sound of his voice rising and falling. And she suddenly realised he wasn't talking; he was praying.

Serge Papon, who had as much time for the Church as he did for stray dogs, was praying. The shock was enough to make her look. She craned her head around the door frame until she could see him, sitting with his back to her beside a bed, head bowed while the stiff fingers of his right hand counted out the rosary beads as he recited the Hail Mary.

More audacious now she knew he couldn't see her, Annie

shifted her position a little, trying to see who was in the bed. But all she could see was a pale hand on top of the bedcovers, its thin fingers resting gently on Serge's left hand. His broad back was obstructing the rest of her view.

Consumed with curiosity, Annie leaned back out of sight and quietly pushed the door open a fraction with her fingertips, holding her breath all the while. She waited a second and then she peered in once more but it was no good. She still couldn't see anything. Feeling like a voyeur, she was just about to leave when Serge fumbled the beads and dropped them to the floor. With a grunt he bent over to pick them up and Annie could see all too clearly who he was visiting.

She wheeled away from the door and was halfway down the corridor before she released the breath she'd been holding. Her legs trembled with shock, adrenalin pumping far too fast around her body, but she didn't stop. She needed to get out into the fresh air.

At last an exit came into sight and she stumbled towards it, pushing the door violently in her haste to be out of the hospital. She staggered into a small courtyard, the biting cold a welcome slap in the face, and collapsed on to a wooden bench. Her eyes stared unseeingly at the magnificent panorama of the mountains beyond St Girons as she sat there, waiting for her heart rate to drop and her senses to come back to normal.

Jesus! She hadn't been prepared for that.

It had been his wife in the bed. But that hadn't been the shock, although having heard she was visiting family up in Toulouse, the last place Annie had expected to see her was in the hospital. No, the shock had been her appearance. Annie had seen enough ailing beasts in her lifetime to know when death was imminent. And the sight of Thérèse Papon's face, skin stretched tight across the bones and tinged with grey, had been enough to tell her that the woman she'd once hated with an intensity that she now marvelled at was very close to death.

Annie let out a deep sigh, her breath collecting in front of her in swirls of moisture. God, thirty-five years ago and it still felt so raw, so recent.

It had been the transhumance and she'd been left at the farm alone while Papa and Maman escorted the cows up to the higher pastures. Normally Annie had accompanied Papa, the long trek up the mountain to the meadows being a highlight of her year. The early start had never bothered her and she'd enjoyed the camaraderie with the neighbouring farmers as they worked together to ensure the animals reached the plateau safely. There was always plenty of chat and lots of laughter punctuated by the odd bit of cursing when a sheep ran off up a hillside forcing someone to send a dog after it, or a cow got stubborn and refused to go on.

But the best part was when they finally reached the summer pastures, the lush grass stretching out before them abundant with wild flowers and the sun shining down from above the mountains where the last vestiges of snow clinging to the sides glistened and shimmered. It was an absolute paradise and every year Annie felt jealous of the animals that got to spend their summers in such a setting.

Tired from their exertions, everyone would sit down for lunch in the shade of one of the shepherds' huts where bread and cold meat passed from hand to hand, a round of local Rogallais cheese following, its edges rough from the cuts of numerous hunting knives, and for dessert, a croustade from the bakery in Massat, the blueberries oozing out of the flaky pastry with every bite. A bottle of wine or two would be shared and afterwards the men would stretch out on the grass and doze as the air grew heavy and the cicadas sang, while the women would gather in small groups, their voices a quiet murmur. And then Emile Galy would start playing softly on the harmonica, the notes rising gently, mournfully, on the slightest of breezes and intertwining with the deeper sound of the cowbells until Annie, her legs tired and her eyes heavy, would wonder sleepily if this pastoral music could be heard back on the farm.

That year, thirty-five years ago, she should have had the chance to find out as, for the first time in her adult life, she hadn't made the trip to the mountains. She hadn't been well enough. She'd told her parents it was a stomach bug and they'd believed her. But she'd been lying.

As she'd cleaned out the byre following the departure of the cows, the smell making her delicate stomach roil, she hadn't even given Emile Galy and his harmonica a second thought. She'd been too preoccupied by a different topic. She'd been to the doctor the week before and he'd confirmed her growing suspicions.

She was pregnant. And unmarried. What on earth was she going to do now?

She hadn't got very far with the answer, given the limited choices available to her, when she'd heard footsteps and a woman's voice calling her name.

'Annie? Annie? Are you there?'

She'd poked her head out of the barn and seen Thérèse Papon picking her way delicately across the farmyard, trying to avoid the worst of the cow shit, looking totally out of place in her pretty dress and high heels. What on earth was she doing here? Usually when she had a message for Papa about the next council meeting she just called.

Annie gripped the pitchfork tighter with a sense of fore-boding and waited.

'Annie? Oh there you are!' Finally spotting her, Thérèse

179

crossed the short distance to the barn and embraced her, the strong smell of perfume instantly making Annie feel sick.

'Papa's not here . . .' Annie began, fighting the waves of nausea but Thérèse put a hand on her arm to stop her.

'It's you I've come to see, Annie.' She cleared her throat, her hands playing nervously with the straps of her handbag. 'I er . . . I need to talk to you. Alone.'

Annie's heart thundered in her chest. There was only one thing she could think of that demure Thérèse Papon could have to say to her and she didn't want to have that conversation. She felt her mouth go dry.

'You see . . . I know. About . . . about . . .' Thérèse's voice quavered and Annie waited for her to say his name. But instead she gestured vaguely at Annie's midriff, her eyes fixed firmly on a bale of hay in the corner.

'I know you're pregnant.'

Annie drew a sharp intake of breath and reached out to steady herself on the manger. She'd deliberately chosen a doctor in town rather than the family doctor in Massat hoping for anonymity. But somehow Thérèse had found out.

'How on earth . . .?' she managed.

'My cousin. She's the receptionist at the doctor's you went to.' Thérèse shrugged her shoulders in a half-apology but Annie knew all too well how people talked in small communities. It was all she'd thought of for the last week.

'She was shocked. Wanted to know if I had any idea who the father might be.'

And with that Thérèse Papon let her gaze rest fully on Annie for the first time, her grey eyes full of pain and a sadness that racked Annie with guilt.

'I think I do know, don't I, Annie?'

Annie groaned, the pitchfork slipping from her grasp as her

limbs went numb and her knees buckled, only the support of the manger keeping her upright.

How long had Thérèse known? It couldn't even be called an affair. In her world where men usually only noticed the curve of a cow's rump or the gait on a horse at the sales, Annie had been flattered by the attentions of the deputy mayor. It had spiralled out of control once. Only once. And she'd become pregnant.

'It's OK. I understand,' Thérèse continued softly. She laughed drily. 'He can be very persuasive.'

Her gaze dropped once more to the floor as though she was summoning resources for her next sentence while a heavy silence filled the barn.

'I'm sorry, Annie. It's not easy for me to say this,' she finally said. 'But I don't think I have any other option. You have to end it.'

'It's finished . . . it never began . . . I'm sorry . . .' Annie stammered, ashamed and cheapened by Thérèse's dignity and desperate to reassure her that the relationship was over.

Thérèse shook her head sadly and turned to look at Annie once more, this time tears visible in her eyes.

'That's not what I meant,' she whispered. 'The pregnancy. You have to end the pregnancy. You must . . . you must have an abortion.'

'NO!' Annie drew back in shock, her hands instinctively clutching her belly in protection of a life that ten minutes ago she'd been regretting. 'I can't. I WON'T.'

'Please, I'm begging you,' Thérèse pleaded, her calm demeanour slipping as her hand gripped Annie's arm with a strength that belied her petite frame. 'You've got to understand. We couldn't . . . I can't have children and we've lived with that. But if he finds out that you're having his . . . his baby . . .'

She choked on the last word and collapsed into silence, her face distraught. She took a deep breath and continued in a voice trembling with emotion.

'It's all he ever wanted. A baby. He'll leave me. If he knows. If he finds out he's the father. Please Annie, please. For me.'

She fumbled with the clasp of her handbag and pulled out an envelope, thick with money.

'I'll pay,' she said, grabbing Annie's hands and thrusting the envelope into them. 'Take this and go to England. It's legal there. No one need ever know.'

Annie jerked her hands away and threw the envelope to the ground, backing off in horror as Thérèse crumpled to the floor and lost the last of her composure, crying openly, her hands covering her face.

With a calm she didn't feel, Annie addressed the broken woman, making a snap decision about her life that only moments before she couldn't have contemplated.

'I won't have an abortion,' she said, her voice shaking. 'But I promise you this. Serge will never know he has a child.'

And with that she turned and ran to the house leaving a sobbing Thérèse kneeling on the ground, 500-franc notes strewn on the straw around her.

That night Annie had confessed to her parents. Shocked and disappointed, they'd accepted her tale of a reckless liaison at the county fair with a passing fair worker and had pressed for no more details. But they'd agreed with her that she couldn't stay in Fogas to have the baby. She'd left the next day for her cousin's house over near Perpignan and had stayed a year.

It had been twelve months of abject misery. Burdened by a difficult pregnancy and the shame she could never escape, she'd wilted in the heat of the Mediterranean summer like a Pyrenean wildflower in full sun, pining to be back at the farm surrounded by green pasture and the peaks she knew so well.

When she'd finally returned to her beloved mountains with her baby girl, her parents had welcomed her home, lavishing love and attention on the tiny infant. But outside of the family, Annie found the rumours and gossip overwhelming. She'd resigned from the Conseil Municipal, started shunning all social events and had immersed herself in the running of the farm. And she had never taken part in the transhumance again. Her father had never passed comment on her reluctance to be part of the commune but to his dying day he'd failed to understand why she'd hated Thérèse Papon, generally agreed to be one of the nicest women in the village, so intensely.

And right now, sitting on a freezing cold bench thirty-five years later, Annie couldn't quite understand it either. She'd never worked out whether she'd hated the woman for forcing her into exile or for forcing her to make a decision; one that perhaps she might not have taken if Thérèse Papon hadn't backed her into a corner.

Annie stood up slowly, her hips stiff and her knees creaking, and followed the path round the hospital towards the car park. Christian and Véronique would be wondering where she'd got to. And she hadn't even made the appointment with the dentist. Ah well, time enough. She'd pop in next week. Maybe go and see Thérèse while she was there. After all, she owed her a debt of gratitude. If it hadn't been for her, maybe Véronique would never have been born.

Annie shook her head at the complexity of human life and headed towards the car.

If human life was complex, the afterlife seemed to be no less so. Josette looked up from the accounts she'd been trying to get sorted for the last hour as Jacques jumped down off the fridge and wandered through the shop to the bar, shoulders slumped and head down.

He'd been giving her a hard time all day, moping around like a sullen teen, his face as miserable as a wet weekend. No doubt he was now going to sulk in the inglenook.

Josette threw down her pen in exasperation. She leaned back on the stool so she could see him through the doorway and her annoyance instantly dissipated. Head propped on his gnarled hands, he was blowing into the fire, each breath making it flare up violently. He kept it up for a few minutes before even that seemed to bore him and he just sat, staring morosely into the flames.

She knew what was up with him. In life, he'd always been involved. A long-time council member, he'd been the person everyone came to for help, whether for straightforward issues like planning permission or for more serious matters like disputes between neighbours. Everyone had known that, no matter what the predicament, Jacques Servat would do his best to sort it. And more often than not, his best had been more than enough.

But now, when the commune seemed to be falling apart around them, he was powerless and Josette shared his frustration.

Six days on from the storm many homes were still without electricity, telephone lines remained down and some water supplies hadn't been re-established. The post office was closed indefinitely after the fire, pensioners in the area, many of whom couldn't drive to Massat or Seix, were having difficulty getting their pensions and the roads were so bad with fallen trees and landslides that the school bus had refused to drive up to Fogas and the post was being left at the épicerie. And as for poor Véronique, no one could say how long it would be before she could go back to her apartment and no decision had been taken about how to rehouse her in the meantime.

The problem was, nobody seemed to be taking control. The council were all at loggerheads after the acrimonious vote to close the Auberge, Pascal Souquet was a complete incompetent and the mayor was never available. Céline, the secretary at the town hall, was running out of excuses for his repeated absences and people were muttering about his behaviour, implying he was having an affair while his wife was away. And as for Christian Dupuy . . .

Josette suspected that while Jacques was chafing at his own inadequacies, his bad mood was sharpened by disappointment in the man he'd expected so much of. As deputy mayor, Christian should have been doing more but he seemed to have switched off as though the way he'd been manipulated over the Auberge had left him wary. He remained reluctant to help the Websters, suspecting them of deliberately releasing Sarko from his field, and had even talked of resigning from the council at the next meeting. Whenever that was! It was supposed to have been tomorrow night but had been cancelled at the mayor's behest with no explanation.

Josette hung her head in her hands.

Basically the commune of Fogas was in complete chaos.

Monique Sentenac had been the first to utter the word *karma*. The wind which had roared through the valleys on New Year's Eve had definitely had something of the wrath of God about it and it was true that the Auberge had been one of the few buildings spared. And while Josette didn't subscribe to Biblical vengeance and wasn't expecting a cloud of locusts to descend on Fogas any time soon, the sordid business over the Auberge did seem to be at the root of much of the trouble that had come the commune's way.

Accepting that she wouldn't get anything more done, she closed her ledger and was putting it away under the counter when she heard the spluttering cough of a tired engine and

Christian pulled up outside. She glanced over at Jacques who'd jumped up and was staring out of the window, a frown in place of his usual welcoming smile as he watched Christian getting out of the car.

Josette knew what he was thinking. The future of the commune depended on the big farmer. But how could they persuade him to get involved once more?

The bell farted rudely as Christian and Annie entered the shop, Véronique hobbling in after them on her crutches.

'Welcome home!' Josette cried and hurried round the counter to gather Véronique in a warm embrace. 'How are you feeling?'

Véronique pulled a face. 'A bit tired,' she said with a droll smile. 'All the excitement of being out of hospital!'

'Well you know where your room is, if you want to go and lie down.'

'Actually, I thought I'd go and have a quick look at . . . the post office . . . my apartment. You know?'

Josette shot a look at Christian who was shaking his head vigorously behind Véronique's back. Even after six days, the sight of the ragged gap where the building had once been, charred rafters protruding from piles of rubble, was still shocking. For Véronique, seeing it for the first time, it would be traumatic.

'Are you sure you want to do that?'

Véronique nodded resolutely, tipping back her head and thrusting out her chin in defiance.

'Yes, I'm quite sure. I want to see it for myself.'

'Well I'll come with you then,' Christian offered, holding open the door for her to exit.

Annie and Josette watched them turn up the alley towards what had been the post office, their progress slow thanks to Véronique's crutches.

'I'm not sure that's a good idea,' Josette confided to Annie. 'It'll only distress her.'

Annie shook her head in disagreement.

'She'shhhgotoshhheeitshhhhometime,' she noted before adding with her usual understatement, 'She's hhhinforahello fashhhurprrrise!'

'What's that?' Josette's attention was diverted from the retreating figures as Annie laid the present she'd been carrying down on the counter.

'It'shhhfrrromChrishhhtian. ForrrVérrronique. Havealook.'

Josette peeled back the paper, her eyes widening in bewilderment at the disjointed statue.

'What on earth . . .?' She looked up at Annie who was grinning widely, and then back at the Gothic saint. 'It's . . . it's . . .'

'Hideoushhh!'

Josette rapidly folded the paper back over.

'That's one word for it!'

'ShallItakeituptoherrrroom?'

'Yes!' Josette quickly agreed. 'That would be best.'

'Afterrrallyoudon'twanttoscarrreofffthecushhhtomers!'

Still cackling, Annie scooped up the statue of St Germaine and made her way to the stairs at the back of the building. Josette only just had time to register the sudden presence of Jacques by the fridge when the door rattled and Monsieur Webster entered the shop.

'Bonjour!' he called out, a big smile on his face.

'Bonjour, monsieur. How are you today?'

'Good, very good,' he replied, bringing over some bread to the counter. He added a packet of biscuits and some milk and then asked for some *saucisson*.

'And how's the Auberge? Any news?' Josette asked as she wrapped up the sausage.

Paul's grin got even wider.

'Yes. Good news. Maybe we can receive help. Money help. From the government.'

'Grants? You're applying for grants?' Josette could see Jacques clapping his hands enthusiastically in the background. 'What a good idea!'

'Yes. Grants. It is Stephanie's idea. Without her . . .' Paul shrugged, looking every bit a Frenchman.

Jacques was listening intently now, and at the mention of Stephanie he nodded his head. At last someone in the commune was trying to do something.

'We are crossing our fingers!' Paul continued, holding up his hands as evidence. 'There is an inspection next Tuesday. We have to keep like this!'

'Well good luck. Let us know how it goes.'

He gathered up his shopping and turned to leave. Josette was too busy watching Jacques, his face lit up for the first time in days at Paul's good news, to see what happened next. But suddenly there was a crash and the bell that had been on the door for decades fell to the ground, narrowly missing Paul's head and shattering into a thousand pieces.

'Gosh! Are you OK?' Josette enquired as Paul looked around him in surprise at the bits of plastic strewn across the floor.

'Yes, I'm fine. But I think it is dead!' he announced sombrely, pointing at the debris.

Judging by the frown on Jacques' face, he'd come to the same conclusion and wasn't best pleased. Josette on the other hand was secretly elated that the bell had chimed its last. Finally she'd be able to install a new one without worrying about hurting Jacques' pride.

She nipped into the bar to get a broom and when she got back Paul had already begun to pick up the biggest bits from the floor. Within minutes they'd cleared up the mess.

'Thanks for your help,' Josette said as Paul gathered up his shopping once more.

'Oh, it's nothing. But perhaps I help you more?'

Josette looked at him enquiringly.

'I have one . . . how do you say . . . of these.' He gestured at the pile of plastic as he searched for the word in French.

'A bell?'

'Yes! I have a bell. But more modern. No wires. I not need it and I put it on the door if you want?'

Modern. That was the only word Josette needed to hear. Ignoring the glowering Jacques, who hated change, Josette quickly accepted.

'Oh yes! That would be lovely. Thank you.'

Paul was clearly glad to have been of help.

'OK. After the inspection. So, next Thursday? The afternoon. It is good?'

'Perfect! I'll see you then.'

Paul said goodbye, formally shaking her hand before he left and she had to hide a smile at his typical English reserve. He was a lovely man and it only made the way the commune was treating him seem even more unjust. And Josette more guilt-ridden for her part in it all.

Helpless to change the course of events for which she felt so responsible, Josette wished that Christian would take the time to get to know his new neighbour. Maybe then they could sort this mess out. But Christian had never met him and after the incident with Sarko, didn't seem inclined to ever make the effort.

And then it came to her, the realisation that there was something she could do after all, something so simple and yet . . . it might just work.

What she needed to do was bring the two of them together and Paul had just handed her the perfect opportunity. No one could refuse to help out an old widow, could they? She grinned at her own cunning and scanned the shop, looking for the excuse she needed. The fridge? No, that would need immediate attention. Christian would be suspicious if she asked him to delay. The glass knife cabinet? She glanced up and saw Jacques leaning against the wall and felt guilty for even considering it. No, not the knife cabinet, he would never forgive her . . . but what else was there?

Of course! She snapped her gaze back to Jacques and crossed the floor, startling him with her sudden movement. He leaped out of the way as she leaned in to inspect the old cheese cabinet he'd been resting against. Handmade by some distant ancestor of Jacques, the wooden box was already at a bit of an angle where it had started to ease away from its wall supports a long time ago. Perfect.

In a hurry now to get the thing done before Christian got back, Josette scurried to the counter and grabbed an old claw hammer from the drawer. Carrying her stool over to the cheese cabinet, she stood up on it and placed the claw of the hammer between the wall and the wood. She pushed with all her might but nothing happened. Ignoring Jacques, who was flapping around the shop in a state of agitation at her perceived vandalism, she gave it one more go and this time was rewarded with the crack of wood splitting. One more heave and the cabinet lurched drunkenly, all the cheese inside sliding to one end.

That ought to do.

She'd only just put the stool and hammer away, Jacques still open-mouthed with incredulity, when Christian and Véronique came in.

'You look shattered,' she commented as a very pale Véronique collapsed gratefully on to the stool. 'You've overdone it.'

'It was worse than I thought,' Véronique whispered,

clearly still affected by what she'd seen. 'There's nothing left. Nothing . . .'

She shook her head in disbelief.

'Wellwedidtrrrytowarrrnyou!'

Josette wheeled round to see Annie standing in the doorway of the bar. How long had she been there? Josette hadn't heard her come down the stairs. Had she seen?

'Comeonlove,' she added with more sympathy. 'Letmehelp youuptobed.'

She held out her arm and helped Véronique on to her crutches and up the stairs.

'Poor thing,' Josette remarked, trying not to stare at the cabinet, or at Jacques who was fuming silently on the fridge.

'Yes, it really shook her up. But I think it's for the best in the long run.' Christian consulted his watch and swore softly. 'I'm late. I promised Maman I'd be back in time to help her fix the hen house. We're still missing several chickens following the storm. Reckon they got blown all the way to Foix!

'Before you go . . .' Josette began, nerves making her stutter. 'Do you think you could, . . . it's just . . . the cheese cabinet.'

'What's wrong with the . . .' Christian tailed off and stared at the lopsided box, the rounds of cheese all squished up at one end. He frowned.

'That's funny. I never noticed it earlier. How long has it been like that?'

Josette, never the best of liars, wasn't prepared for the question.

'Just . . . er . . .'

'Atleashhhtaweek! Showshhhowmuchattentionyoupay,' grumped Annie, her sudden bark making Josette jump.

'A week? Can't believe I didn't notice. Sorry Josette, you should have said.'

Josette felt mean in the face of his genuine concern.

'Well I can't do it now. Would tomorrow be OK?'

'No! I mean, thanks but really it's not that important. Why don't we leave it until next Thursday afternoon?'

'Are you sure? You don't want me to do it sooner?'

'Youhearrrdwhatsheshhhaid. Nowshhhtoppeshhhterrr ingthewomanandtakemehome. Jushhhtabouthadashhhm uchofyoupeopleashhhIcantakeforrroneday!'

'OK! OK! Next Thursday it is!' Christian held up his hands in mock surrender and backed out of the shop, grinning good-naturedly at Annie's gruff tone.

Annie leaned over to kiss Josette on the cheeks, her eyes twinkling with devilment.

'Thanks!' whispered Josette.

'ShhheeyounextThurrrshhhday!' Annie cackled and squeezed Josette's arm before heading out to the car which was stuttering and choking into life outside.

As they drove off, backfiring into the distance, Josette sank on to the stool, tired but elated. She noticed Jacques slip off the fridge and drift towards the broken cheese cabinet. He stared at it for a few seconds and then turned to her and nodded his head, approval on his weathered face, before he slipped into the bar and settled himself at the inglenook. It wasn't long before his head was on his chest.

At last, thought Josette, reaching under the counter. I might get those accounts done!

14

Madame Dubois, chief hotel inspector for the Ariège Department, was hopelessly lost. Or rather not lost as such, as her sat nav was still gamely telling her to drive straight on, but she was rapidly losing faith in it as her Renault Twingo bounced over the unmade road, engine struggling as the incline got steeper. She twisted the heating up further, wiping her gloved hand across the windscreen in an effort to improve visibility, but it was useless. The problem was the white mist outside, clinging to the car and obscuring all but the immediate view. Which was of pine trees. Lots and lots and lots of them.

Trying not to think about what could be lurking in the woods, she drove on, her fingers gripping the steering wheel. Although Ariège born and bred, she was made apprehensive by the isolation of the mountains, coming as she did from the more populated, relatively flat lands beyond Foix. She didn't know how the people in these parts slept at night knowing there were bears wandering around. And snakes. And wild boars.

She shuddered and turned the heating up full blast, praying that the car would make it to the top of whatever godforsaken col she was climbing. As if in response, there was a loud bang and the car bucked beneath her as a back wheel hit a pothole, bouncing her in her seat and causing her to almost veer off the road. She swallowed nervously and cursed herself for not taking the main road from Foix to St Girons instead of trusting her new sat nav. She should have known that in terrain like this, distance was meaningless without a sense of altitude. Technically the route she had taken was the shortest, but only because it came over a mountain on a track not meant for vehicles.

She was seriously contemplating turning back despite the poor visibility when she noticed that the engine had stopped screeching like an amorous cat. The road was finally flattening out. At least she'd made it to the top. But what about the other side?

Peering through the windscreen she could just about make out parking spaces and a small clearing containing what looked like a large noticeboard surrounded by picnic benches. Relieved, she pulled over and got out to stretch her legs and as the mist parted, she was afforded a stunning view of the sharp edges of the Pyrenees splayed out in front of her. She barely had time to take it all in before the clouds closed over again, shrouding her in their silent, opaque world once more.

Hugging her coat tightly around her, she hurried over to the noticeboard, anxious to be back in the car as fast as possible. It was a tourist information point and according to the map, she was at the top of the Col d'Ayens but how that related to where she needed to go, she didn't know. She scanned the board and her eyes were caught by the small silhouette of a bear in the bottom right-hand corner.

Recommendations in the event of meeting a bear.

Contrary to her best instincts, Madame Dubois read on, the skin tingling at the back of her neck.

If you come face to face with a bear help it to identify you:
  Express yourself calmly by moving or speaking
  Move away gradually
  DO NOT RUN.

A sudden rustling in the dense forest beyond the noticeboard was all it took. Madame Dubois, nerves on edge and eyes wide with fear, screamed in terror and ran as fast as she could all the way back to her car, completely ignoring, as would any sane person, the advice she'd just read. She slammed the door shut and locked it just in case.

Still panting from the unexpected exertion, she reached for the map that was tucked into the back pocket of the passenger seat and unfolded it, her hands shaking and her eyes darting. wildly over its creased surface as she searched for the Col d'Ayens, desperate to be out of this savage wilderness.

'Good God!' she muttered, her finger finally pinpointing her location. She was in the middle of nowhere, straddling a mountain perched above her destination. But the good news was that the road down was at least marked on the map. All she had to do was follow it to the valley floor and turn left and she would be on the main road.

Turning off the redundant sat nav in disgust, she started the car and eased back on to the track, eyes staring out into the dense swirls of mist as she negotiated her way out of the forest.

By the time she regained civilisation, small hamlets appearing alongside the now tarmacked road, her nerves were frayed and her temper was far from suitable for conducting an inspection.

Direction Départementale de la Concurrence, de la Consommation
et de la Répression des Fraudes de l'Ariège
Mme Brigitte Dubois

Paul lowered the business card and looked at the person who'd just handed it to him. A sparrow of a woman, immaculately attired in a jacket, skirt and prim blouse, all in muted hues of brown, half-moon glasses perched on her nose, she was the archetypal government official. The only things out of place were her hair, strands escaping from its barrette as though she had been doing exercise, and her shoes, which were covered in mud and dead leaves. One of those shoes had started tapping the floor in impatience as she stood in front of him, glaring over her glasses at her clipboard which she held fast across her chest like a shield.

Paul's heart sank. The inspection rested on the shoulders of this woman and already he felt like they'd failed, just in the way he'd shaken her bony hand.

'So, are you ready? Let's get this under way,' she snapped and Lorna and Paul jumped to attention as she pulled a tape measure out of her briefcase, thrust one end at Paul and strode across the dining room with the other.

'How many covers?' she demanded as she consulted the tape and scribbled furiously on her clipboard.

'Sorry?' Lorna replied, struggling to follow the rapid French.

'How many covers? In the restaurant?'

'Oh, ermm, forty here. And forty on the terrace.' Lorna gestured towards the covered area outside where the tables and chairs were all stacked to one side, withered leaves gathered beneath the legs and puddles of water spotted here and there. Madame Dubois swept the area with a glance and raised a sceptical eyebrow, clearly unable to see its potential.

'It's winter,' Paul felt the need to explain. 'And we're closed.'

'FORTY covers,' she stated, pursing her lips as she wrote it down. 'And what are your qualifications?'

Lorna and Paul looked at each other, neither sure they'd understood correctly.

'Your qualifications?' Madame Dubois repeated with a loud sigh. 'Which of you is the chef? And what diplomas do you have? Did you study hotel management? Where and to what level?'

'Well . . . I'm the chef but . . . no . . . we have nothing,' Lorna stuttered, her palms starting to sweat under the fierce gaze of the inspector. 'No qualifications.'

'*NO* qualifications?' Madame Dubois' pencil-thin eyebrows rose incredulously along with her voice. 'You've bought a hotel and restaurant and you have no experience? No training?'

'Well . . . I am cook in school kitchen before . . . in England . . . but—'

Madame Dubois didn't give Lorna time to finish, cutting her short with a disparaging look.

'And you?' she barked at Paul, her pen at the ready.

'I'm an electrical engineer.'

The pen froze in mid-air as Madame Dubois' face puckered in disbelief.

'I do not understand,' she muttered, skimming through the pages on her clipboard. 'There is nowhere to note this. You do not fit my boxes!'

Lorna shrugged apologetically, embarrassed by the woman's open derision. Madame Dubois seemed to find their precious dream of being their own bosses and running their own business ridiculous. And standing in the dining room, being grilled by this representative of French bureaucracy, Lorna was beginning to suspect the woman was right.

Maybe they had been idiotic, giving up steady jobs to come over to France with a basic grasp of the language and no previous experience of running a hotel and restaurant. Paul

197

looked as though he too was questioning their decision. At that precise moment, they were both wishing they'd never set foot in the commune of Fogas.

'Bonjour! Sorry I'm late!'

In a whirl of colour, Stephanie breezed through the back door, letting it slam in her wake as she threw her bags on to the nearest table and discarded her coat on a chair.

'I'm Stephanie Morvan. Lovely to meet you,' she stated, striding across the room and shaking the hand of Madame Dubois with such energy that even more of the inspector's hair was dislodged from its clasp.

As the inspector did her best to tuck away the errant strands, Stephanie turned to kiss Lorna.

'She is very brown, no? 'Er clothes, 'er shoes. She even 'as a brown aura!' she whispered in English.

Lorna stifled a snort as Stephanie whipped back to face the inspector.

'So, how are we getting on?' she demanded with a smile. 'Everything going well?'

Madame Dubois indicated her clipboard with a sniff.

'This is all highly irregular!' she said, tapping the board with her pen.

'What is?'

'They have no relevant qualifications.'

'Poof!' Stephanie waved an elegant hand in the air, sending a scale of bracelets jingling down her arm. 'Qualifications! They're highly overrated. Do you think Escoffier, the emperor of chefs, had qualifications? Or Taillevent, the creator of our national cuisine? Who dared ask them for flimsy pieces of paper when they had such talent! Such passion!'

Clearly in her element, Stephanie was prowling up and down in front of the inspector, her hands flashing as though weaving a spell around the poor woman.

'When did we French allow the mere notion of a piece of paper to become more important than desire? Than ability? Pah! We are becoming worse than our Anglo-Saxon neighbours with their love of conformity and precision.'

By now Madame Dubois was nodding enthusiastically as Stephanie continued to rant.

'Do you think the people who created this great Republic were asked what qualifications they had for leading a revolution? Or that Pasteur's discoveries hinged on him having the right diplomas?'

Stephanie stopped abruptly in front of the inspector and threw both arms in the air.

'Passion! That is what we French know is important, don't you agree, Madame?'

'Yes, yes. You are right!'

'And these people,' Stephanie continued, turning to gesture at Paul and Lorna who were mesmerised by her performance. 'These people have come all the way from England to live here, in France, because they are passionate about running a hotel and restaurant.'

She encircled Madame Dubois in one of her arms and gently led her towards the hallway, her voice returning to its normal levels.

'So, later we will decide what to put on your piece of paper about qualifications. For now, let us continue with the inspection.'

She ushered the now placid inspector out of the room and up the stairs, winking at a bemused Lorna as she went.

With Stephanie at the helm, the inspection went like clockwork. In less than an hour every bedroom had been measured and assessed and they were all back downstairs sitting around a dining table over coffee enjoying the *moelleux an chocolat*

Lorna had made that morning. 'This is very good!' enthused Madame Dubois, finishing off her last morsel of cake and closing her eyes momentarily as she savoured the taste, as though this too was part of the inspection.

'And now,' she continued with a slightly ironic smile, 'time for the paperwork!'

She placed her clipboard on the table, the pages now covered with crossed boxes, and Lorna felt her heart thudding with anticipation.

'As I mentioned upstairs, there are one or two items which need attention. The carpets need replacing in the hall and Room Three, the bed in Room Four needs to be replaced and Rooms Three and Six must be repainted to remove the water stains from the ceiling. Finally, there must be one lamp per occupant which means you must provide extra lamps in Rooms One, Two and Three and Rooms Two and Four need curtains. OK?'

Paul and Lorna nodded. They'd done a quick tally upstairs and had reckoned they could just about find a thousand euros which should cover everything.

'Once you have that work done, contact me and I'll revisit. After that I see no reason why you shouldn't gain accreditation.'

'Brilliant!' Stephanie exclaimed while Lorna just beamed, her hand clasped tight in Paul's under the table.

'Before you get too excited, let me explain a bit more about the accreditation system,' Madame Dubois cautioned. 'A hotel must have at least seven rooms in order to gain a star rating. As you only have six guest rooms at present, which is the minimum for hotel classification, then I cannot award you any stars.' She glanced at Paul and Lorna to make sure they were following her and then continued. 'Once you've converted the attic space into your own living quarters and developed the seventh bedroom however, then I will be able to award you a one-star classification. Until then, you will simply be an Hôtel de Tourisme. OK?'

Paul and Lorna both nodded, not caring about whether or not they had a star. All that mattered was getting the accreditation.

'That's enough to start the paperwork for the grant application,' Stephanie said, voicing their thoughts, her eyes alight with excitement.

'You're applying for grants?' queried Madame Dubois as she started filling out the inspection report. 'In that case you need to get a move on as the end of January is the deadline.'

'The end of January?'

'Yes, the EU funding for this year has been withdrawn so only applications submitted by then will be considered.'

'We'd best get painting then!' Stephanie laughed as Madame Dubois put down her pen and gathered her papers together.

'One last thing and then we're done,' she said, looking out over her glasses at Lorna and Paul. 'I just need to see a copy of your fire and safety certificate.'

And just like that, the flicker of hope that had been growing in strength over the last few days was extinguished. Lorna went pale while Stephanie just swore quietly.

'Is there something wrong?' asked the inspector, aware of the sudden change of mood.

'We must be having this certificate for the accreditation?' asked Lorna, finally finding her voice.

'Yes, of course. All hotels accredited by the department have to have passed the inspection.'

Paul threw himself back in his chair while Lorna hung her head.

'There is no point,' she said, her shoulders slumped in despondency as she gestured at the neat pile of papers in front of the inspector. 'We can't doing it.'

Madame Dubois, all the irritation resulting from her horrendous journey long since gone, felt real concern.

'What's the problem?' she asked Stephanie who was drumming her fingers on the table in annoyance.

'Well, first of all they failed the fire and safety inspection and the mayor closed them down. They now have no income so they need the grants to do the work necessary for the repeat inspection. But to get the grants they have to be accredited by the department . . .'

She spread her hands.

'. . . and they can't get accreditation if they don't have a fire and safety certificate,' Madame Dubois concluded, nodding her head in comprehension. 'It's a vicious circle.'

Stephanie let out an exasperated sigh.

'Only in France!' she muttered.

'I'm sorry. Really I am,' Madame Dubois said as she placed her papers in her briefcase. 'But there is nothing I can do to help you. Is there no way you can get the work done before the end of the month?'

Paul laughed sarcastically.

'Not without a miracle!'

'And the mayor? He won't revoke the notice of closure?'

'They haven't been able to contact him,' Stephanie explained. 'They finally managed to get an appointment to see him this Thursday but I can't see him changing his mind.'

'Local politics?' queried the inspector quietly and Stephanie nodded.

Madame Dubois closed her briefcase and sat for a few seconds with it on her lap, genuinely upset by the predicament facing the English hoteliers.

'Well,' she said, standing to leave, 'all I can suggest is that you set a date for both repeat inspections a few days before the end of the month. That way you should be able to get the paperwork for the grants submitted in time.'

She held up her hand as Lorna started to protest at the futility of carrying on.

'I will get the accreditation pre-approved so all I have to do on the day is sign the papers. In the meantime, maybe some-thing will turn up. I wish you the best of luck!'

They all rose to shake the inspector's hand, thanking her for her time.

'Hopefully I will see you again soon,' Madame Dubois said before the door closed behind her, leaving them in a silence heavy with disappointment.

'I am sorry. It's my fault—' Stephanie began but Lorna quietened her with a hug.

'Don't you dare take the blame!' she exclaimed. 'You're the only one around here trying to help us.'

'But it is no good. I 'ave failed.'

'Lorna's right, Stephanie,' Paul replied. 'You've done all you could and we're grateful.'

'So what will you to do now?' She slipped into her coat and picked up her bags.

Paul tipped his head thoughtfully to one side.

'Well, we still have one more chance. We can appeal to the mayor to revoke the notice of closure on Thursday.'

Lorna snorted.

'Seriously, it's worth a try. If he agrees we can go to the bank manager again for a loan. If he knows we have an income he might change his mind.'

'And the work? You can to do it before January end?' Stephanie asked.

'Maybe. Maybe.'

Stephanie shrugged.

'Like the little brown inspector, I wish you luck!' she said and with a final embrace for both of them, she left.

Lorna watched her walk down the back steps before she turned to Paul.

'Are you serious?' she queried. 'Do you really think we still have a chance?'

Paul slipped an arm around her shoulders.

'Not a chance in hell,' he murmured. 'I just couldn't bear to see Stephanie so depressed.'

Lorna's eyes were full of sadness.

'So we'll put it up for sale then?'

'We have no option.'

He kissed the top of her head and they stood looking out across the river to the bare trees and the bleak mountains, harsh in the late sunlight. Somehow, Paul mused, their dreams germinated in the warmth of the summer sun had been shrivelled by the reality of winter.

Madame Dubois gunned the engine and crashed the gears as she approached the roundabout at Kerkabanac, her exasperation affecting her driving which wasn't brilliant at the best of times. She glanced to the left to check for traffic and out of the corner of her eye she saw the sign, a rustic wooden rectangle in green and cream with ornate writing:

Auberge des Deux Vallées – Hôtel/Restaurant

She grimaced and snapped her head back the other way, pulling out rather sharply in front of a motorcyclist. She acknowledged his annoyance with an apologetic wave and tried to concentrate on the road ahead.

But it was useless. Her mind kept returning to the quandary faced by the English couple and her frustration mounted. If the mayor had decided to close them pending the fire and safety certificate then that was his right, no matter how unjust it seemed. Or how corrupt. And if he really wanted to stymie their chances, he could delay the second inspection until after the deadline for the grants.

They really didn't have a hope.

The inspector shook her head in disgust at the behaviour of her fellow countryman, her foot pushing down on the accelerator in response. Soon the river was whipping past, the rocks on her left a mere blur as she got more and more annoyed, unused to feeling so impotent. By the time the blue light started flashing in her rear-view mirror she'd managed to get up to 100 km an hour which, as the officer explained as he stood with her on the roadside, was some feat on the winding gorge road.

'I'm only going to give you a warning this time,' the young policeman said as he towered over her. 'But you really should be more careful.'

'I'm sorry, really I am.' Madame Dubois did her best to look contrite, which given her present mood was quite an achievement. 'I promise I won't do it again, Officer . . .'

'Officer Gaillard.' The man held her door as she got back behind the wheel and suddenly she saw the family resemblance.

'Officer Gaillard? Major Didier Gaillard's son?'

'Afraid so.' He gave a crooked smile as he felt the scrutiny of his father's acquaintance.

'Well you're a credit to him,' she responded. 'Tell him Brigitte Dubois said hello next time you see him.'

She closed the door and slowly, ever so carefully, pulled away from the verge and down the road. He followed her at a distance the whole way into St Girons and she didn't speed once. As he passed her at the turn-off for Foix he sketched a wave and was gone.

But it had set her thinking.

With one half of her mind on her driving, the other was busy planning.

Major Didier Gaillard. Of course, why hadn't she thought of him before? As the person overseeing all fire and safety inspections in the Ariège he had the power to call an inspection when he saw fit, regardless of any objections from the mayor of the commune.

Perhaps he would be able to help. They could organise an inspection of the Auberge des Deux Vallées behind the mayor's back so at least the English hoteliers would be able to complete the paperwork on time if by some fluke they managed to find the resources to finish the outstanding work by the end of January.

Half an hour of careful driving later, Madame Dubois was at the Fire Department's head office in the centre of Foix. She entered the foyer and was directed upstairs to the first floor. Boxes of papers stacked on the edge of each tread and more spilling out across the hallway blocked fire escapes and generally created a hazardous working environment; what an irony that this was the department with the remit for upholding safety in the workplace.

'Brigitte!' Major Gaillard exclaimed as she appeared in the doorway of his office. 'It's been ages!'

He kissed her on each cheek and she inhaled the subtle scent of an expensive aftershave. He hadn't changed. Maybe slightly greyer at the temples and a few more lines on his weathered face but he still looked fit and the twinkle hadn't disappeared from his eyes.

'Hello Didier,' she replied, a bit shy as he gestured for her to sit down. 'How are things?'

He smiled sardonically as he resumed his seat and spread his hands to encompass the avalanche of paperwork spilling over his desk and threatening to slide onto the floor.

'Busy!'

'And Colette?'

He dipped his head and the smile disappeared. 'We're divorced. You know how it is. The kids left home, we grew

206

apart . . .' He shrugged as if suddenly conscious of the cliché he was living out.

Brigitte didn't know how it was at all, never having succumbed to marriage despite several offers. She felt an awkwardness descend and blurted out the first thing that came to mind.

'I met your son earlier, over near St Girons.'

'Nicolas? Not in an official capacity I hope?'

Now it was Brigitte's turn to shrug as she gave him a cheeky smile.

'He let me off with a warning.'

Major Gaillard barked a laugh as she turned on him the demure look that had been so successful on his son.

'Still the same old Brigitte. So what brings you here?'

'Well, I've got a favour to ask. It's a bit of a long shot but you might be able to help.'

'Fire away.'

'Do you know the Auberge des Deux Vallées in Fogas?'

A cloud passed over his face as he recalled the sour taste the inspection had left in his mouth.

'Only too well I'm afraid. The mayor is a bit of a rogue.'

'So how would you like to help out the owners?'

Intrigued, Major Gaillard leaned forward over his desk and sent a cascade of papers on to the floor.

'Tell me more!' he said, ignoring the mess.

Brigitte carefully outlined her plan and by the time she left the Fire Department thirty minutes later, she was feeling a lot more optimistic about the fate of the English people she'd met that day.

Passion, she thought as she got back into her car. Stephanie Morvan was right. There was a lot to be said for it.

15

'Do you want me to turn the heater on in the mayor's office?' asked Céline, the long-suffering secretary at the Fogas town hall.

Pascal Souquet bridled instantly at the perceived slur. Had it really been necessary for her to point out just whose office it was?

'No!' he snapped 'I've no intention of letting them stay long!' He walked past her and closed the door behind him, thus missing the dramatic eye-roll performed by his subordinate whose letter of resignation was ready and waiting should the odious deputy mayor ever succeed in his political aspirations.

But Pascal was oblivious as he paced the floor in the arctic temperatures of the large room that was normally the domain of Serge Papon, the bare floorboards creaking beneath his impatient feet. His feelings about today's appointment were mixed. On the one hand he was peeved at being summoned at the eleventh hour by the mayor to stand in for him yet again. It had become a frequent occurrence over the last few weeks and the mayor had offered no excuses for his sudden absences, although rumour was rife given that his wife was away. But despite his annoyance, Pascal relished being left in charge, especially with the meeting he was overseeing this morning.

He strode over to the window and surveyed the village of

Fogas as it meandered down the road, feeling the tingle of ambition race along his veins.

How long, he wondered, until he could take complete control? The next municipal elections were five years away. He wasn't sure if he could stand the imbecilic machinations of Serge Papon that long. Or the bumbling goodwill of Christian Dupuy.

Such peasants.

He turned from the window and rubbed his hands to stave off the cold.

Of course, as Fatima had pointed out, there was another possibility. Perhaps the present mayor had run his course? His conduct of late was causing unrest in the commune as the already slow service at the town hall became even more snail-like. Philippe Galy had been on the phone just yesterday, irate because the scheduled council meeting had been cancelled at short notice thus delaying his planning permission for the second time.

Not that the commune needed another gîte. Left to his own devices, Pascal would veto the request but Fatima had counselled him to be careful, advocating that Philippe Galy remained an unknown on the Conseil Municipal so his future vote should be wooed, not scorned.

She had a point. But how he hated having to consider these little people.

Still, if the mayor kept up his erratic behaviour, Pascal might find himself installed in this office permanently instead of as a last-minute stand-in. And then the path would be clear for him to go even further, maybe on to the Conseil Général in Foix or even as far as the Conseil Régional in Toulouse. And with that kind of power he wouldn't have to consider anybody. Except Fatima of course!

Voices in the office next door brought him back to the present and he seated himself behind the large desk in front of the window, doing his best to look like he belonged there despite feeling somewhat dwarfed by the dimensions of the room. He could hear Céline telling someone to go on through, too lazy to get up and show them in no doubt. Then there was a knock on the door and Monsieur and Madame Webster entered.

'Bonjour,' Monsieur Webster greeted him, a note of surprise in his voice at seeing the deputy mayor waiting for them.

Pascal waved a regal hand at the two chairs opposite the desk, making no attempt to stand.

He watched them sit, awkward and unsure of themselves. How he was going to relish the next few minutes, the power of having them beg, because he was sure that was why they were here.

'So, where is the mayor?' Monsieur Webster asked in the blunt manner typical of second-language speakers who haven't acquired the vocabulary of diplomacy.

His anticipated pleasure short-lived, Pascal spat back, 'He's unavailable!'

'Unavailable?' Madame Webster chipped in, further irritating Pascal, her consonant-laden accent turning the strains of romance inherent in his language into a clunking, lumbering cacophony. He ignored her.

'How can I help you?' he enquired, steepling his long fingers in front of him as he leaned back in his chair.

But Madame Webster persisted, her voice more strident than before.

'I'm sorry. We have an appointment with the mayor. Please explain, he is where?'

Pascal turned his head slowly, expecting her to quail before him. Instead she leaned even further across the desk and out of the corner of his eye, he saw Monsieur Webster place a restraining hand on her arm.

'As I said,' he replied in icy tones, 'he is unavailable. Now, how can I help you?'

'It's about the notice of closure,' Monsieur Webster began as his wife reluctantly settled back in her chair, clearly annoyed. 'We want asking the mayor to turn it over.'

Pascal smirked.

'I think you mean *overturn* it?' He paused as though considering the possibility, letting the tension grow. And then he took great delight in dashing their hopes.

'Not possible, I'm afraid.'

'Not possible? Why?'

'Quite simply, your Auberge does not meet French safety regulations. Under the circumstances, we would be irresponsible to allow you to keep trading.' He shrugged indifferently.

'And this is the mayor's opinion too?' interjected Madame Webster.

Pascal's nostrils flared.

'Madame,' he stated in his most haughty manner. 'Please rest assured that the mayor and I have discussed this issue at length and that I represent him here today when I say to you that a revocation of the notice of closure is not possible.'

'Did you catch all that?' Lorna asked Paul, who made a fifty-fifty gesture with his hand.

'Think it's basically a no!'

Still bristling from an accumulation of slights, Pascal's blood pressure rose even further at the rapid exchange in English which he couldn't understand. How dare they! Making him feel like a foreigner in his own country.

'Anything else?' he asked, the condescension dripping from him.

'Yes. One more thing.' Monsieur Webster consulted the notepad on his lap and read out the sentence he'd prepared. 'We would like to request a second fire and safety inspection.'

Pascal bit back a smile. Fatima had been right. She'd predicted they'd ask for this having heard on the grapevine that they were applying for grants from the Chambre de Commerce. And while the mayor had versed him in what to say if they asked for the notice of closure to be overturned, he hadn't said anything about a second inspection. So as far as Pascal was concerned, he was free to do as he saw fit. Well, as Fatima had advised him to anyway.

'Of course,' he replied haughtily. He made a great show of consulting the diary on the desk, running his fingers down the days as he turned over pages. Finally he looked up at the couple, anticipation on their faces. 'Wednesday May the twentieth? How does that sound?'

'Ah, no, that's not possible. We would liking it before January the twenty-eighth please.'

Pascal feigned surprise.

'That's impossible. We need to give the inspection party at least three months' notice.'

'But . . . but,' Monsieur Webster spluttered, struggling to find the words. 'This is an emergency. Please help us. If no inspection . . .' He stopped and looked to his wife for assistance.

'If no inspection before January the twenty-eighth then we must be selling,' she stated clearly, fixing the deputy mayor with a frank stare.

Enjoying himself immensely, Pascal creased his brow with mock concern as though their plight could touch his cold heart. Then he spread his hands in that classic Gallic gesture of fatalism.

'There's nothing I can do.'

'Oh for God's sake!' Lorna exclaimed, finally losing her tether with the arrogance of the deputy mayor. 'We're wasting our time here. Let's go.'

She stood up abruptly and slung her bag over her shoulder. As her husband opened the door for her, she turned back to the deputy mayor.

'Goodbye *Monsieur* Souquet,' she said, her deliberate emphasis underlining the fact that he was merely deputising. As the door closed in their wake, Pascal could hear Céline's hyena-like laugh echoing around the building in response.

'What a jerk!' Lorna fumed, as Paul negotiated the difficult bends on the route down to La Rivière. With the mood she was in they'd decided it was best if he drove.

'Couldn't agree more,' Paul replied. 'Only thing is, I don't think the mayor would have been any more helpful.'

'No, but at least he's not a condescending prick!'

Paul laughed without humour. 'No, he's just a manipulative bastard!'

Recognising the truth in his words, Lorna slumped in her seat, exhausted by the interminable battle that they seemed to have been waging from the day they set foot in the commune of Fogas.

'So they won't revoke the notice of closure which means there's no point approaching the bank again,' she said wearily.

'Nope.'

'And without an inspection before the end of January, getting a grant is out of the question.'

'Not that it was feasible anyway. We'd never have found the money to replace the boiler and oil tank in time for the deadline.'

'I guess not. But still . . .'

'I know.'

'So what now?'

Paul shrugged. 'Not a lot of choice really.'

Lorna turned to stare at the forest as though its mossy

depths could reveal the solution to all their problems. But all she felt was carsick as the trees blurred and her head started to reel.

'Tell you what,' Paul continued in a chipper tone Lorna knew was for her benefit. 'We'll take the rest of the day off. Maybe go over to Foix or even up to Toulouse.'

Lorna mustered a smile. 'That'd be great.'

'Shit!' Paul thumped his head in annoyance. 'Sorry, I've just remembered. I've agreed to pop into the épicerie to fit the new doorbell this afternoon.'

'Can't we go afterwards? How long will you be?'

'Half an hour max.'

'Then we'll go as soon as you're done.'

'You sure? I could always cry off.'

Lorna shook her head, not having much enthusiasm for the proposed outing anyway.

'It's fine. Fit the bell. God knows we need the brownie points around here.'

At last the car came to the junction with the main road and Lorna was glad to be out of the narrow valley and the depressing gloom of the forest in winter. As she turned her head to the left, she could see the Auberge, sunlight making its rugged stones seem warm and inviting, a welcome sight for weary travellers.

Lorna felt tears slide down her cheeks.

The plan that Josette had concocted so hastily a week and a half ago now seemed to be falling apart at the seams. Monsieur Webster, or Paul as he insisted on being called, had arrived straight after lunch and had set to work immediately. He hadn't seemed keen to talk and when she'd enquired about the inspection two days before, he'd merely grimaced and said, 'No good.' She'd pushed him a bit but he'd offered nothing more, except a comment about needing some carpets and curtains, clearly not wanting to discuss it.

Consequently, half an hour later, he was just about finished and there was still no sign of Christian. Jacques, keeping look-out at the window, was getting more anxious by the minute.

'It is finish I think,' Paul announced. 'Do you want to trying?'

He gestured for Josette to join him at the front of the shop and at his urging she tentatively opened the door.

'DING DONG DING DONG . . . DING DONG DING DONG.'

Jacques clapped his hands over his ears as the raucous peal of bells sounded in the small interior of the shop.

'Oh! It's a bit loud,' Josette exclaimed and Paul nodded, making an adjustment to the chimer which he'd fixed on the back wall behind the counter.

'It's Big Ben!' he said with a grin. 'But no worry. You have a choice,' and he proceeded to play the five different bell chimes for Josette, giving her the perfect excuse to stall him. As the notes of the last one faded she did her best impression of a dizzy old lady.

'Oh, I can't decide!' she lied. 'Can you play them again please?'

Paul was going through the repertoire for the third time, with no sign of impatience, when Jacques started flapping his hands at Josette. She looked out of the window to see the Panda crawling up the road towards them, its spluttering engine getting louder by the second. It pulled up outside the épicerie and Christian got out, swearing and cursing at the car and giving it a kick for good measure.

He stormed into the shop, obviously in the foulest of moods, and didn't even notice the sweet sound of birdsong that greeted his arrival.

215

'Bloody car!' he fumed as he scooped Josette up into a big hug. 'Sorry I'm late. Couldn't get the stupid thing to start.'

When he noticed Paul packing away his tools, he stiffened, turning to Josette with a questioning gaze.

'I don't think you two have met,' she managed, trying to steady her voice in the face of Christian's annoyance. 'Monsieur Paul Webster, may I introduce Monsieur Christian Dupuy.'

Paul already had his hand stretched out, eager to finally meet the big man with the curly blond hair who'd been so friendly to him and Lorna from afar. But as he registered the name of this latest acquaintance, a look of puzzlement crossed his face as he had difficulty reconciling the name with the person.

'Christian Dupuy?' he questioned. 'The deputy mayor?'

Josette nodded.

Paul said no more, simply shook hands with Christian and continued tidying his toolbox.

'*Et tu* Josette?' Christian muttered as Paul took the step-ladder through to the bar.

'I don't know what you mean,' she retorted with fake indignation.

'Of course you don't.'

Josette bit her lip as Christian crossed to the wonky cheese cabinet, no sign of a twinkle in his eyes. Perhaps she'd gone too far.

'So, you have choosing the sound?'

She swung round to see Paul standing with his toolbox in hand, ready to go.

'Oh! Yes, sorry. It's fine as it is,' she said, flustered, and feeling like an interfering old woman. 'Thanks for all your help. How much do I owe you?'

Paul put out a hand to stop her opening the till.

'No need.'

'Oh, but I must give you something! Just a moment.' She disappeared into the bar, leaving the two men in an awkward silence.

'So,' thought Paul. 'This is the man who caused all our problems.' He had no desire to punch him, partly because of the height difference, but also because . . . well, it just didn't seem to matter any more. Not now it was all but over.

Christian felt a twist of guilt as he saw Paul's worried profile. Stephanie had told him about their attempts to get funding to carry out the repairs to the Auberge and from all accounts, they'd failed. Yet another setback. It really wasn't in his nature to watch a neighbour struggling without offering help but the nagging doubt about the Websters' involvement in Sarko's release had made him take a step back.

He was just contemplating asking Paul about it outright and resolving the matter there and then when his phone rang.

When Josette came back into the shop, a bottle of wine and a box of chocolates in her arms, Christian was hanging up, looking even more vexed than before.

'So sorry Josette, I have to go. Sarko's escaped again. I'll pop down later to finish this.'

And with that he was out of the door and into the car, leaving Jacques hopping in the doorway, Josette looking upset and Paul with a bemused expression.

'What did he say?' Paul asked Josette. 'Something about the President. He *escapes*?'

Josette smiled. 'No, not the President. It's his bull.'

The door crashed open, the bird chorus tweeting in response, and Christian thundered back into the shop.

'DAMN that piece of shit!'

'Won't it start?'

Christian shook his head in exasperation.

'And my bloody phone has just run out of battery too. What a shit day!'

'There is problem?'

Christian took a deep breath before answering the Englishman. It was unfair to take this out on anyone, least of all someone about to lose their business and their home.

'My car won't start,' he explained. 'And I need to get home, urgently.'

'I can helping? I take you in my car?'

Even Jacques froze as the two men regarded each other across this tentative bridge of friendship that Paul had thrown over the deep divide that separated them. Josette hadn't realised she was holding her breath until Christian spoke and she felt the air ease out of her lungs.

'That would be very kind. Thank you.' With fingers thick and strong, his palm as rough as rope, he clasped Paul's hand as a smile transformed his face from fierce to friendly.

Paul grinned instinctively and the two of them headed down the road to the Auberge, Paul a little perturbed at how he was going to stop Lorna from leaping at the man's throat when she found out who he was.

'Well, I think that worked out OK in the end!' Josette acknowledged with a sigh of relief.

Jacques nodded, clearly elated. But when the door blew open and the birds started tweeting again, he grimaced, gesturing for Josette to change the sound.

'I can't!' she explained, walking towards the chimer. 'I don't know how to. You'll just have to live with it for now.'

'Live with what?'

Josette spun round. 'Annie! I didn't hear you come in!'

Annie gestured at the open door.

'You do rrrealise talking to yourrrself is one of the firrrst signs . . .' She tailed off and simply circled a finger at her temple.

Josette threw a murderous glance at Jacques who was enjoying every minute of her discomfort.

'But you sound . . . different,' Josette commented, anxious to change the subject.

Annie bared her teeth and what teeth they were! A gleaming set of new dentures, top and bottom.

'Thought it was about time I smarrrtened up my image,' she said, her speech much improved but her local accent still intact. She gestured towards the Auberge. 'See you had a bit of success therrre! Just met Chrrristian and Monsieurrr Websterrr going down the rrroad all chatty.'

'Here's hoping,' Josette replied, crossing her fingers.

'Well in that case, let's celebrrrate. I'll make coffee and call Vérrronique down, you open that box of chocolates.'

It was only then, seeing the chocolates and the wine still sitting on the counter, that Josette realised she'd let Paul go without giving him anything at all.

16

'WHAT did you say his name was?' Lorna hissed at Paul as Christian tried to pretend he wasn't there, doing his best to blend in with the wood panelling which ran around the walls of the dining room. Even though he couldn't understand the words, he knew enough about women to know when one was pissed off.

'It doesn't matter who he is. He needs our help.'

'HE needs OUR help? What about the help we need and all because of him! Driving past and tooting all friendly-like while stabbing us in the back!'

'Look, you don't have to come, OK? We won't be long.'

Lorna grabbed her coat and the back-door key.

'I'd best bloody had come. You might give the Auberge to him while you're at it!'

Paul ruffled her hair affectionately, knowing of old that her bark was usually worse than her bite. Even so, he gestured for Christian to go first out of the door with himself between them.

The drive up to the farm beyond Picarets was conducted in silence. Lorna was too busy trying not to be carsick in the back seat to carry on her tirade and Christian and Paul were both too awkward for small talk. Finally Christian gestured for Paul to pull over and they all got out.

'Oh, I know where we are!' Lorna exclaimed, her relief at being out of the car overcoming her annoyance. She pointed at the track on the nearby hillside. 'It's where we saw that man being chased by the bull.'

Paul looked over at the empty field opposite, a tangled mess of electric fence wire signalling the route of escape. 'It must be the same beast.'

Christian had walked down the road towards the farm in the distance to meet an elderly man coming towards them. Thinner than Christian, he was slightly stooped with age and his curly hair was more grey than blond. Even so, it was easy to see the family resemblance as they conferred quietly, the older man gesturing at the woods as though to indicate the possible location of the bull.

When they reached Lorna and Paul, Christian introduced his father, André, who took Lorna's outstretched hand, and kissed it profusely.

'Enchanted to meet you,' he said, his eyes dancing with devilment.

'Come on Papa, stop flirting, we've got a bull to find,' quipped Christian, trying to keep his tone light. He shook Paul's hand in farewell. 'Thanks for the lift. It was much appreciated.'

'But we can helping? We look for the bull?' Paul offered and to his amazement, Lorna joined in.

'Yes, yes. We look too.'

Christian scratched his head, reluctant to turn down the offer of much-needed help.

'OK,' he finally responded. 'He's this high, brown and, well, he's a bull so be careful.'

'We know,' Paul said. 'We see him before.'

Lorna laughed at the memory and Christian's face darkened at what appeared to be her cavalier attitude to an incident he suspected they'd caused.

Completely oblivious, Lorna continued. 'It is strange. The man opens the gate and vrooooommmm!'

She imitated the movement of the fleeing bull but Christian was still concentrating on the beginning of the sentence.

'The man?' he asked, his voice sharp. 'Which man?'

'The man with the orange beret. You know him? He's like this . . .' She curved her arms out from her body to resemble his physique.

Christian and his father exchanged glances and something in Christian's memory clicked into place: a piece of orange felt dangling on a horn, a man seen on hunting day without his beret . . .

'Bloody Bernard! I'll kill him!'

'You are not knowing?' Paul asked. 'So why he opens the gate?'

'Why indeed!' Christian rubbed his chin and let his eyes wander over the mountain peaks on the horizon as though coming to a momentous decision as his perception of the last two months shifted in response to this new information.

'Tell you what,' he said, turning back to Lorna and Paul. 'You help us look for Sarko, and I'll tell you all about it over dinner.'

His father looked flabbergasted at the invitation. In his opinion, bringing guests home for a meal of his wife's preparing was one way to ensure they never became friends.

'Sarko?' Lorna asked, oblivious to the family politics. 'Why you call him that? You like the President?'

André Dupuy, a lifelong socialist, grimaced and shook his head.

'Not at all. He's called Sarko because he's short, stubborn and fancies himself with the ladies!'

Even though they couldn't catch all the words, Lorna and Paul got the gist and they were still chuckling as they headed off into the woods to search for the missing bull.

★   ★   ★

Dinner at the Dupuys' was like nothing Lorna had ever experienced. With Sarko the bull safely escorted back to his field a couple of hours after they'd started the search, they'd arrived at the farm just as the sky was darkening, the tips of the mountains black silhouettes against the last of the daylight.

Josephine Dupuy, a short, robust woman who barely came up to Christian's shoulder, hadn't appeared daunted at the arrival of extra guests for dinner. Giving them a warm welcome, she'd set another two places at the large table in the main room which seemed to serve as kitchen, dining room and lounge and within minutes of entering, Lorna felt at home, sitting in an old armchair by the woodburner in the corner with a tabby cat on her lap.

André Dupuy had insisted on them having an aperitif, pouring a generous measure of whisky for Paul and a kir for Lorna, saying mysteriously that they would need the extra fortification which had made Josephine hit her husband with a tea towel. As the banter continued around the fire, Lorna felt herself relax and realised that she hadn't felt this content for weeks, which, considering whose house she was in, was rather extraordinary. It was amazing that she felt so welcome here when Christian Dupuy had been the cause of so much of their misery.

'You look miles away!' Christian commented as he watched Lorna stroke the cat.

She felt caught out, but the alcohol made her brave.

'I wonder why . . . why you demand inspection for the Auberge.'

'Ahh!' Christian had been expecting the question and turned his whisky glass around in his hands, contemplating it intently while organising his thoughts.

'I didn't order the inspection,' he finally replied, giving her a frank look. 'Well, technically I did, but I was manipulated into it.'

'I don't understand.'

'Neither did I until today!' Christian took a deep breath and started telling them the tale of their short time in the commune of Fogas and the way the mayor had used them all to get the Auberge back on the market. When he was finished, even André and Josephine were having difficulty taking it all in.

'So he never intended the commune to buy the Auberge?' André asked.

'No. I think he knew that would be difficult to explain away should his brother-in-law end up owning it.'

'So why . . .?' Paul's language skills abandoned him as he strove to make sense of the revelations.

Christian gave a self-deprecating smile. 'He knew me too well. He gambled that I would object to the compulsory purchase and suggest an alternative . . . which I did.'

'The inspection!' Lorna exclaimed.

Christian nodded. 'My idea. To save you from being bought by the commune. Only I didn't know that I was playing straight into Serge Papon's chubby little hands. I'm so sorry. I thought I was doing the right thing. And when Josette and I tried to stop him closing the Auberge after the inspection, he made sure I wasn't able to put forward an argument to the council.'

'You mean the rogue got Bernard to let Sarko out to deliberately keep you from the meeting?' Josephine asked, a dangerous edge to her voice.

'Well, of course I can't prove it. But yes, I think so. He thought if I was there I'd persuade the others to vote against the notice of closure.'

'We never have a chance!' Lorna declared. 'Not from the beginning.'

'No. None of us did.'

'So what will you do now?' asked André, looking at Paul with sympathy.

'They should keep fighting!' Josephine brandished her fist. Paul shook his head.

'We are finish fighting. We have no money for the work. We can't getting grants. Tomorrow we put the Auberge up for to sale and the mayor, he wins.'

Christian felt a sting of reproach in the glance his mother gave him.

'There must be something you can do?' she demanded. 'There must be some way round this?'

'I'm sorry but I can't overturn the notice of closure and I certainly don't have enough money to cover the cost of the work . . .' Christian paused as he heard his words echo back in his head. He might not have the money, but as for the work . . . Suddenly his mind was racing.

'Actually, there might be something left to try. Do you think you could give me twenty-four hours?' he asked Paul, refusing to elaborate further.

Paul nodded. One more day was hardly going to make a difference to their plans.

'I'll contact you tomorrow then. Let's drink to a happy outcome!'

They all raised their glasses and as they did so, André started sniffing the air. 'Is something burning?'

'Shit!' Josephine jumped up and scurried over to the oven where she pulled open the door, thick black clouds of smoke issuing forth. 'Oh no! I think I've burnt it!'

'How can you burn boeuf bourguignon, Maman?' Christian asked incredulously.

She shrugged, wafting away the worst of the smoke with her tea towel.

'I don't know. I think it's this oven.' She looked up with a cheeky smile. 'At least the dessert isn't homemade.'

Christian rolled his eyes mournfully while André simply reached for the whisky bottle and topped up Paul's glass.

'Like I said,' he muttered. 'Fortification!'

The meal was memorable in many ways. The burnt boeuf bourguignon, which Lorna would have thought was impossible to achieve, had an acrid flavour which had permeated the vegetables and the sauce, and the potatoes served with it were as hard as rocks. The bread however, which came from the bakery up the mountain, was delicious and afterwards they were all able to fill up on *tarte au citron*, the sharp tang of the lemons serving to alleviate the taste of carbon which had lingered after the main course.

But if the food wasn't up to standard, the atmosphere more than made up for it. The Dupuys were relaxed in each others' company and there was a constant flow of conversation as they argued amicably about politics, eagerly seeking the views of their foreign neighbours on everything from the French health service to their stance on the President.

With her plate finally empty, Lorna wiped her mouth with her napkin and sat back, feeling totally content.

'I can eating nothing more!' she announced, patting her stomach as a compliment to the chef.

André let out a dry bark. 'With my wife's cooking, you're lucky if you can eat anything at all!'

Josephine held up her hands in surrender. 'OK, I admit it! I can't cook.' She looked over at Lorna, her eyes twinkling. 'Perhaps you should stay and teach me. Maybe open a cooking school. Goodness knows but Stephanie could learn a thing or two about baking cakes!'

They sat chatting until a distant peal of church bells sounded the hour and Paul looked at his watch. Realising with astonishment that it was ten o'clock, he suggested it was time for them to go.

'I'm sorry about all the politics at the table,' Christian said, as he escorted them to the doorway and bent down to kiss Lorna on each cheek. 'Papa thinks he's the next José Bové. But at least they weren't telling you how much I need a wife!'

He shook Paul's hand and thanked him again for his help.

'We thank you too,' Paul replied. 'For a lovely meal!'

Christian laughed and slapped Paul on the back.

'So it's true what they say about Englishmen always being polite!'

He watched them pull out of the drive and then re-entered the farmhouse. Before they were even level with Sarko's field, he was on the phone.

'Hi René. It's me. Have you got a minute? It's about the Auberge . . .'

Annie Estaque was on the crest of the hill at the back of her house gazing at the stars, all sharp edges and cold light against the frosty night sky, when the sweep of headlights came around the corner, the beams struggling to penetrate the dark before being swallowed by the dense forest.

Who could that be at this time of night?

She waited, eyes focused intently on the road, until the car appeared again around another bend and her face split into a broad smile.

The English! Stephanie had rung to say she'd seen them up at the farm with Christian and André earlier in the afternoon and here they were, just heading home. Annie didn't wear a watch but she knew it must be after ten, having heard the bells across the valley some time ago.

Well well well. Not only had they helped look for the bull, they'd also endured one of Josephine's meals. It looked like Josette's plan had worked and hopefully Christian would now get his finger out and get something organised.

227

Quite what he could do though, she had no idea. She'd exhausted her last avenues that morning, plucking up her courage to visit Thérèse Papon at the hospital. The woman had looked even more fragile, but had managed a smile of genuine pleasure at seeing Annie, hesitant and nervous in the doorway.

Annie had apologised for the intrusion, saying she would leave if Thérèse wanted her to, but she'd simply held out her hand and Annie, holding the thin fingers gently, the contrast against her own broad hands stark, had sat beside her and prattled on for ages. She'd told her about the damage the storm had caused, she'd answered her questions about Véronique and the fire at the post office and she'd even told her about her new teeth which had elicited a shaky laugh. And then she'd told her about the Auberge and the people there, how good they would be for the commune and their need for the notice of closure to be lifted. Thérèse had listened intently and Annie knew that she'd done all she could.

Finally, Thérèse's eyelids had started to droop and Annie stood to go. She was putting on her coat when she heard a hoarse whisper and Thérèse's bony fingers had clutched at her sleeve. Annie bent down to hear what she was saying.

'Tell him,' Thérèse whispered.

Annie felt the shock ripple across her face.

'When I'm gone, tell him,' Thérèse repeated, her eyes focused on Annie with an intense energy. 'He has a right to know.'

Annie had nodded, incapable of uttering a sound as she held the hand of the woman she'd been so distant from for thirty-five years and yet whose life had been so intertwined with hers. She'd walked quickly down the corridors and out of the hospital to the bus stop in a blur, fighting to keep her emotions under control.

Now she craned back her head once more, her eyes read-justing as the last of the light from the car disappeared down the valley. She watched the night sky turning slowly above her, the warm body of one of her dogs leaning against her thigh as he kept guard, and she marvelled not for the first time at the size of the universe and the tiny speck she was within it.

17

On the surface, Friday 16 January was like any other day in the commune of Fogas. Josette sold the usual amount of bread, cigarettes and vegetables, the only notable exception being the two bottles of wine, a tin of cassoulet, and a set of laces bought by a couple of hardy tourists visiting the area for winter walking. But she'd spent the best part of the day staring out of the window towards the Auberge, not sure what she was watching for. Stephanie's call last night had given her hope but she still couldn't see what Christian could do at this late stage. As for Jacques, the anxiety had worn him out and so he'd taken up his usual position in the inglenook, his head soon heavy on his chest.

Almost two weeks into her stay at the épicerie, Véronique had passed that Friday sitting in the window of the bar, her leg up on a chair and a book open on her lap. With no news from the Conseil Municipal as to how she was to be relocated while the post office and apartment were rebuilt, she was slowly going mad. She was frustrated at living in someone else's house, constantly on her best behaviour. Although Josette had made her more than welcome she still felt like an intruder and she was seriously worried about the number of times she'd overheard Josette talking to herself.

As she continued staring down the road, waiting for the appearance of the little blue Panda that was the highlight of her day, she scratched absent-mindedly at the itch under the plaster that still persisted. Six more weeks before she could have the cast taken off. She groaned, unaware that she was disturbing Jacques' sleep, and turned back to the book on her lap. It took only a few sentences of heavy Marxist theory before her eyes wandered back to the window.

Meanwhile Stephanie spent the day in the garden, making the most of the relatively mild weather by rebuilding her polytunnel, trying not to think how bleak the future looked for her and Chloé in Picarets. She'd had a call from a friend up in Brittany offering her a job in a garden centre in Finistère complete with a place to live and she was giving it serious consideration. As a gust of wind tugged at the plastic in her hands, for a brief moment she thought she could taste the tang of sea salt on her tongue. She shook her head at her own nonsense, pushed her wayward hair back behind her ears, and focused on her work.

With the polytunnel finally in place, she stood up, hands on hips, and stared across the garden to the white peaks of the mountains behind the house. Could she go back? The call of her native land was strong but so was the pull of the mountains. It would be hard to leave Picarets for so many reasons. She had friends here, as did Chloé. But most of all, she felt safe in the tiny hamlet. There was no way they could be found by her ex-husband with his violent temper and lightning-fast fists. But without work, it wouldn't be feasible for her to remain. Not fair on Chloé either. So returning to Finistère was tempting, but was it wise?

While Stephanie wrestled with her future, Christian was busy rebuilding the hen house that Maman had been nagging him about since the storm. He worked at his usual pace, methodical and focused, no haste and no hurry, everything done with purpose and with care. But his mind was racing and he was willing the hours to pass. As the final nail went into the felt-covered roof he cocked his head and heard the bells chiming the hour. Not long now, he thought, as he put away his tools and stored them in the back of the Panda. A change of spark plugs and leads had given the little car a new lease of life but even so, he felt the need to caution it.

'You'd better bloody start tonight!' he threatened as he walked towards the house to get ready.

Her house still full of builders working on the damaged gable wall, Annie had had a noisy and disrupted day. She was beginning to wonder if she'd been foolish to try and stay in the house throughout the work. There was dust everywhere, a fine white powder which continued to drift down from the ceiling long after the workmen had left for the night, covering every flat surface. If she sat still long enough they'd discover her in the morning, a replica of Lot's wife sitting at her kitchen table.

Savouring the idea of a weekend without them, she watched the workmen's white van meander down the mountain under the darkening sky as the clock started chiming in the house behind her. She fed the dogs and then made herself a coffee, her ears pricked for the rattle of the tired Panda engine. When he went past she'd call Josette and maybe between them they could work out what he was up to.

Up in Fogas, Serge was standing at his bedroom window when the light began to fade. He made no move to turn on a lamp; he didn't want to be seen. When Céline's white Peugeot drove past he left his vigil and headed downstairs. He waited another half-hour for it to get truly dark, then he slipped into his coat and quietly let himself out the back door. The two houses next to his were both second homes and the owners were away so he was confident he wouldn't be spotted. All he had to do was cross their gardens and he would be in the car park behind the town hall.

The first garden proved no problem, separated as it was from his by bushes and trees. But the second had a chicken-wire fence and Serge wasn't as young, or as slim, as he used to be. Using a compost bin as a ladder he managed to haul himself over the fence and slide down the other side, landing with a thud on the pile of debris which the builders had left behind when they'd replaced the annexe roof after the storm.

He dusted off his trousers and, keeping to the shadows, worked his way around the building to the side entrance. A quick turn of the key and he was inside. He locked the door behind him and stood for a minute as his eyes adjusted to the gloom of the interior. Somewhere above him a pipe clanked and a floorboard creaked in response and then everything fell silent.

Feeling his neck prickling, Serge edged over to the stairs and used the handrail to guide him up to the first floor which was in total darkness. He groped his way through Céline's office and into his own and once inside he flicked on a lamp, safe in the knowledge that the shuttered windows would prevent his presence from being noticed by the world outside. As a pool of white light pushed back the dark, he inhaled deeply, the room smelling as always of old floor polish, dust and a slight tinge of damp. To Serge Papon it was the musky aroma of power and the space settled around him like a mantle.

Now to work. The first thing he saw on his desk was a letter from the Fire Department in Foix. He tapped it on his left hand as he regarded it thoughtfully and then slid a thick finger under one end of the envelope and ripped it open.

As he'd expected. A notice of inspection for the Auberge des Deux Vallées for 26 January.

Serge laughed, the sound ricocheting around the empty room in the shadows beyond the lamplight. So he'd been right! Major Gaillard was joining in the fun. That made it all the more interesting. His suspicions had been aroused when he'd made his daily call to Céline only to be told that a Monsieur Peloffi had left a message to apologise in advance for not being able to make the twenty-sixth.

At first nonplussed, he'd asked Céline to check the calendar. Nothing was scheduled. But knowing that Monsieur Peloffi had been a member of the original inspection party, and with his political instincts as sharp as ever, Serge had deduced that somehow, behind his back, a second inspection had been organised. His initial instinct had been to postpone it, as was his right as mayor. But that would only arouse suspicions and from what he'd heard, the English owners didn't have the financial resources to be ready by 26 January. No, it was better to let it go ahead.

And then he'd visited Thérèse in the hospital and everything had changed. With a slight flush in her normally wan cheeks, she'd started asking him about the Auberge straight away. Clearly someone had been telling her about the goings-on but she wouldn't say who and he was at a loss to work it out. On her strict instructions, he'd told no one about her illness and as far as their friends and neighbours were concerned, she was visiting family in Toulouse. But no matter. As usual, she'd taken the plight of the poor English couple to heart and wanted to know if he could do anything to help.

Throughout their married life, Serge had always accepted as a given that his wife's perception of him was governed by her own gentle disposition. She was incapable of suspecting him of subterfuge and believed that he had everyone's best interests at heart. Which on the whole he did. But he'd never felt hindered by her trust in him; in fact on more than one occasion he'd used it to his advantage. Today, however, he'd found her innocent belief hard to take and her plea had struck a chord.

That, plus he sensed it was politically expedient for him to change direction midstream now that Major Gaillard was involved.

He reached into his pocket and pulled out another envelope. It had taken him the best part of the afternoon to produce the letter it contained using Thérèse's ancient computer, his stiff fingers jabbing at the keys as he sought to find the right words. He placed it in the middle of the desk and then had second thoughts. Céline would notice it there on Monday morning and that wasn't what he wanted. So he leaned down and casually dropped it under the desk, as though it had been knocked there some time ago. He'd have to hope she didn't spot it, until the time was right!

Checking first that nothing was out of place, he turned off the light and felt his way carefully across the room and out into the corridor, Major Gaillard's letter still in his hand. He would risk Céline realising it was gone. He didn't want anyone else to see it. He'd pop in to the town hall on Monday and set the trap in motion and by the twenty-sixth, the matter would be resolved. And who knew, maybe Thérèse was right. Maybe it was best for the commune this way round after all. But at least he'd done his utmost to make sure it was also best for him.

Serge Papon eased open the door and let himself out into the cold night air. Within a couple of minutes he was back in his house, greeted by the same silence that always greeted him these days. He took off his coat and sat next to the fire, his pleasure at outmanoeuvring a political opponent already fading as he stared at the flames and wondered what on earth he was going to do when she was gone.

★   ★   ★

In La Rivière it was already dark, the rear window of the Auberge now a rectangle of black, simply throwing back a reflection of the large room. Paul pushed his face against the cold glass, trying to see something, anything. But all he could make out was a couple of lights dotted across the hillside in Sarrat. Even the river, swollen in recent weeks by the winter weather, was only discernible by the constant murmur as it passed over the weir.

With an air of resignation he pulled the curtains shut, as though calling an end to what had been a long day of waiting.

'Looks like he's not going to call,' he said wearily.

Lorna looked up from the laptop. She'd tried to warn Paul not to get his hopes up; after all, what could Christian Dupuy achieve in a day that they hadn't been able to sort out in two months? But after last night, Paul had placed all his faith in the farmer.

It had been a fantastic evening with the Dupuys, no question, but it had made their inevitable decision harder to bear. It would have been easier to leave the Auberge with bitterness in their hearts, blaming those they didn't know for the predicament they were in. Now they knew the truth and that there were people in the commune who really cared about them. And that made Lorna's present task a lot more difficult.

'What do you think? Have I covered all the points?'

Paul skimmed over the For Sale notice on the computer screen. 'I'd buy it,' he said sadly.

'I'll post it then?'

Paul nodded and with an air of ceremony, Lorna pressed *Enter* and the Auberge was officially put up for sale on the Internet. She stood up and he pulled her into a fierce embrace.

'We gave it a go,' he muttered into her hair. 'No one can say we didn't try.'

She hugged him even tighter, burying her head in his chest until all she could hear was the blood pounding through her ears.

Thud thud thud thud . . .

She closed her eyes, immersing herself in the beat of her heart and the comfort of Paul's arms around her, trying to shut out the stress, the disappointment, the uncertainty of their future and the sense of failure that seemed to accompany her every waking hour. Finally, as though through water, she became aware of the muffled sound of Paul's voice above the persistent thudding.

'Lorna?'

She lifted her head, the pulse still throbbing in her ears. Thud thud thud . . .

'There's someone at the back door.'

THUD THUD THUD!

The shutters over the back door were rattling as the knocking became more determined. Paul hurried over and opened the door and the second he lifted the latch on the shutters they were torn open by two massive hands and Christian's curly mop of hair appeared in the room.

'Haven't sold it yet have you?' he asked, striding into the room, crackling with energy, followed by two smaller, squatter men, one of whom was carrying a toolbox.

'This is René Piquemal,' he said indicating the older of the two, whose swarthy round face was accented by a drooping moustache.

'And this is his brother-in-law, Claude. And they,' Christian announced with a flourish, 'are going to solve all your problems!'

Josette was beside herself with excitement. Her plan had worked. Véronique had called her into the bar the minute she saw the two sets of headlights turning into the Auberge.

'It's got to be Christian!' Josette exclaimed.

'But what can he do?' mused Véronique. 'It's not as if he's loaded with money!'

'And the other car? You couldn't see whose it was?'

Véronique shook her head.

But they didn't have to wonder for long.

Within minutes Annie was on the phone, having spoken to Stephanie who'd been called by Christian. He'd wanted a list of the essential work for the fire and safety certificate and he'd told Stephanie his plan. It was ingenious.

Now Josette and Véronique were stationed at the window, staring down the road into the dark while Jacques loitered in the shadows.

'I feel useless,' Véronique muttered, scratching at her cast. 'I'd love to be down there helping out.'

'You're not the only one,' Josette agreed, one eye on her husband who'd started pacing up and down the floor, his face furrowed in thought.

'There must be some way we can get involved? Something we can do?'

But Josette couldn't come up with anything that would justify them turning up at the door.

'I think we'll just have to stay put,' she said to Véronique who was scowling like a small child, her insatiable curiosity having to remain unappeased. 'We'd only be in the way.'

As she glanced back out the window, Josette saw the lace curtain that decorated the bottom half of the glass shift in the breeze and then resettle. Turning to see if she'd left the door open by mistake she jumped slightly. Jacques had crept up alongside her.

'You OK? You look like you saw a ghost.'

'Yes, I'm fine,' Josette managed, as she glared at Jacques. 'Just a silly old goose walking over my grave.'

The curtain moved again. Only this time she could see it wasn't a draught. It was Jacques, his lips pursed as he blew as hard as he could, making the curtain float in front of them.

'What on earth . . .' Véronique was staring now at the fragile lace which was dancing before her eyes as though it had a life of its own.

'It's just a draught.' Josette tried to grab hold of the curtain and silently threaten her idiot husband with a frown at the same time.

'Behave, for goodness sake!' she finally hissed.

'What? Did you say something?' Véronique was regarding her warily and Josette had to think fast, to cover her slip.

'I said maybe there's something we could take . . .'

Jacques hit his forehead in frustration. He was pointing openly now at the curtains, pleading with his wife to understand him.

'Of course!' Josette threw her hands into the air in revelation. 'Something to take! The curtains!'

'What? I don't understand.'

Josette rushed over to the phone.

'Just let me call Stephanie and I'll explain,' she said as she began dialling. 'And then we'll be paying a visit to the Auberge.'

Jacques retreated to his seat in the inglenook, feeling a contentment that he hadn't known since his last mouthful of Josette's cassoulet. Everything was going to be OK. The commune was in safe hands.

Down at the Auberge things were happening. Lorna was racking her brains as to what she could cook for her three impromptu guests while Claude was wandering around flicking fuses off and on and testing every socket in the place. Meanwhile, Christian, René and Paul were down in the cellar inspecting the boiler and the oil tank.

Having introduced René and Claude with such hype, Christian had sensed Paul and Lorna's scepticism and hurriedly offered an explanation. He began by throwing an arm around Claude's shoulder.

'Claude here is an electrician and he has come all the way from Seix to carry out a diagnostic test on your electrics.'

Christian encompassed René with his other arm.

'And René is a local plumber. He is going to install a new boiler and oil tank this week. Then you can pass the inspection.'

Paul struggled to respond.

'But . . .' he stammered, 'we don't having much money. We can't paying.'

Christian held up a hand.

'We know. René has agreed to do the work for the cost of materials only. What do you reckon René? Total price?'

The plumber tugged his moustache and screwed up his eyes as though calculating the size of the building.

'I reckon I could do it for two and a half thousand all in.'

'Two and a half thousand?' Paul's voice rose an octave. 'That's so cheap! And the electrics?'

Claude smiled shyly. 'Free,' he said.

'Well, not quite free,' Christian butted in hastily. 'The problem is, we can only work at night. We're busy in the day plus we don't want people to know we're here. It's politics!' He pulled a face and then continued. 'So, our payment will be a meal tonight and every night we work, if that's OK?'

'That's it?' Lorna asked. 'A meal?'

She nodded eagerly at Paul and he took each man's hand in turn as he shook on the deal.

'But why?' Lorna asked as the men prepared to set to work. 'Why you help us?'

René looked embarrassed as he rubbed the floor with his foot, his eyes cast downwards.

'I voted to close the Auberge,' he said quietly, 'despite Christian and Josette trying to persuade me otherwise. Then Christian called last night and told me what he'd found out. About the mayor. About the bull. Everything.'

He shook his head in disgust. 'It's totally wrong what happened to you. So, I'm here to make amends.'

'And Claude? He doesn't even living here. Why he helps?'

'Ah, Claude!' intoned the plumber disdainfully while his brother-in-law's face creased into dimples. 'It's simple. Last winter when we were out hunting he shot me by accident so he owes me one.'

'He shoots you?' Lorna exclaimed. 'Where?'

Claude giggled and Christian smothered a grin. René rubbed his backside and glowered at the pair of them.

'Suffice to say, it's a good job I've got plenty of natural padding!'

And with that the men had started work, leaving Paul and Lorna to discuss the unexpected turnaround in their fortunes.

'Two and a half thousand euros for the boiler and oil tank. I can't believe it. We'll be able to open within weeks.'

'You're forgetting the inspection,' Lorna cautioned. 'Monsieur Souquet said we'd have to wait until mid-May for the next one. I don't suppose he'll change his mind.'

'No, but the mayor might! He may even lift the notice of closure if he knows the work is done. We'll see him next week and not take no for an answer.'

'We'll still miss the deadline for the grants though.'

Paul chewed his lip. 'Yes, there's no way we'll make that. But with an income and good bookings, the bank might give us a loan to do the roof at a later date.' He gave a broad smile, his optimism contagious. 'At least we now have a fighting chance.'

A loud crash and muffled cursing from the cellar

interrupted them and Paul hurried off to join the men while Lorna ransacked the kitchen, looking for inspiration. Twenty minutes later, she remembered the chorizo, lurking at the back of a cupboard, that she'd bought to try out a new recipe but had lost the enthusiasm for when everything started to go wrong. Perfect. She started preparing the meal and was almost ready to start cooking when she heard raised voices in the dining room. Paul poked his head around the kitchen door.

'Feeling miraculous?' he enquired.

'Miraculous? What do you mean?'

'Well, are you able to turn that into a meal for eleven?' he asked, pointing at the pile of sausage, tomatoes and onions on the chopping board.

'ELEVEN?'

Paul grinned and held the door open for Lorna to see.

'Bonsoir Lorna!' shouted a chorus of voices as she looked in amazement at the group of people crowding the big room. Stephanie was there, with Annie from up the hill, Josette from the shop, the postmistress, whose name she didn't know, still on crutches after the fire, and an older man and woman she'd never seen before.

'We came to help,' Josette announced, her face barely visible behind a mound of material spilling over her arms. 'And we brought some things that Stephanie said you needed for the Hôtel de Tourisme inspection.'

Lorna relieved her of her load and saw that it was two pairs of curtains.

'For the bedrooms,' Josette explained.

One by one they came forward, each with something different. Stephanie had several pots of paint, all white, which would cover the stained ceilings, and the man, whom she introduced as Alain Rougé, had brought an assortment of lamps, more than enough for their needs. Annie explained that she had two

242

rolls of carpet from her house in Stephanie's car; they had been slightly damaged in the storm and were going to be replaced by the insurance company. She thought they might do for now. Then the older lady, who was called Monique Sentenac, said that she had a bed out in the car. She apologised that it was a bit old-fashioned and hadn't been used in twenty years, then muttered something about a curate which made everyone laugh. And finally the postmistress, whose name was Véronique, hobbled forward awkwardly as she tried to manage her crutches and carry something at the same time.

'I lost everything in the fire,' she said. 'So I brought you this instead.'

Lorna took the large bundle she was carrying and laid it on the table. She peeled back the blanket it was wrapped in to reveal one of the most grotesque statues she'd ever seen. It looked like a shepherdess with leprosy sporting a gruesome neck wound and accompanied by a deformed lamb. Even so, Lorna's eyes welled with tears.

'It's St Germaine,' Véronique explained. 'She brought me luck, so maybe she will do the same for you.'

'Thank you!' Lorna gave the woman an impetuous hug.

'What's this?' Christian's voice boomed from the back door. 'Giving my presents away already, Véronique?'

'Don't worry Chrrristian. It's just a loan,' Annie cackled. She whispered to Lorna, 'You'll be glad to know she wants it back afterrr the inspection!'

'So,' Josette clapped her hands, bringing order to the rapidly descending chaos. 'What can we do to help?'

Within minutes they were all working away. Carpets were carried upstairs, the bed was assembled, curtains hung, the lamps distributed and St Germaine placed on the plinth in the hall. By the time Lorna announced dinner the Auberge was a hive of activity.

'English cooking!' René said with a hint of trepidation as he took his place at the table. 'Well at least Christian won't be disappointed!'

'Pah!' Annie snorted. 'Chrrristian thinks Madame Loubet was a good cook!'

'Madame Loubet? That old bat?' Alain exclaimed. 'Worst food I've ever had in my life.'

Christian blushed as he sat down between Stephanie and Véronique.

'I thought her cassoulet was good,' he protested.

Catching the gist of the banter, Lorna couldn't resist joining in as she placed the large pan of chorizo bean stew in the centre of the table, while Paul poured generous glasses of red wine for everyone.

'Her cassoulet? It is good?' she asked innocently.

'Bloody good!' Christian announced, feeling like he could recapture some of his lost pride. 'You can't beat honest home cooking.'

Lorna returned to the kitchen and came back out carrying a huge tin.

'A present,' she said, putting the catering tin of cassoulet down in front of Christian. 'Madame Loubet leaves it here.'

Soon everyone around the table was in uproar. And then Véronique noticed the expiry date on the side and the laughter started all over again.

Above the noise Lorna became aware of a shrill ringing. The phone. She raced over to the bar but couldn't hear over the commotion. Seeing her predicament, Paul shouted for silence, much to Christian's relief, and they all fell quiet as Lorna's voice carried clearly across the room.

'Could you repeat please?' She listened carefully and then covered the mouthpiece and looked over at her neighbours, her new friends and her husband.

'They see the advert on the Internet,' she explained. 'They ask if the Auberge is still for sale! What do I say?'

A split second of silence followed and then Christian roared, 'Tell them NO!' and everyone joined in, shouting and laughing until Lorna had to retreat into the kitchen to make herself heard.

'I'm sorry,' she said, trying to keep the laughter out of her voice. 'But the Auberge is not for sale.'

She hung up, grabbed a basket of bread and another bottle of wine and went to join the party.

18

For the commune of Fogas, the week that followed passed in a web of intrigue and deception. For Serge Papon, that was nothing out of the ordinary. The Monday after his late night visit to the town hall he called in again, but this time he made sure as many people as possible saw him.

In the car park, he took the time to speak to Bernard about the new snow-plough attachment which had finally arrived and was resting beside the tractor, the last one having met its end in an encounter with a stone wall which Bernard refused to take the blame for. Then he listened patiently to Madame Aubert. The old widow, who lived on her own at the entrance to the village next to the stone wash-basins which had once served as the communal laundry area, harangued him for several minutes about the fact that she couldn't get her pension in La Rivière and demanded to know when the post office would be reopening. He smoothed her ruffled feathers with a few lies and a couple of promises he had no way of keeping.

In the hallway he met an irate Philippe Galy who was incensed that the last council meeting had been postponed and threatened to take legal action against the commune if his planning permission was held up any longer. The mayor commiserated with his predicament and calmed him down by guaranteeing a meeting within seven days. He insinuated that the permission was all but approved, even though Serge had

246

done no more than shuffle the paperwork around his desk since it had first arrived there in December.

Confident that he still possessed the delicate touch that had kept him in power all these years, Serge entered Céline's office with an affectionate embrace for his secretary. Reeling from the shock of seeing him in the flesh after so long and from inhaling the pungent fumes of his aftershave, Céline didn't know where to start. She grabbed a pile of papers that needed his signature and as the mayor began working his way through them, signing each one with a flourish, she read out the messages that had come in that day. Soon she was near the bottom of the list.

'Erm . . . what else? Oh, yes. Philippe Galy's just been in. He's demanding to know when the next council meeting is.'

'I've just seen him,' Serge responded without looking up. 'It's all sorted.'

Céline crossed off another item and moved to the last one.

'And finally, Pascal called,' she said, her voice lacing his name with venom.

'I thought he was on holiday,' Serge barked, his attention now focused on his secretary.

'He is. He'll be back next Monday. He was just checking everything was OK.'

'He called from the Alps to ask if everything was OK?'

Céline did a good impression of Pascal's simpering smile and the mayor relaxed. It was time to set the trap.

'I meant to ask, Céline,' he said, his tone serious and concerned. 'Did the simpleton remember to give Monsieur WebSter the letter I left on the desk for him last week when he stood in for me?'

Céline frowned. 'I can't be sure. I don't recall him mentioning it. Was it important?'

'Very.'

'I'll just check your desk. No one's been in there since he used it last Thursday.'

'Would you? I'll finish these off while you do.' Serge held his breath while Céline trotted across the office and into the large room next door. When he was sure she was out of sight, he drew an envelope out of his pocket and slipped it into the pile of post waiting to be collected. Unlike the letter lying under his desk, which hopefully Céline wouldn't spot, this one needed to be delivered immediately. It informed the owners of the Auberge about the impending inspection. But this way, with the secretary out of the loop, come 26 January there would be no record at the town hall of the event and that was the way he wanted it.

'Where was it exactly?' Céline's voice called from beyond the doorway.

'On my desk, in full view,' he answered, praying that she didn't look too hard.

'Well it's not there now.' He heard the welcome sound of her footsteps as she came back into the office and closed the adjoining door.

'He must have delivered it,' she said taking the signed papers from the mayor's hands. 'Not like him to get something right!'

Serge said his farewells, promising Céline that he'd be back in the office by next week at the latest. She asked archly if that was because he was expecting his wife back and he managed to give her a boyish grin in response. It quickly disappeared as he headed down the stairs, leaving in its place the haunted look of a man who has witnessed the worst life can offer and is condemned to live with it.

Treachery didn't come quite so easily to Christian Dupuy and by Wednesday evening he was feeling the strain. Every night, under cover of darkness, he'd joined René at the

Auberge and they'd worked on replacing the old boiler and oil tank. Others from the commune had come along to help, leaving their cars at the far end of the village to avoid detection. So far, no one had been spotted but it was only a matter of time and Christian really didn't want to be there when the mayor found out what was going on behind his back.

With his hair standing on end from stress-induced head scratching, he clambered out of the Panda at the rear of the Auberge, glad to see René's van already there, tucked out of sight of the road. He stretched his tall frame, his muscles protesting at the thought of another four hours' work. But still, they were nearly finished. With Paul able to do all of the wiring, the three of them had virtually installed the new boiler and it would be ready for testing tonight. Which was just as well as apart from the woodburner in the corner of the dining room, the Websters had been three days without heating since René had disconnected the old system and in these temperatures, that wasn't funny.

But Lorna hadn't complained. She'd not stopped smiling since they'd turned up last Friday and every night she'd provided a meal for whoever happened to be there. Some nights it was ten people sitting around the big table, sometimes just six or seven, Monique Sentenac quite often busy at her hair salon and Josette and Véronique having to take it in turns to help out because as Josette pointed out, everyone would be suspicious if the shop was closed on a regular basis!

Christian felt a sense of pride at how his neighbours had rallied to the cause. The stained ceilings had been covered with a fresh layer of paint, the carpets fitted and the bed put in place. But even when the work necessary for the inspection was finished, still people came. They cleaned the windows and washed the old curtains, cleared the cellar of rubbish accumulated over the years and helped Lorna wash and iron piles of dirty bedlinen left behind by the Loubets. After five days, the Auberge was barely recognisable.

Feeling less fatigued, he sprinted up the steps and opened the back door.

'Bonsoir!' The assembled group of people at the bar were making far too much noise to hear him. Stephanie was jigging up and down on the spot, René was thumping Paul on the back, Annie was cackling away and Véronique, who was embracing Lorna, looked positively . . . Christian's mind went blank as it refused to complete the sentence. He blinked and looked at her again, her tight-fitting jumper and flared trousers a vast improvement on the shapeless skirts and cardigans that had been consumed by the fire. As his eyes involuntarily skimmed over her curves, he had a flashback to the hospital and that glimpse of her perfect . . . And just at that moment she glanced up, her eyes met his and his face started to burn.

'Christian!' Stephanie screeched, spotting him hovering in the doorway. She bounded across the floor and flung her arms around him and, glad of the distraction, he swung her around. It was only as he put her down that he caught sight of Véronique, her expression of joy from minutes earlier replaced by a strained smile.

With a sense of betrayal he couldn't begin to understand, he eased away from Stephanie and addressed the others.

'Why the celebration?'

Lorna handed him two letters which he quickly skimmed. The first was from the chief hotel inspector explaining that there would be a second inspection for the Hôtel de Tourisme accreditation on 26 January, which was fantastic news. But it was the second letter that really changed things.

'I don't believe it!' he exclaimed. 'The mayor has ordered a second fire and safety inspection for the same day. Why would he do that when Pascal said it wasn't possible? Surely it's not in his best interests?'

Paul shrugged. 'I do not care! Now we can getting grants and maybe we can fixing the roof!'

'I'm going to start the paperwork tonight,' Stephanie butted in, 'and that way we should have everything in place in time.'

'But look at this bit.' Christian pointed to a line in the middle of the text and began to read out loud.

'With reference to my letter dated the fifteenth of January, I hereby inform you that I have successfully arranged a re-inspection of the Auberge des Deux Vallées by the Fire and Safety Committee on Monday the twenty-sixth of January . . .'

Christian consulted his watch for the date, making a quick calculation as he did so.

'The fifteenth was last Thursday. Did you receive a letter from the mayor last week?'

Paul shook his head. 'No, nothing. We go to the town hall that day and he isn't there, only Pascal Souquet. He gives us no help and no letter.'

'That's what I thought.' Christian's forehead creased in frowns. 'So what's he referring to?'

'He's probably just confused,' said Véronique. 'After all, it seems he has a lot on his mind with his wife away!'

René let out a ribald laugh but Annie was quick to reproach her.

'Véronique! You should know betterrr than to sprrread gossip!' she said sharply.

'How can you defend him, Maman? After everything he's done?'

Annie pursed her lips and made a huffing noise.

Christian, however, wasn't convinced.

'The old fox is up to something. I just don't know what.'

Lorna put her hand on Christian's arm. 'Maybe he changes his mind? For us, we do not ask. We are simply grateful.'

'Yes, of course, you're right.' Christian didn't want to throw more cold water on their enthusiasm. 'It's excellent news.'

'Not if we don't get finished it's not,' René put in gruffly. 'Come on, no more slacking.'

And with that the group broke up and everyone headed off to work, their effort over the last few days seeming even more worthwhile with this unexpected news.

But Christian wasn't as light-hearted. He knew the mayor of old and wasn't prepared to trust him one iota. He decided to put the matter aside as he concentrated on building the fireproof wall that had to be erected around the new boiler. But his mind refused to let go. The problem was, he couldn't see how the mayor's abrupt about-turn could be anything but beneficial to everyone in the commune. And that was precisely what made him suspicious.

While Christian was doing his best to negotiate the intricate twists and turns of the mayor's thought processes, the mayor was wishing, for the first time in his existence, that life was a bit less complicated. Not that much was simpler than death and that was the reality he was facing.

It was the night before the inspection and he was stationed at his wife's bedside. For the last week he'd kept his vigil next to her as he watched her condition deteriorate. Now, barely able to speak, she was slipping in and out of consciousness and her breathing had become shallow and harsh. He hadn't needed the doctor to warn him that she didn't have long to live.

As the light outside began to fade, the sound of her laboured breaths intertwined with the patter of raindrops against the windows, he wondered whether she was in pain. The nurses had assured him that the medication was strong enough to ease her suffering but even so, he worried. She was so frail, Serge was almost convinced that she would float out of the room but for the weight of the rosary beads looped around her fingers, anchoring her to the Earth like a spiritual ballast. He placed his hand on top of hers where it lay pale and listless against the bedcovers, his own, although misshapen and battered from years of labouring in the tungsten mines up in Salau, ruddy with health by comparison.

Twenty-five years. He stroked the backs of her unresponsive fingers. A quarter of a century since he'd been elected mayor. He'd rejected the agricultural life of his father and his ancestors, scornful of the meagre living to be had from a pocketful of land that was mostly mountain. Instead he'd opted for a more secure existence. Mining was hard, physical work, and by the time the mines had started to fail and he'd been laid off in the mid-eighties, part of him had been relieved. Within six months of his redundancy he'd managed to elevate himself to mayor, narrowly beating old Henri Estaque in the elections, and his political career had taken off. But all the contriving and the manipulation which had become second nature to him could do nothing for his wife now.

Frustrated beyond measure, he paced the room to the window where the mountains were hidden behind a mass of rain clouds which were growing more menacing by the second. Below, the lights of St Girons splattered across the narrow plain, reaching out away from the Pyrenees and towards the flat lands as though running before the storm. He rested his forehead against the glass, the cold a welcome relief from the suffocating stuffiness of the hospital ward, and he contemplated all the small adjustments he would soon have to make, all of the tiny details of a shared existence which would have to be modified. Only by thinking about the minutiae could he begin to grasp how comprehensively his life was about to change.

'Monsieur Papon?'

The nurse was standing in the doorway, a firm but sympathetic look on her face.

'You should go home now. It's time you got some rest.'

'Five more minutes,' he pleaded and she checked her watch and nodded her consent. The door swished closed behind her.

Thérèse had been adamant from the day of the diagnosis that she didn't want this illness to disrupt their lives. A private woman anyway, she'd been loath to be the subject of gossip no matter how well intentioned, and so she'd insisted that he tell no one. Not even her sole remaining sister. She'd rejected the offer of being cared for at home, saying she didn't want their house turned into a hospital or the memories of the life they'd made there together submerged by a lingering sense of death. And when he'd suggested that he stay overnight in the hospital as her illness got worse, she'd really put her foot down.

The memory of her indignation made him smile ruefully, a rare flash of the inner strength that few knew Thérèse possessed. But it also left him in a quandary. Should he respect her wishes and leave even though she wasn't conscious? Or should he behave in his usual selfish fashion and do exactly as he wanted, which was to stay here by her side?

A sound from the bed caught his attention.

'Thérèse,' he whispered, taking hold of her hand once more. Her eyelids flickered and opened, her eyes struggling to focus on him.

'Go home,' she murmured, as her fingers curled around his.

'Are you sure?'

She blinked, the closest she could come to a nod.

'OK. If that's what you want,' he said with an air of resignation. 'I'll see you in the morning.'

He kissed her sunken cheek.

'Serge . . . I'm sorry.'

'*Sorry*? What do you have to be sorry about?' He fought back tears and gently squeezed her hand. 'You're the only true thing in my life.'

Her eyelids flickered in response and he could see she was trying to shake her head.

'So . . . sorry . . .' Her voice faded and she lost her tentative grip on consciousness.

He stood over her for a few minutes, watching her chest rise and fall, until he heard the pointed cough of the young nurse.

'You really should go home,' she said, her face softening. 'I'll take good care of her tonight.'

He nodded numbly and stumbled towards the door.

'You'll call me, if . . .' He ran out of words but the nurse understood.

'If there's any change we'll call you straight away.'

Somehow he made it to the exit where groups of visitors were clustered around, many inhaling gratefully on their first cigarette after hours inside, others like himself shuffling stupefied towards their cars.

He tried to concentrate on the road on the way home, but it was difficult. The sense of shame triggered by her words had magnified until it was all he could think of. Her apologising to him! After all the affairs he'd concealed from her, the schemes he'd concocted, the way he'd taken her for granted. He shook his head to dispel the images and gripped the steering wheel tighter.

His mind was still churning when he turned the last corner before La Rivière, and the Auberge des Deux Vallées came into view. The first thing he noticed was the lights. It seemed like every room in the place was illuminated. He slowed down and just as he pulled level he saw a man lean out of a downstairs window to close the shutters. Their eyes met through the falling rain, and Serge knew instantly what the man's presence signified.

A dry chuckle escaped his throat. So that was their game eh? The owners of the Auberge, not averse to a bit of trickery themselves, had roped in some outside help. He doubted they could have achieved much in the time frame and with their finances. Still, it showed initiative. Maybe they'd fit in well after all.

He finished the journey with a lighter heart, the tortuous road up to Fogas not troubling him at all, and by the time he reached his house, the only one in the village with the shutters wide open and in total darkness, he was anticipating the day ahead. He was especially looking forward to telling Thérèse that, despite it failing the inspection for a second time, he'd relented and allowed the Auberge to be reopened and it appeared as though the English couple were here to stay.

'SHIT!' Christian exclaimed and jerked his head back through the open window of the Auberge, his curls damp with rain.

Véronique, resting on a bar stool with her broken leg propped on a chair, nearly fell off her perch as he slammed the window shut, still cursing.

'What's the matter?'

'The mayor. Damn it! The mayor just saw me. He was driving past as I leaned out to do the shutters. Shit!'

An edgy silence filled the room, broken only by scratchy accordion music coming from the radio in the background.

'Are you sure it was him?' René asked, his half-rolled cigarette suspended in mid-air.

'There's no mistaking that face.'

'Well maybe he didn't see you,' proposed Stephanie.

'He saw me all right. He actually grinned, the bastard.' René inhaled sharply.

'That's not good,' he said. 'That's not good at all.'

'Oh forrr heaven's sake!' Annie declared in exasperation. 'What can he do to us? It's not as if we'rrre brrreaking the law.'

Paul shifted anxiously, striving to follow the heated exchange and beginning to suspect that by helping him out, his neighbours had caused trouble for themselves.

'Damn it!' Christian slapped himself on the forehead. 'And after it was all going so well.'

'It's not your fault,' Véronique interposed. 'He was going to find out tomorrow morning anyway. And look on the bright side. Now we don't have to hide our involvement any more, we can all be here for the inspection!'

'She's right.' René licked the edge of his cigarette paper, inspected the finished result and popped it in his top pocket for the drive home. 'Don't know about the rest of you, but I'll be here at nine a.m. tomorrow.' He turned to Paul and Lorna. 'If that's OK with you?'

'Excellent,' said Lorna. 'And you too Christian? I make a big meal . . .'

Christian grinned sheepishly while everyone else burst out laughing. With the boiler up and running on Wednesday night, Christian had been teased about his presence at the Auberge every night since, with René implying it had more to do with the evening's meal than the evening's work.

'Hush!' Véronique signalled for them to be quiet as she struggled off her stool to reach the radio and turn up the volume. 'Did she just say what I thought she did?'

A young woman's voice bubbled out of the speakers. The French was rapid and the voice incredibly high pitched, but it was clearly an advertisement for a local business. Lorna couldn't understand why Véronique thought it was so important until the last few words tumbled out of the radio.

'. . . *at the Auberge des Deux Vallées, La Rivière, telephone . . .*'

'That's us! That's an advert for us! On the radio! Who on earth . . .'

But it was no good asking the others. They all seemed equally surprised, animated by their brush with fame, even if it was only Radio Couserans. Only Véronique stayed quiet, her eyes shrewd as she watched Christian, his earlier expression of unease replaced by one of satisfaction. Sensing her scrutiny, he walked over, picking up her crutches on the way.

'You about ready to go home?' he asked nonchalantly.

'You're a good man, Christian Dupuy.'

'Don't know what you mean,' he protested.

'Of course you don't.'

He shrugged as if still in ignorance and then grinned. 'Will this save me from eternal damnation then?'

Véronique screwed up her face as though seriously considering the question. 'No,' she finally conceded with a laugh. 'I don't think so. I think you're condemned to spend eternity in the flames of hell. But if you help me down the steps, I'll pray for you.'

Laughing with her, he took her arm and guided her across the room, the others saying their goodbyes and promising to come down the following morning. They left the warmth of the Auberge, moaning at the cold and the wet outside, as they dashed for their cars. With secrecy no longer an issue, René sounded his horn as he left, while Stephanie hollered a last goodbye as she followed the spluttering, backfiring Panda out on to the road.

'Wow, what a night!' Paul said as he closed the door.

'What a week more like.'

They stood there in silence for a moment as the sheer size

of their achievement sank in. On the bar was a folder containing all the paperwork necessary for the grant application which Stephanie had slaved over for four nights. On the back wall was the new thermostat for the central heating system that René and Christian had installed. Upstairs the bedrooms were pristine, new curtains hand-hemmed by Véronique and Josette, carpets fitted by Alain Rougé, and the windows, thanks to Annie and Monique Sentenac, sparkling. And presiding over all, of course, was St Germaine in pride of place on her plinth in the hall.

'Madame Dubois won't know the place,' Lorna said with a shaky laugh.

'*I* don't know the place!' Paul shook his head in wonder. 'It feels like we're almost there. Only two more inspections to go.'

'And at least this time, we know what we're letting ourselves in for.'

With a sense of immense satisfaction, they turned off the lights and headed upstairs to bed.

Outside the rain was getting heavier, the pitter-patter of drops changing to a pulsating beat that drummed down on to the roof of the Auberge. Grey slates gleamed in the light from the street lamps, the water cascading over them, running in rivulets, searching for an opening, an easy descent, the slightest of gaps would suffice. In one or two places it started to seep under the slates, trickling down the inside of the roof and dripping into the carefully placed buckets below. Splish, splash, the water fell, safely contained. Apart from in one corner where there was no bucket, no tarpaulin, because until the storm on New Year's Eve, there had been no leak. Here the rain fell quietly, leaching into the rough floorboards and oozing down into the ceiling below.

At first the plaster coped, simply swelling as the moisture

soaked into it, a brown blotch spreading out over the fresh paint. But as the rain persisted, it reached saturation point, the sodden chalk no longer able to hold its own weight. With a muffled thump, a huge part of the ceiling collapsed, scattering dust and debris over the new bed and the hand-hemmed curtains, and knocking one of the lamps off a bedside table.

Down the corridor, in the only room that was occupied, no one stirred. All was quiet. In the early hours of the morning on the day of the inspection, the rain finally stopped. But the damage was already done.

19

It was Lorna who made the discovery. An hour and a half before the inspection was due to start she was going from room to room, turning on radiators and checking that everything was as it should be. She took her time, partly to quell the nervous anticipation that was causing her stomach to flutter, but also because she was still marvelling at the transformation that the Auberge had undergone. The dismal day in mid-November when they'd discovered the leaking roof and the appalling kitchen seemed a distant memory as she ran her hand over the newly painted walls of one of the bedrooms and admired the curtain-framed windows in another, the glass glittering in the bright sunlight. When she got to the last door on the landing, she was feeling almost serene. She reached out to turn the handle and then paused, her nostrils twitching at the musty smell that hadn't been there the night before. She didn't think anything of it. Until she opened the door.

'OH MY GOD!' she screamed, hands in her hair as she tried to take in what she was seeing.

Her cries were heard by the people assembled downstairs around the coffee machine and they all started running. Paul and Stephanie flew up the stairs two at a time, Christian leaving René gasping as he tried to keep up, while Annie and Josette moved as fast as their age permitted. By the time Véronique arrived, having hopped her way up, she was at the back with her view completely blocked.

'What's happened?' she asked, trying to see over Christian's broad shoulders.

'The ceiling's fallen down!' Josette whispered in horror.

'It's a disaster!' Stephanie declared. 'Here, have a look,' and she edged aside so that Véronique could take her place.

Inside, the newly decorated space was unrecognisable. A large part of the ceiling had been replaced by a ragged, gaping hole which revealed the still-damp, rough boards of the attic floor, chinks of dusty sunshine filtering down between them. About a third of the plaster had come down, smashing on to the floor and covering the furnishings with the accumulated dirt of many years. One of the curtains was ripped in half where a lump of debris had caught it as it fell while the other was filthy and caked in grime. The bed, what Véronique could see of it, looked to be undamaged, just in need of a good clean but as for the carpet . . . A huge wet patch was visible where the rain had continued to fall after the ceiling had collapsed and it squelched as Paul and Christian picked their way through the mess. But it was the smell that was worst of all. The heavy, dank odour caught at the throat and made breathing difficult.

They'd never get the room ready in time.

As if reading Véronique's thoughts, Paul signalled to Christian and they came out of the bedroom, closing the door behind them.

'I think we must cancelling the Hôtel de Tourisme inspection,' Paul said, putting an arm around Lorna who was grey with shock. 'We must having six rooms minimum for accreditation.'

'What about your bedroom?' Véronique suggested but Lorna was already shaking her head.

'When we arrive, we choose worst room to live in. The ceiling, it is like this,' and she made a sagging gesture with her hand and sighed heavily. 'It will not pass.'

'But the grants . . .' spluttered Stephanie. 'You won't be able to get the grants.'

Paul gestured at the closed door. 'But it is impossible to fix.'

'He's right.' Christian scratched his head, and ran a hand over his brow, feeling the dejection of the people around him who'd worked so hard to make the inspection possible. 'There's nothing we can do. At least the fire and safety inspection can still go ahead and we'll pressure the mayor into overturning the notice of closure once you've passed.'

'All that hard work was for nothing,' Stephanie muttered, not ready to look on the bright side. 'Why did it have to be that room? Why couldn't the ceiling have fallen in on your room or . . . I don't know . . .' Realising she might seem to be wishing Paul and Lorna dead, she hastily cast a black look up and down the landing and plumped for the only alternative. 'The laundry! Why couldn't that have been the room damaged? It doesn't even get inspected!'

'It's not part of the inspection?' Véronique queried.

Lorna shook her head.

'How big is it?'

'The same size as the bedrooms.'

'Can I have a look?'

Lorna indicated for Véronique to go ahead, exasperated by her digressions. The others watched bemused as she flung open the laundry and hopped inside. Her voice emerged, muffled.

'There *is* something we can do, you know.' She reappeared in the doorway looking triumphant. 'We can move the laundry.'

'Move the laundry?' Christian was a bit slow on the uptake. But Paul had no trouble understanding.

'Yes! Of course! An excellent idea. We can moving the bedroom here.'

'All we have to do is empty the laundry into the bedroom and bring the bedroom furniture into here,' Véronique explained. 'We'll have to give it a clean of course! And then we simply deal with the rest of the mess after the inspection.'

'Do we have time?' Josette glanced at her watch.

'We'll bloody make time!' declared Annie, rolling up her sleeves and marching into the laundry where Véronique was already beginning to move out piles of towels and sheets. Josette hurried after her, deciding that for once, the shop would open late. René, stunned into a rare silence by a combination of the devastation and the race up the stairs, went into the bedroom and started dusting off the bedside tables while Christian and Paul embarked on the difficult task of clearing off the bed.

'What can I do?' Stephanie asked Christian.

'You and Lorna can wait downstairs and if the chief inspector of hotels turns up early, try and stall him.'

'How do we do that?'

'I'm sure you'll find a way. Just make sure it doesn't involve violence!'

Stephanie batted her eyelashes as she leaned against the door frame and pouted sexily.

'That's it!' Christian laughed. 'Look, it's working already.' He pointed to René who'd stopped wiping down the furniture and was regarding Stephanie, as she twisted a curl sensuously around a long finger, with the look of a starved dog.

'Only trouble is, you sexist morons,' drawled Stephanie, preparing to follow Lorna downstairs, 'the chief inspector's a woman!'

In the end, Stephanie didn't have to use her powers of feminine persuasion. With fifteen minutes to spare, the laundry had been reincarnated into a cheerful bedroom. The bed, flanked by two bedside tables with mismatching lamps, looked none the worse for its recent immersion in plaster. The original bedding was beyond use so now it was covered in a vibrant yellow bedspread and at the window hung a pair of matching curtains, all hastily fetched from Chloé's bedroom. Stephanie had also brought down a vase of early daffodils which she'd placed on a table in the corner and she'd hung bouquets of dried lavender in the corridor to detract from the pervasive smell of damp. The door on the damaged room had been firmly locked.

'Brilliant,' Christian congratulated Véronique as they both sat slumped on a bar stool sipping coffee, tired out by the physical effort. 'And incredibly crafty too. Didn't know you had it in you!'

Véronique dipped her head at his praise.

'She's a chip off the old block,' Annie muttered, taking the time to pat her daughter affectionately on the back but without elaborating which side of the block she was referring to.

'He's here!' René's high-pitched squeal came from outside where he'd been smoking a guilty cigarette. Now he was frantically trying to stub it out while opening the front door at the same time. 'He's here, he's here!'

Responding to the panic in René's voice, everyone gathered near the bar, herding together with a primitive sense of group safety. Paul was amazed to realise that only Monique Sentenac and Josette were missing, both having apologised for not being able to lend their support at the most crucial stage. Well aware of the political risk those present were taking, Paul felt a rush of affection for his neighbours, who over the last ten nights had become friends.

'You can going, if you are quick,' he said, pointing at the back door and gesturing for them to hurry.

René's eyes darted towards the escape route as though

calculating whether he could move fast enough to be out the back door before the mayor arrived at the front but Annie merely snorted.

'No good rrrunning now!' she declared. 'Too late. He knows we'rrre involved.'

With her words hanging over their heads like a death sentence, they waited, the booming voice of the mayor getting ever closer until his thick fingers could be seen stretching out to grab hold of the door handle.

'This is it!' muttered Christian, and he felt someone squeeze his hand in solidarity. He barely had time to register it was Véronique before the mayor stepped into the room.

'Bonjour Monsieur, Mad . . .' The mayor's greeting died on his lips as he took in the group before him. 'Messieurs, Mesdames,' he corrected himself, sounding far from good-natured. Casting a steely eye over everyone in turn, as though committing their act of treason to memory, he dismissed them with a toss of his head and walked over to Paul and Lorna, his hand outstretched.

'Monsieur WebSter, Madame WebSter. I trust you are both well?'

'Fine thank you,' Paul managed while Lorna was trying not to breathe as the mayor's aftershave enveloped her.

'I think you know everyone here.' The mayor indicated the members of the inspection party who'd followed him in and seemed equally surprised by the presence of so many people. Madame Dubois separated herself from the others and came forward to shake hands, leaning in to whisper to Lorna as she did so.

'Did you manage to get everything done?'

Lorna gave the briefest of nods and Madame Dubois' face lit up.

'Excellent!' She melted back into the group.

'So. Where do we start?' the mayor asked.

Paul decided to take the initiative. 'Well, perhaps Major Gaillard likes to see the new boiler? Or perhaps the new oil tank?'

The mayor blinked slowly but that was his only visible reaction.

'And I take Madame Dubois to the bedrooms,' added Lorna. 'Everything is completed.'

The two inspectors readily agreed and as he felt the power draining from him, the mayor's face turned puce. Although he'd suspected something was up when he'd driven past last night, he hadn't realised the extent to which he'd been out-manoeuvred. He'd never thought that they would get all the work done in time. And even though he'd come to the conclusion that it was best if the Auberge reopened, having his authority usurped in this way, and by so many, infuriated him.

The trilling of his mobile saved him from having to comment. He strode to the furthest end of the room while everyone else broke into conversation. When he returned minutes later, his face was ashen.

'Erm, unfortunately I have to leave,' he said, his sombre tone cutting across the chatter. 'Urgent business.'

'But the inspection?' Paul suspected more subterfuge. 'You must being here.'

The mayor spread his hands, for the first time in the memory of all those present, lost for words. Watching him struggling to respond, Annie felt a wave of pity, for she suspected that the call had been from the hospital.

'I'm sorry,' he said, genuinely upset. 'I really am sorry.' He hurried out of the Auberge, his car soon speeding past towards St Girons.

Meanwhile Major Gaillard started putting away the paperwork he'd had to hand.

'You are leaving also?' asked Lorna, her voice shaking.

'Sorry, but we can't carry out the inspection without the mayor. It's invalid.' He shrugged his shoulders as if to acknowledge that they'd all been outwitted by a grand master.'

Stephanie threw up her arms in rage. 'I don't believe it! What a nerve! He's blatantly scuppered the inspection yet again. The man has no scruples.'

As others started muttering in agreement, Annie, who'd kept her counsel for so long, stepped forward and spoke, her brusque tone carrying over everyone else.

'His wife is dying,' she said, chastening them with the truth. 'That's why he had to go in such a hurry.'

No one moved. Only the clock was audible in the background as it marked the passing seconds. And then Christian found his voice.

'I can't believe it. Thérèse is dying? I thought she was in Toulouse?'

Annie shook her head. 'She's in the hospital in St Girrrons.'

'But . . . how long has . . .' Christian faltered, not sure what he should be asking as pieces of the jigsaw that was the mayor's erratic behaviour fell into place.

'She was admitted on New Yearrr's Eve. She didn't want anyone to know and I only found out by accident. So when you all starrrted gossiping about Serrrge, he couldn't say anything.'

Her words fell heavy on them all as they realised the burden he'd been under and how they'd unwittingly added to the load.

'So despite his naturrral inclination to chicanerrry, I think forrr once he had no intention of trrrricking you. In light of that, let's see if therrre's any way we can get this blasted inspection done.' Annie turned to Major Gaillard. 'Why does the mayorrr have to be herrre? Won't someone else frrrom the Conseil Municipal do?'

'I'm afraid it has to be the mayor. He called the inspection in the first place so he has to be here.'

'No! Not the mayor!' interjected Lorna. She pointed at Christian. 'He called the inspection.'

A buzz of excitement went around the room as people grasped the implication of her words and no one noticed that Lorna had just managed to use the past tense correctly for the first time.

'Is that right?' the fireman asked Christian. 'Is your name on the notice of inspection?'

Christian pulled a wry smile, acknowledging the irony of the situation. 'Yes, my name is on it. The mayor saw to that.'

Major Gaillard smiled as Lorna produced the initial letter of notification from a folder on the bar, and triumphantly pointed at the relevant text.

'Well then, what are we waiting for? Let's get started!'

Pascal Souquet was apprehensive and he didn't know why. The week skiing in Les Houches had been exquisite. His sister and her nauseatingly successful husband had invited them to their luxurious chalet where they'd entertained a succession of high profile guests from the Parisian elite and Pascal had been in his element. Intelligent conversation, erudite discussions, excellent wine. Not once had he heard the word bluetongue, there'd been no arguments over the best method to train a hunting dog and he hadn't so much as smelt a pastis. But after only a day back in Fogas already he could feel life chafing at him, irritating his skin like an ill-fitting collar.

First there'd been the incident at the town hall. Céline had been her usual insolent self, compelling him to make a mental note to find out how difficult it would be to fire her when he took over. She'd barely greeted him and had then interrogated him about some letter he was supposed to have given to the

Websters before he went on holiday. Apparently it was very important and the mayor had been asking about it.

Pascal had been adamant that no such request had been made of him and no such document existed. But she'd persisted, muttering under her breath. Finally she'd marched into the mayor's office where Pascal was working and started looking for the letter, rummaging around on the desk and flicking through piles of papers until she'd knocked his coffee flying. The hot liquid had spilled over the edge of the desk on to his legs, scorching him through his trousers and as he leaped into the air in pain, he'd caught her giggling behind her hand.

Trying to cover up her impertinence, she'd bent down to retrieve the fallen cup and when she'd stood back up, there was a letter in her hand and a smug expression on her face.

'You must have knocked it on to the floor the last time you were in here,' she said as she brandished the envelope like the spoils of war. 'The mayor won't be pleased when he finds out they didn't get it. You'd best drive down to the Auberge and deliver it right now.'

He didn't have his wife's perspicacity or even the benefit of it as she was still on holiday in Les Houches, making the most of the fresh snow with her mobile out of range. But Pascal could sense something wasn't right as he drove down the road to La Rivière. He was too dense to work it out, so he began to get worried.

Now, parked outside the Auberge, his anxiety was intensifying, because parked next to him was a vehicle from the Fire and Safety Department in Foix. And the other side of that was a blue van. Not just any blue van. A police van. There were several other cars too, as though a large group of people were visiting the Auberge.

Pascal chewed on the edge of a manicured nail as he wondered what it could mean. And the more he chewed, the more the evidence seemed to point to one thing: an inspection. But it couldn't be. Even Céline wouldn't be so insubordinate as to not tell him if something that monumental had been arranged in his absence. Plus the mayor's car was nowhere in sight and without him an inspection was impossible.

Aware in some part of his subconscious mind that he was about to walk into a well-laid trap, Pascal got out of the car, letter in hand, and made his way to the front door.

'Bonjour,' he called out, hearing voices from the kitchen.

Madame Webster came hurrying out and as the kitchen door swung closed behind her, he caught a glimpse of Major Gaillard, chief fire and safety inspector for the Ariège. And standing next to him, telling an anecdote that had the fireman laughing loudly, was none other than his fellow deputy mayor, Christian Dupuy.

Like a rabbit cut off from his burrow, Pascal froze, the envelope in his outstretched hand. He could sense danger, but he still couldn't make out what form it would take. Nor how to avoid it.

'What do *you* want?' Madame Webster asked, obviously having taken lessons from the Céline School of Decorum. She saw the letter and as her fingers closed over it, Pascal instinctively tugged it back, finally realising how the trap would be sprung.

'It is for us, no?' she demanded, pulling the letter more firmly towards her.

Pascal knew he was doomed.

'Is that all?' Madame Webster asked, the envelope tucked against her chest.

He nodded mutely.

'Maybe you are wanting to know,' she said, her voice rich with victory. 'Today, we pass the inspection. Tomorrow we are opening the Auberge.'

Pascal swept out of the building with the most dignity he could muster. He collapsed into his car, her words echoing in his ears. Suddenly he knew all too well why he was nervous. Somehow he had well and truly messed up. And Fatima was going to kill him.

It was some time before anyone got round to opening Pascal's letter. Lorna had propped it against the coffee machine and gone back to join the others in the kitchen where Monsieur Chevalier of the Veterinary Department was finishing his test of the chip-pan oil. It was all a matter of routine as the main stumbling block of the previous inspection had already been overcome and Major Gaillard had announced, to loud cheering, that he was more than happy to award the Auberge a pass. Likewise with Madame Dubois. She'd raised an eyebrow at the change in room layout upstairs but if she suspected anything, she never said a word. She had however discreetly enquired as to the status of the statue of St Germaine in the hallway and had shown immense relief when Stephanie had explained its presence was merely temporary.

With the inspections all completed and the paperwork finished, everyone was gathered in the dining room which was filled with noise and laughter as people prepared for the meal that Lorna was busy cooking in the kitchen. Christian, Alain and one of the policemen, under Stephanie's increasingly exasperated directions, were moving furniture to create one long table down the middle of the room, while Annie and Madame Dubois were setting out cutlery and glasses. Amidst all this, René was handing out aperitifs and Véronique, leaning heavily on the arm of the gallant Major Gaillard, was limping round with a tray of appetisers which was emptying fast.

As she passed him, Véronique offered Paul the last goat's

cheese and walnut tart from the tray. Realising he was starving, he accepted and as he bit into it, the sweet taste of the honey Lorna had bought the day before from Philippe Galy softening the sharp edge of the cheese, it seemed to finally sink in: his wife was a chef in a restaurant. No! Not just a chef in a restaurant. A chef in a FRENCH restaurant. And for the first time, as he watched the good-humoured mayhem before him, he actually felt like they could make it work.

That was when he caught sight of the envelope. He picked it up, slid his finger under the edge and pulled out the paper within.

'What's that?' Christian asked, spotting the town hall's insignia on the top of the letter as he took a seat at the bar in front of Paul. 'Is it from the mayor?'

Paul nodded concentrating on translating. Then he whistled softly and passed it to Christian to read. When he'd finished he looked at Paul, one eyebrow arched.

'When did you get this?'

'Monsieur Souquet gives it to Lorna earlier. But look.' Paul pointed at the date in the top right hand corner and Christian nodded.

'Yes. This is the letter the mayor was referring to in his notice of inspection last week. But why didn't you get it on the fifteenth?'

'Perhaps Monsieur Souquet keeps it deliberately? Who knows? But it changes everything. I go to tell Lorna.'

Christian twisted his beer glass in his hands as he mulled over the contents of the letter.

'A penny forrr them,' Annie rasped in his ear making him jump.

'You really don't want to know.' Then he explained.

'So the mayorrr had rrrevoked the notice of closurrre on the fifteenth of Januarrry and Pascal didn't give them the letterrr?' Annie asked incredulously.

'That's how it seems.'

'So they could have been open all this time? And the inspection wasn't needed.'

'Apparently.'

'You don't believe it?'

Christian looked cynical. 'It's all a bit too neat.'

'In what way?'

'Well, the mayor supposedly changed his mind and decided to revoke the notice of closure and then ordered the second inspection. Meanwhile, Pascal either forgets to deliver the letter informing Paul and Lorna of the change or he decides not to. Either way, he now gets the blame and the mayor comes out smelling of roses.' Christian shrugged and took a sip of his beer. 'Like I said, it's all a bit too convenient.'

'Will you say anything?' Annie asked as Paul showed the letter to Stephanie who was already cursing Pascal openly.

'I can't prove it. And anyway, I think he had the commune's best interests at heart in the end.'

Annie snorted.

'I'd love to know what made him change his mind though,' Christian mused. But Annie, suspecting it might have been a who rather than a what, kept quiet. 'Anyway, I'd best go and rescue your daughter,' he said, tipping his head to the far corner of the room where Major Gaillard was showing a lot of interest in Véronique, her status as a fire survivor no doubt having a certain appeal.

'Doesn't look like she needs rrrescuing from herrre!' quipped Annie as she gathered up the bin bag at her feet and walked out of the door.

'That's precisely the problem,' Christian muttered.

Glad to be out in the fresh air after a whole morning inside, Annie dawdled as she took the rubbish to the bin. She watched the river roar past, the swirls and eddies incessant as the water tumbled over the weir and off towards St Girons. She was just about to go back inside when she saw a small silver Peugeot coming up the road as though the driver had had one drink too many and was driving extra carefully to compensate.

It was Serge Papon.

He came to a halt in front of her, winding the window down as he did so. She didn't need to ask. One look at his face was enough.

Thérèse Papon was dead.

'Did they pass?' he asked, as though biting back emotion.

'Yes.'

He nodded and made as though to drive off but Annie placed a hand on his arm.

'Don't go, Serrrge,' she said softly. 'We know. About Thérrrèse. Now's not the time to be alone.'

When he put the car into gear she was sure he was going to ignore her but instead he parked it next to the Auberge and got out. Tucking his arm through hers, Annie led him towards the steps.

'Here's to passing the inspection,' Paul said, handing Lorna a glass of kir.

She raised her glass and took a grateful sip. With the *pot-au-feu* on a low simmer and the French onion soup finally ready to be served, she surveyed the dining room with an expression of bemused happiness. The long row of tables dominated the space, laden with baskets of fresh bread and the bottles of Ariège wine which René had brought with him as an opening present. It certainly tasted better than the stuff they'd discovered in the cellar! Someone had lit the woodburner in the corner and the fire reflected off the place settings, sparks of light glinting off the knives and forks and dancing on the glasses, giving the whole place a festive air.

'I can't believe it,' Lorna marvelled. 'It feels so unreal after all the hassle. To think we've finally passed!'

'And we have the grant application in. This time next year we should have a new roof!'

'We couldn't have done it without them,' she said, looking round at the people who'd helped. Véronique was chatting away to Major Gaillard, while René and Alain were having a ferocious discussion with one of the policemen which Lorna suspected was on the subject of bread-making machines. Christian had been cornered by Madame Dubois who was clearly flirting with him, the big farmer looking awkward and uneasy at the attention. Chloé, who'd just got in from school, was stroking the cat and listening to Stephanie, who was deep in discussion with Monsieur Chevalier. Whatever they were talking about, her hands were in constant motion, her bracelets jingling in time with her voice.

'Do you feel like we're part of this?' Paul asked in a whisper as he put his arm around his wife.

Lorna nodded, her throat tightening with emotion.

'Well wait until they've tried your *pot-au-feu*! Then we'll really be accepted into the community!' Paul lifted his nose and sniffed appreciatively at the mouth-watering aroma wafting out of the kitchen. 'How soon can we eat?'

'We really ought to tell Stephanie first, don't you think?'

'What, now? Before lunch?'

'Why not? It's the perfect time.'

Paul turned to face the room. 'Excuse me!' he shouted, loud enough to be heard by everyone. As the talking ceased he raised his glass.

'To our new waitress!' he declared. 'Stephanie Morvan!'

Stephanie opened her mouth but nothing came out.

'You don't want working here?' Lorna teased.

'You're giving me the job? Seriously? I've got the job?'

'When can you starting?'

'Now!'

Everyone cheered while Stephanie turned to Chloé and scooped her up in her arms, hugging her tightly.

'We don't have to leave,' she whispered into her daughter's hair. 'We can stay here.'

Chloé leaned back to see her mother's face, her expression solemn.

'I never planned to leave anyway, Maman. This is where we belong.'

In total agreement, Stephanie planted a big kiss on her cheek, much to Chloé's mortification, and it was only as she put her back on the ground that she saw Annie in the doorway with Serge Papon leaning on her arm.

The room fell silent at the sight of the old man, his age suddenly apparent as he stood there, unsure of his welcome and awash with grief. Christian made the first move, walking over and taking Serge's hand, the broad expanse of his palm engulfing the twisted fingers of the older man.

'I'm sorry,' he said simply. 'She was a good woman.'

Serge nodded, unable to speak. Then Lorna, her eyes filled with tears for a woman she hadn't known, gently took him by the arm and led him to a chair at the table.

'Stay with us and eat,' she said. 'You can't going home.'

'Thank you,' Serge managed.

'She's a good cook,' René blurted out nervously, feeling the tension. 'Even though she's English.'

'René!' Véronique admonished while everyone else laughed, including Serge, and the mood lightened a little as one by one they all sat down.

'But it's true,' René spluttered, keen not to have offended. 'She cooks French food. She even uses recipes by Jamio Le Vert.'

'Who?' asked Stephanie as she sorted out an extra place at the table, already assuming her new role.

'You don't know him? Jamio Le Vert? He's French!' René exclaimed with Gallic pride. 'Very famous. My wife swears by him.'

'I think,' said Lorna, who was trying not to laugh as she ladled out the soup, 'you are meaning Jamie Oliver.'

'Yes, that's what I said. Jamio Le Vert.'

The place was now in uproar as everyone realised René's mistake.

'He's English you idiot!' Christian called out and René looked aghast as bowls of soup topped with melting cheese were passed down the table amid great laughter.

'What do you mean, *English*? My wife has been feeding me his food for years and she told me he was French!'

As the extent of his wife's betrayal became apparent, René got more and more indignant, and everyone just laughed the harder. Sitting in the midst of the commotion, Annie realised that someone was missing. She called Chloé over and whispered in her ear and with black curls flying, Chloé scampered out of the front door and up the street to the shop.

'Josette,' she called out as she crashed through the door, setting the birds off tweeting furiously.

Josette came rushing in from the bar.

'Goodness, Chloé, is everything all right?'

'Annie says you're to close up and come down to the Auberge for a meal. We're celebrating.'

'Celebrating? They passed the inspection then? Well I'd best do as Annie says! Wait here for me, love, I'll be down in a minute.'

With her heart lighter than it had been in a long long time, Josette hurried up the stairs to fetch her coat. It was fantastic news. All the stress had been worth it. And Jacques would be so happy.

As she came back down, she could hear Chloé chatting to someone in the bar and she uttered a rare curse. That's all she needed. A lone customer in search of a lunchtime drink. Well, for once they'd just have to go elsewhere. She was about to close.

But when she stepped into the bar Chloé was alone, except for Jacques sitting by the fire, a huge grin on his face. Relieved that the customer hadn't waited, she took Chloé by the hand and prepared to leave.

'Josette,' Chloé asked as they got to the door. 'Isn't Jacques coming with us?'

Josette froze and looked down at Chloé's earnest face.

'What do you mean, love? Jacques died last year.'

'I know,' said Chloé, pointing at the inglenook where Jacques was laughing silently. 'But he's back. Look.'

'You can see him?'

'Yes.' She waved and to her delight, he waved back.

'Well,' said Josette, struggling to keep her voice steady, 'not everyone can see him, Chloé. So I think we should keep this as our secret. OK?'

Chloé shrugged with the nonchalance of a nine year old. 'Whatever. But if he's not coming, maybe we should leave the shutters open so at least he can see out.'

'That's a great idea,' agreed Josette, and with one last backwards glance of affection for her husband, she followed Chloé out of the shop and locked the door.

Jacques stood up to watch them go, lingering at the window as they walked towards the building which had been at the centre of the maelstrom that had threatened to engulf them all. A huge sense of satisfaction filled his heart as he contemplated the outcome of what could have been a disaster for the Commune of Fogas.

When Josette and Chloé reached the Auberge, they turned to wave one last time. Then Jacques resumed his seat by the fire, his head soon growing heavy as it dropped towards his chest.

'Life is good,' he thought as he slipped towards sleep. 'And death is not too bad either.'

Acknowledgements

This book is the creation of one mind, but the product of many souls. For reading, editing, cups of tea and encouragement, I owe a bottle of Ariège's finest and a tin of cassoulet to the following:

Claire, Brenda, Matthew, Karen, Ellen S, Micheál, Ellen Mc, Simon, Peter, Gary, Anne, Ali, Jenni, Swati and Alice.
And a special thanks to the three Graces, without whom this book would still be a pile of A4 pages in a bottom drawer:

Judith, Sue and their catalyst, Meg.